ADVANCE PRAISE FOR
Margaret and the Mystery of the Missing Body

"What if all those nineties book series about girlhood had been truly honest about the process of growing up? You'd get this wonderful book: a comforting facade that opens into an entrancing and wildly innovative gut renovation of the genre, with an interior that lays bare the hidden workings of life I wish I'd known on my own first run through adolescence. Brilliant."

—TORREY PETERS, author of *Detransition, Baby*

"*Margaret and the Mystery of the Missing Body* is queer dynamite. I devoured this book in one sitting, completely engrossed by the wild plot and by Megan Milks's stellar, singular voice. This is a book of bodies, sure, but it's also a book about the messiness of them, their complications and intractability, their frustrating unknowability. Their mutability. Their wonder. This novel is a bright spot of brilliance. I absolutely adored it."

—KRISTEN ARNETT, author of *With Teeth*

"I tore through this book in a day and was still thinking about it weeks later. It's the smartest novel I've read in a long time and the most politically astute. *Margaret and the Mystery of the Missing Body* is a coming-of-age novel about growing up through coming-of-age narratives, then reappropriating those narratives from the inside and writing your own freedom. It's also compulsively readable, hugely moving, and more fun than the pop classics it makes free with. Magnificent."

—SANDRA NEWMAN, author of *The Heavens*

"*Margaret and the Mystery of the Missing Body*, a thrilling and surprising crystallization of the best and worst parts of growing up in the nineties, lit up all of the pleasure receptors in my brain. It's intimate, fearless, and a fun house of form and style. Megan Milks is a supremely generous writer whose work is daring and alive."

—PATRICK COTTRELL, author of *Sorry to Disrupt the Peace*

MARGARET
AND THE MYSTERY OF THE
MISSING BODY

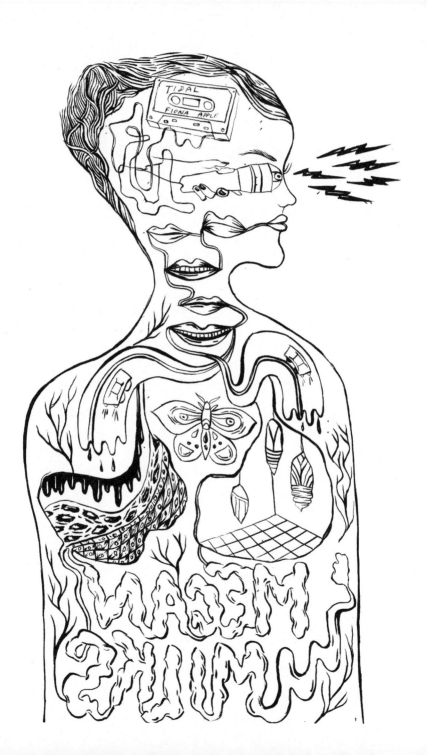

MARGARET
AND THE
MYSTERY
OF THE
MISSING
BODY

MEGAN MILKS

THE FEMINIST PRESS
AT THE CITY UNIVERSITY OF NEW YORK
NEW YORK CITY

Published in 2021 by the Feminist Press
at the City University of New York
The Graduate Center
365 Fifth Avenue, Suite 5406
New York, NY 10016

feministpress.org

First Feminist Press edition 2021

Copyright © 2021 by Megan Milks

This book was made possible thanks to a grant from New York State Council on the Arts with the support of Governor Andrew M. Cuomo and the New York State Legislature.

This book was published with financial support from the Jerome Foundation.

First printing September 2021

Cover design by Xander Marro
Text design by Drew Stevens

Library of Congress Cataloging-in-Publication Data
Names: Milks, Megan, author.
Title: Margaret and the mystery of the missing body / Megan Milks.
Description: First Feminist Press edition. | New York, NY : Feminist Press, 2021.
Identifiers: LCCN 2021013657 (print) | LCCN 2021013658 (ebook) | ISBN 9781952177804 (paperback) | ISBN 9781952177811 (ebook)
Classification: LCC PS3613.I532274 M37 2021 (print) | LCC PS3613.I532274 (ebook) | DDC 813/.6--dc23
LC record available at https://lccn.loc.gov/2021013657
LC ebook record available at https://lccn.loc.gov/2021013658

PRINTED IN THE UNITED STATES OF AMERICA

For Caroline

"Picking locks is a glorious thing."

—KAI CHENG THOM,
Fierce Femmes and Notorious Liars:
A Dangerous Trans Girl's
Confabulous Memoir

Adolescence: We all go through it, some of us again and again. It's a transitional space, a waiting room, this long, shapeless stretch between youth and adulthood, naivete and knowledge. It's the private heat within which our goop becomes what it wants to become. It's the mystery of the banana, the magic converting its peel from pale green to a brash and confident yellow. It's the burrow of dirt into which the earthworm worms to improve itself in secret. It's the passage from this into that, from here to there, to some kind of passing maturity. Adolescence is the hallway. The between, the almost, the not-there-yet.

Margaret is spending hers driving.

Every morning she guides her LeSabre down the long pebbled driveway of her home, then left past the massive clay edifice that is Shady Bluff's namesake, or so she has supposed since childhood (it is, rather, a pile of dull dirt), another left, and another, out through the snaking back roads of South Chesterfield, Virginia, past the flicker of tobacco fields and forest, two winding rights and a hard left to go north, up a frightful hill and all the way down to its bottom, to park in the muddy overflow lot allocated to lowly juniors like her. Then again hours later, from that same parking lot to (once a week) the way-out field where her environmental science group counts insects in weekly grids, and back to school to drop off her friends Davina and Richie; or (once a week) heading north on the parkway and through the tolls, to the difficult, one-way streets of Richmond for two hours of symphonic band. And (always) back to Shady Bluff. On the weekends, it's the back roads the other way, across the train tracks and into Petersburg for her two long shifts at the mall, and home again, to Shady Bluff. Or not yet. More and more she drives past the entrance and keeps driving. If it is always inevitable, she might as well delay getting home.

From here to there and home, always home, to Shady Bluff, where she has lived for most of her life, and keeps living, while around her the neighborhood changes, grows, *develops*. There's a new, uglier entrance sign now, and a major expansion just down the street from her house. Acres of forest have been razed to make way for a west wing with twelve lots. What with the steady stream of trucks and plows and porta-potties, not to mention prospective buyers cruising slowly, too slowly, only to stop in the middle of the pavement, Margaret has been feeling like a castaway prop in someone else's future.

The disconnect unsettles her. Not long ago she would have been thrilled at the prospect of a new wing, imagining what the construction might dig up: time capsules and ghosts; if they were lucky, some skeletal remains. Then would come new homes, which would mean new clients, new cases, which would mean more Girls Can Solve Anything business.

But Girls Can Solve Anything is dead. That's the problem.

She won't think about that now. She only thinks about that on Tuesdays between 5:30 p.m. and 6:30 p.m.

It's too early still, yet she's late. After a bloated school day followed by debate and then field hockey, bodies all around,

Margaret is running behind. She should have been home an hour ago, should have been home and gone, hi Mom, bye Mom, grabbing M&M's and Doritos for club time. She should be surreptitiously creeping up on her target site and parking discreetly, should be readying the CD, unlatching the glove compartment to extract her ball cap and binoculars, her shades. Should be opening her candy, her chips, placing one bag at her left hip, the other at her right, should be waiting for the digital clock to flip to 5:30, and then, exactly then, she should press Play.

That was the plan. The plan has been foiled.

Today's snacks are from Wendy's, a capitulation to her lateness, and they are sitting in a greasy bag atop her JanSport, emitting fumes of meaty impatience. Fiona Apple's *Tidal* is in position in the portable CD player, the cassette adapter at rest in the mouth of the deck. Everything is ready but Margaret, who, fifteen minutes from her destination, is still moodily maneuvering her Buick along the back roads. Today's crime scene is supposed to be Mrs. Stillwater's house, which she has been putting off revisiting, as she's put off revisiting all cases that took place in Gretchen's neighborhood. It's risky, she knows, but it's clear: if there are new clues to be found, it will be there.

5:28. Of course she's behind. She's self-sabotaging.

Yes, the delay will cut into her club time, and yes, she will be despondent the rest of the week. That will be fine: it's her punishment.

She can at least start the album on time. Margaret presses the flimsy cassette until the deck is activated, and chews. She reaches for the orb of her portable Panasonic, which has been flung to the edge of the crimson passenger seat. Her stretch pulls the steering wheel with her so she's out of the

3

lane just a little—who cares, no big deal, nothing's coming, oops, a turn. She straightens to swing her car through it, a move that brings the CD player into reach, well done, and she feels around the lip of the dome for the right button, and . . . got it, now she's pressing it: Play.

Finally. Thank you. *God*. Deep breath as she relaxes into the thumping beat of "Sleep to Dream," which introduces Fiona in her lowest register, voice hardened, over it, done. Margaret is appeased but still trembling. What a fucking day. It had been a tough field hockey practice and then she— didn't know *what* happened, some sort of nervous collapse, and it had taken forever to get herself out of the locker room and into the car. Now she has a vicious, all-over headache and she's hungry—madly, slobberingly hungry. She hasn't eaten in hours, not since a small, neat lunch of yogurt and bread at eleven, and now the salty onion smells are spiraling up through her nostrils and drilling into her brain.

You need to eat now, the smell spiral declares.

She's not allowed to eat until she parks at the crime scene.

Now, it repeats, more loudly this time.

Those are the rules. She has to follow them.

You won't make it to Mrs. Stillwater's, the smell spiral hisses. *You will not survive so long in this car.*

Fine. It will be another failure.

The woods on the right cut out, replaced by rustling tobacco, her signal to slow down. On the left is the horse farm where she took lessons in a short-lived stab at being a horse girl, after GCSA's shattering demise. Here, she thinks. Now. It's not the plan, but it is true that unexpected detours can occasionally rustle up new evidence. The horse farm might trigger memories that might trigger other memories, key information she's left unexplored.

4

The truth is it's taking all of her energy not to reach in and pluck a french fry from the bag. Just one single, solo salty fry, dissolving upon her tongue like the Host. This is the body of a potato, she imagines. Don't do it, Margaret. Wait.

She pulls into the lot beside a mud-streaked pickup. Grabs her mini-binoculars and tucks her hair into her dad's old VT ball cap. Slumps low in her seat. She eats. She allows herself one fry and one good suck of the Frosty, by now mostly liquid, before unwrapping the double cheeseburger and bringing it between her teeth.

She keeps the car running, track two rippling softly in the background. With its rolling piano, "Sullen Girl" is *Tidal*'s most tidal-like song, ebbing and flowing like the waves invoked in the chorus. It's a brave choice, she thinks, she always thinks, to follow up the confident romp of "Sleep to Dream" with a solemn—arguably *sullen*—piano ballad, but it is a solid and beautiful song that anticipates the tremendous range and depth of the album as a whole. And its hypnotic undertow never fails to sweep her into the churning waters of her own memory, where she might retrieve new, unnoticed clues.

With her binoculars, she scans the corral for Munchy the ill-behaved pony (her other hand feeling around for the fries). The homeliest, chunkiest pony, Munchy was the least sought out steed by far, but Sharon the stable owner had taken one look at Margaret and said she could handle him. Was that a jab about her size? Did Sharon think Munchy's bad behavior would be somehow suppressed by Margaret's considerable heft? If so, Sharon had been wrong. Week after week, Munchy had resisted each one of Margaret's commands. *No*, he told her, again and again. He wasn't going to hop over some dumb plastic bar just because she was steering him toward it. On the contrary, he would halt abruptly instead, thrusting her from the saddle as he did so. Nor was he going to break into a joyful canter in response to her thwacking him with a crop. No, no. Munchy was going to eat grass, insisting, by scraping her calf against the rough fence, that she please remove herself from his back, thank you very much. That was her last lesson. At the time, she had been outraged. Horses were supposed to do what you said, she complained to her mother. She has since come to respect his refusal.

No sign of Munchy in the corral, but there's Whisper cantering evenly under a long-bodied girl whose thick braid drops like a tail, a horse tail, from the shelf of her velvety helmet. Margaret's sole experience with the magnificent white mare called Whisper was a dream, her brisk trot like riding the wind. But though Whisper performed beautifully, unimpeachably, her snide snorts communicated something that smelled like disdain. Was Margaret too heavy? Too clumsy and uncertain in the saddle? *You do not deserve me*, Whisper was telling her with each moist grunt. And she didn't. Margaret deserved Munchy, dowdy Munchy, who was rude. So Margaret quit, much to her mother's relief: riding was expensive, untenably so.

Margaret recognizes Sharon's son Buddy, who whistles approvingly from outside the ring as Whisper's rider guides her through a double jump. None of the girls are familiar, which is no surprise. Her time here was brief and she never fit in with these braided, leggy horse girls, their shiny boots and soft nutters. They roundly refused Margaret and the tales she endeavored to share with them. Even the one about horses (Girls Can Solve Anything #27: Jina and the Case of the Ghostly Gallop) did not win her any friends. Years later, the shame of their blatant rejection still sears. She slumps down farther in her seat. If anyone catches her here, like this . . . she won't let anyone catch her.

She has since stopped talking about mysteries and her club, a decision arrived at in a desperate attempt to increase her friend quotient (success). Indeed, she has largely stopped thinking about them, with the exception of these club hours, which she maintains for precisely that purpose. On Tuesdays from 5:30 p.m. to 6:30 p.m., when she *should* be at her best childhood friend Angie's, she lets it all flood back: those salad days, how she misses them, her best friends and their mysteries, her bygone youth, when real things actually happened—especially now, in this in-between state, this sort-of-not-really-adult state, stuck in the sludge of early teenagehood where her peers demonstrate their blooming maturity by being irresponsibly, irredeemably bad: drinking (bad), smoking (bad), cursing (bad), *having sex* (bad bad bad). Not Margaret. Ever the judgy and responsible one, our Margaret. It's precisely these qualities that made her a successful sleuth, head detective—until they didn't.

Now Margaret is whoever, whatever, who cares. What a fall. Once president and head detective of a highly esteemed organization, Margaret is now sixteen and she is lost, ripped from the pages of her girl-group series and profoundly, uncomfortably unmoored.

Why?

She doesn't know. It's still a mystery.

For that, she blames herself. She took time off out of spite and sorrow. Only recently, upon the sad second anniversary of the end, has she reinstated club hours. Now she's revisiting their cases one by one—alone. She'll never recover the lost time, but if she retraces her steps, her choices, the painful and mysterious past (her logic goes), she might discover

7

missed clues. Clues to what *really* happened: why GCSA is over; what Margaret did wrong.

Sometimes she has a clear plan for these Tuesdays; mostly she doesn't. Always, she listens to Fiona Apple, and always, she brings snacks.

Margaret slurps up the last of the Frosty. Here comes "Criminal," in which the tables satisfyingly turn. Where the speaker of the preceding track ("Shadowboxer") was a bruised, recovering victim, in "Criminal" she becomes perpetrator, becomes criminal. It's complex. Margaret believes *Tidal* to be the most remarkable album ever made, a cohesive and affecting work of emotive orchestral pop written while Fiona was in high school; the album thus stands as proof of girl genius. Take the title, a very clever pun. Yet *Tidal* is not simply a playful gotcha, homograph for "title"; it also describes perfectly the album's rises and falls, ebbs and flows. It's a real girl's title, a girl tidal, naming without apology the cyclical waves of emotions so many of us can't help but feel. What a title. It's not quite a joke.

The interesting thing about "Criminal," Margaret thinks, is that while in the chorus the speaker tries repeatedly to convince herself, and the listener, of her remorse, in fact this is mere pretense, as she quickly shrugs off her guilt and submits to the mischievous swirl of melody. That is to say, the speaker is *playing at* feeling guilty. It's a show, a put-on, a pretense supported by the fact that, knobby white girl that she is, Fiona Apple is not actually a criminal nor in danger of being misperceived as such. The truth is that, for some people, being bad is good, and for people like Fiona Apple, it can be very sexy.

Two more horse girls walk past, whinnying affectionately at each other on their way to a waiting minivan.

Gretchen could be a horse girl, Margaret thinks. Or a criminal. Gretchen could be any kind of girl. That was part of her gift as an actor. She could morph into whatever you wanted her to be, such as your very best friend. Then you do one wrong thing and she doesn't speak to you again.

And now, although she is not at Mrs. Stillwater's as planned, Margaret finds her thoughts returning to that first case with Gretchen, The Case of the Stolen Specimens. In particular, she is recalling the Princess Pageant that started it all, that fateful fun-wear competition in which Gretchen stepped onto the stage as a detective wearing a trench coat and carrying a magnifying glass, then—surprise!—morphed into the femme fatale.

"Morph" is not quite right. In Gretchen's scene, the detective was murdered, then supplanted.

Sure, sure, Gretchen had said it was a comment on sexism in noir cinema. But what if it wasn't? What if it was foreshadowing the entirety of Margaret and Gretchen's friendship, their briefly entangled lives? What if Gretchen, with hidden psychic powers, had known all along that she would mortally wound Margaret, head detective, and usurp her role with a new one, the role of femme fatale? Or what if—a better story—what if Gretchen, good friend after all, was only trying to warn Margaret, in the manner of a time traveler stuck in a loop? *Beware, Margaret!* Gretchen may have been saying with that terrible knife thrust. *Someday I'll murder you!*

Stop. The only loop is Margaret's churning mind, where Gretchen fake-stabs herself again and again, then removes her trench coat to reveal her red dress. No, Gretchen isn't psychic or a time traveler, or even a femme fatale. But if there's one thing she is, it's a good actor. Gretchen's uncanny ability to step into different roles with all the right props made her a valuable club asset: she could slide undercover at the drop of a fedora. It also made her suspect—to Margaret, at least, who, aware of her prowess, never could tell where the performances ended.

Gretchen stabs herself again. Reveals the red dress. Now Gretchen is creeping out of her bedroom window under the cloak of night, wearing the same dress, this time with combat boots. Why? What, in this memory, was she doing? Margaret never found out, and her ex-friend's deceptions still sting. That's because Gretchen faced no real consequences for them. It's Margaret who suffered the consequences.

Life isn't fair. Her mother's favorite refrain swings smugly through her mind. Yes, well . . . it *should* be.

But it isn't. And if it isn't, what's the point of fighting crime? Maybe Gretchen—and Angie and Jina, the other GCSA members—were on to something. They had all killed their detectives and grown up; become other, older people. Margaret has tried and tried—tried being a horse girl, tried being a poet (ha)—but hasn't found her next role. She wants one, she needs one: a clear and focused identity, a hard shell to rove around in. But nothing quite feels like it fits.

Maybe the problem is not the fit, she considers, but her expectation that something should. Maybe the solution is it doesn't *have* to; she just needs to *act* like it does. Like Gretchen. Drag it around on top of her like a hermit crab, and eventually she'll grow into it, make it her home.

What about this role—Fiona's pseudocriminal, Gretchen's femme fatale—could she drag that around? It would certainly confer more power. And it's legible. It's available. It's complex, itself a put-on, a performance. She's already been playing it, she realizes: sort of, vaguely, and without recognizing it as such. In short, she hasn't been playing it well.

Margaret has been, in Fiona's words, "careless with a delicate man"—that is, with her Internet paramour TheVoice23. She has led him to believe they are having the kind of relationship that could go somewhere it never will. Now it's over. Done. His fault. With his last mixtape he included a photograph that revealed himself to be a pale and pudgy young man leaning over a guitar and grinning—*grinning*—with mossy teeth and a forehead gleaming with oil. What kills her is his un-self-consciousness, his *apparent happiness*. How? Why does he get to be that way?

Margaret has ceased responding to his chats and emails. She'll miss him, but TheVoice23 has turned out to be, well, not who she thought he was. People rarely are. That's one lesson learned from being a seasoned sleuth: everyone is hiding something.

No matter. Margaret has finally achieved buddy-list status with her actual, IRL crush Stephen Colson (8infinity8)—a sign of real progress—and with TheVoice23 out of the picture (he was practice, really) she can dedicate herself fully to this role.

For most of her adolescence, Margaret has dodged these kinds of things—the development of crushes on boys. Now she's behind, and grateful (for once) for the vicarious experiences of her friends. Her mission is clear: She will secure the attentions of Stephen Colson. And then—

Well, she'll figure that part out later.

She trains her binoculars to the expanse beyond the riding corral. Ah-ha. There he is: Munchy, the cantankerous criminal. Not in the riding arena, steered and spanked, but munching away free in the field. His bad temperament has paid off and he's been dismissed, retired, sent to pasture. His goal all along.

The triumph of Munchy.

What a life it would be, she imagines, spending whole days munching from one end of a field to the other, grinning at cars and pooping while you walk. Margaret shoves the vision away. She could never eat all day. That would be giving up this new plot, the get-Stephen plot, which, now that it's in motion, seems to unfurl before her like the straight-shot highway she's taken to avoiding. Her next-level goal: initiate chat, during which she will demonstrate how clever she can be in disembodied form, as opposed to in flesh, where she's tongue-tied and embarrassing. But she's gathering intel. Figuring him out. In debate today she noted his application of ChapStick five minutes into the meeting, the wag of his knee after he crossed his legs the guy way, his twitchy smiles and hair tucks. Evidence of dry lips and some subtle anxieties. Yes, soon she'll initiate a chat. After the next two pounds.

Margaret wipes her mouth and chin with a napkin, already regretting today's snacks. This is the last time, she tells herself. From now on (she squeezes down on, rejects the clench in her chest), she's done. She's killing her inner detective. She's taking off the trench coat (she removes the ball cap, returns it with the binoculars to the glove compartment) so that she may reveal . . . someone else. Which means that (she holds herself with nobly straight posture) Margaret must let go of club time. She must (her decision is pure and wise; she nods) let go of Girls Can Solve Anything.

She stops the CD. She closes her eyes. Breathes in, holds, releases.

"Goodbye," she whispers.

And just like that, she's done.

Now to get rid of the evidence. She balls up the burger foil and stuffs it in the french-fry tray, which she stuffs in the

Frosty cup, which she stuffs in the bag with the lid smashed inside it. She opens the glove compartment and removes a few balled-up potato-chip bags, then wrestles mini-Snickers wrappers, peanut-butter-cup foils, and other trash from under the seats, cramming it all in the two biggest bags. She steps out of the car and marches across the dirt lot to drop them in the big rubber trash can. Too visible, too exposed. She hides them under a Slurpee cup, sludgy with what she guesses is, gross, chewing tobacco.

The door to the farmhouse creaks open.

She steps away from the trash can. She's caught.

"Can I help you?" The voice is familiar, bright: Sharon's. "Maggie, hello! Don't tell me we had an appointment?"

Margaret thinks fast. "Oh no, I just really need to use the bathroom. Is that all right?"

Sharon nods knowingly. "Sure thing, hon. Come right in," she says in her twangy drawl. "Have you lost weight? You look real good, girl."

"Thanks." Margaret hurries inside. "Sorry. I drank a lot of coke."

Back in her car, she pulls out of the lot, turns left onto Branders Bridge Road. She'll take the long way home, might as well. Home is more miserable now that her brother's friend is dead. They're all on their tippy-toes because, instead of sobbing it out like a reasonable person, Brian flies into a rage with no notice. *It's not fair*, he yells, about stupid things that don't matter, like setting the table, for example, a task that gets transferred to her. She has been waiting for her mother to unleash her *life isn't fair* line, but she seems to use it only with Margaret. Yes, Brian, the world is bullshit, Margaret wants to say. Fiona Apple said it first, and famously.

Margaret has little sympathy. Cory had been *drinking and driving*. Which is illegal for a reason. People don't just make up laws. They're in effect to keep people like Cory from dying. If he had followed the laws, he wouldn't be dead. Simple. He might be standing in their garage right now, where he stood a few weeks ago: Tobacco pouched in his jaw (bad), drinking a Miller Lite (bad), while slitting a dead deer's throat and letting the blood sluice down onto newspapers spread in the center of *her* workout space (bad). His colossal red pickup in *her* spot (bad), Confederate flag (the worst) stretched halfway across the back window, impeding visibility and sending loud, bad signals around town. She guesses the truck is dead too. Coming up on it, that sharp bend, now marked with a wooden cross and a pitiable few dried bouquets, she slows to a creep, grips the steering wheel tight. Keeps driving.

The Case of the Stolen Specimens

CHAPTER 1

"Margaret, come on already," Jina yelled, sounding cross. "We're going to be late."

"It's too hot," I griped. "I can't even *see* straight." We were on the main road now, walking our bikes along the grass to keep a safe distance from cars. Ahead of me, Jina remained unfazed, no visible sweat spots, her warm brown skin practically singing in the sun. Meanwhile my whole surface area was sweaty, swollen, pink. My cheeks were pink. My thighs were pink. I had to walk funny, sort of staggering, so my shorts didn't ride up between them.

"We were supposed to be there by now. Janet's going to flip." Jina stopped and waited for me.

"Their category doesn't start for two hours," I reminded her, making no effort to speed up. "We could be doing research. The new library's *right here*." I gestured to the sparkling new building set back from the road, a major improvement over the decrepit older branch in the center of town.

Jina charged ahead again before I could catch up. "I'm her moral support," she called over her shoulder. "We can go to the library tomorrow."

"Or we could pop in just for a second," I persisted. "Mr. Dillinger might be on the desk. He'll have ideas." If anyone could provide us with a historical precedent for The Case of the Stolen Specimens, it would be Mr. Dillinger. He was our favorite librarian, and older than dust.

"Margaret." She stopped again. "Believe me, I want to figure this case out just as much as you do. But we're not going to figure it out now. We don't have Angie. And we don't have time!"

"Okay, okay. We'll go tomorrow." I gazed longingly at the library as we trudged past. The building promised many hours of absorbing microfiche scanning—*and* vigorous air-conditioning. But Jina was right. We had places to be.

We were on our way to the Princess Pageant at the Chesterfield County Fair: Jina's twin sister, Janet, was competing in the Preteen Princess category, along with her new friend Gretchen. Jina Castle is one of my best friends and her twin, Janet, is, well, not my favorite person. They're both gorgeous, five feet seven and slender, with disarming dimples and dazzling smiles. But that's where the similarities end. Jina typically wears her hair natural, pulled back with a headband, while Janet is obsessed with keeping hers sleek and straightened. Jina likes easy, comfortable things, such as this afternoon's sleeveless red tee over cuffed jean shorts, while Janet wears more "adult" clothing, such as cropped halter tops that she's always adjusting. Jina is nerdy and studious, loves puns and puzzles and playing the piano. And while it's not as though Janet isn't smart, she certainly doesn't apply herself—not in school, at least. Instead she lives for fashion and boys—and the annual Princess Pageant.

"I really hope she wins this year," Jina said. "She'll be so mopey if she doesn't."

"Me too," I said lacklusterly. I suspected Janet was simply "too much" for the pageant judges. It was her fourth year entering, and while she may not be my favorite person, she really does have all the marks of a pageant queen: beauty, confidence, poise, and sophistication—everything but humility, which unfortunately for her is overvalued in this context.

The fairgrounds were rowdy with bodies: bloated adults in damp polo shirts and dumpy shorts, scrawny girls in big T-shirts tucked into the tiniest shorts. Here and there, a screaming, blotchy child, overheated and uncomfortable. I could relate.

We locked up our bikes and surveyed our surroundings. There was so much to see! Wrestling past a row of crowded food vendors, I observed a knot of high schoolers passing around oily funnel cake, clearly up to no good. At the dunking booth, CJ Watson sat shirtless and grinning as a chunky girl hurled beanbags at the target and missed. Was that Brian with his friend Cory up ahead, passing out flyers at the Sons of Confederacy booth? Ugh. My brother, Brian, is the worst. Jina grabbed my wrist and impatiently yanked me along.

The grandstand was set up on the far corner of the field and looked pretty pathetic in the daytime. The pageant crowd was sparse, mostly parents and other family members of the contestants. Onstage, tiny girls formed a row in floofy princess gowns—the Little Princesses, I presumed. "In fourth place, Louisa May Freemont." There was a smattering of applause as a freckled, bucktoothed girl stepped forward. "In third place, Sparkle Jones." My across-the-street neighbor sauntered forward, swallowed up in a big purple dress. "Yay, Sparkle!" I cheered. When the winner was announced, a tiny girl with professional makeup tottered forward uncertainly. A woman in the audience modeled the cupped wave of the pageant queen. The girl mimicked it, smiling big.

No sign of Janet or Gretchen. "They must be inside with the Junior Princesses," Jina said, meaning in the high school's girls' locker room. Their category was two age groups away and, as I had expected, we had plenty of time.

"You go ahead," I told her. "I'll find Angie." Our other best friend was helping her mom with the Canned Foods and Vegetables exhibit.

On my way to the Arts and Crafts tent, I passed the Chesterfield County Police Department booth and gave a friendly wave to Chief Stroud and Sergeant Henry. Their return nods were reserved and somewhat resentful, I thought. Clearly they were still peeved that we had solved last month's mystery at the mall before they could (see Girls Can Solve Anything #2: Jina's Double Trouble). I stopped to pump them for information on our latest case.

"Any new leads in The Case of the Stolen Specimens?" I asked.

"Case of the—? Oh." Chief Stroud shook his head. "Not yet. You girls will be the first to know." Right. I saw the amused glance he exchanged with Sergeant Henry. Well, we hadn't relied on the police before, and we wouldn't start now.

By "we" I mean Angie, Jina, and me. Together, we make up Girls Can Solve Anything (GCSA for short), a club for girl sleuths. Though we've only been in business a few months, we've solved every case thrown at us, and our reputation is spreading like wildfire. But in The Case of the Stolen Specimens, we seemed to have reached an impasse. There had been a theft at the botanical gardens two weeks ago. All kinds of exotic butterflies had been swiped, and in broad daylight! No one had hired us, exactly, but given our success rate with missing-pet cases, we felt we could be of use. For key details we relied on Angie's neighbor Beverly Bunch, who works at the gardens and agreed to give us access to the crime scene. We didn't find much. What evidence we did find, we went over repeatedly with a fine-tooth comb, and still no leads, no suspects. The most we had was a tentative criminal profile: the perp was smart and skilled with a butterfly net. Which could be a lot of people. To narrow it down, we speculated that our suspect likely had a scientific or business interest in butterflies.

I thanked the chief and moved along, stopping at a food stand for a cup of ice water. Since I was there, I got some chocolate ice cream too, then, already cooler and more comfortable, I strolled toward Arts and Crafts. Ahead, a throng of people gathered around a booth. I took a few bites of my ice cream and joined them, wondering what the excitement was about. In the center of the throng, a brawny lumberjack type was ripping into a hunk of log with a chainsaw, slicing off one chunk of woodflesh after another. When he'd hacked out a rough shape, he became more delicate with the saw, his movements yielding curves and textured details; before long, the log was transformed into an owl. I was impressed. You'd never know by looking at him that this big, burly man was an inspired and skillful *artiste*.

My ice cream was melting down my hand. I chomped through the cone and licked the sticky chocolate from my palm.

"Is that Margaret? Margaret Worms?"

Why, yes! That *is* me.

At this point you may be wondering who exactly "me" is. Well, I'll tell you. My name is Margaret. Margaret Worms. I've just turned twelve and I'm about to enter the seventh grade at Chesterfield Middle School. I live in lovely old Chesterfield, Virginia, in a newish neighborhood called Shady

Bluff. Upon first glance, Shady Bluff is just about as normal as it gets. But peel up any corner and you'll quickly find that, under the surface, strange things are constantly happening. Weird things. Wondersome things. Unnerving, upsetting, alarming things that raise all sorts of troublesome questions. That's where the GCSA comes in.

I'm big and tall for my age, which makes sense because my dad's six feet six and has to watch his head wherever he goes. Dad works for a regional grocery chain, so companies send him an endless supply of products in the hopes that he'll sell them in his stores, meaning every few weeks he brings home big boxes full of trial items like pretzel M&M's and lime-dusted tortilla chips, or seasonal candies a season in advance—Halloween Oreos in June, the newest Cadbury egg flavor just in time for Valentine's Day. That's why, when GCSA meets at Angie's house, I'm the one who supplies all the snacks.

As for my mom, she's a stay-at-home mom. She cooks and cleans and irons and does all our laundry and shopping. Mom is pleasantly plump and so obnoxiously friendly that completing a basic transaction at the mall can take forever. Good thing she mostly stays home!

Then there's my older brother, Brian, who seems to get in more and more trouble as he grows up. Lately it seems like every other day he does something wrong, like drinking and driving, or skipping school or work. I don't understand what his problem is. As for me, I'm no trouble at all. In fact, I'm dedicating my life to stopping trouble—that is, crime.

And *that* brings me to the most important of my biographical details. You know Girls Can Solve Anything, the detective club I mentioned? Well, it was my idea, and I'm the president and head detective.

More on all that in a bit.

I spun around, caught. "Mrs. Stillwater!" I exclaimed, excited to see my sixth-grade science teacher, one of my favorites from last year. She let us examine all sorts of interesting organisms, including a worm, a fern, and a crawfish. Used to seeing her in a lab coat, I was taken aback by her unteacherly appearance that afternoon. Her sleeveless shirt revealed chunky, doughy arms; her khaki shorts bunched up unflatteringly. But there was something else: a strange iridescent glimmer to her pale skin, reminiscent of a layer of mica.

Mrs. Stillwater smiled down at me, her eyes magnified by thick glasses. They seemed more bulbous than usual. It was probably the heat . . . These *were* mirage conditions. "Perfect day for ice cream," she said.

I grinned sheepishly and wiped my hand on my shorts. "We biked over here," I said, anxious to explain I'd been exercising. "Janet's in the pageant."

"Ah! Wonderful. Tell her to break a leg. And be sure to stop by the Flowers competition. I have a number of lovelies on display."

"Neat," I said, curious. I hadn't realized Mrs. Stillwater nursed plants. But I had never run into her outside of school and there was no reason I would know anything of her private life. "I will. I was just about to head over there now."

"Well, I won't keep you. How nice it was to run into you, Margaret. Enjoy the fair. And this last weekend of summer."

School started on Tuesday. I groaned dramatically, though in fact I was looking forward to it. "Don't remind me."

She chuckled. As she turned to go, I noticed an ugly bulge of veins on the back of her right leg. It looked painful. I sucked down the rest of my ice water and tossed my trash in a bin.

The Arts and Crafts tent wasn't a tent so much as a large rectangular building made of sheet metal. It housed not only the Arts and Crafts exhibits but all of Canned Foods and Vegetables, Breads and Pies, and Flowers. When I stepped inside, I immediately knew what sector it was by the bakery smell. The array of shapely breads and glazed pies tantalized my senses. I couldn't imagine sampling them all but, boy, did I want to. What a dream job *that* would be, tasting so many delectable treats. But how would one judge them? We all have different taste buds, after all, and qualities such as appearance and flavor, texture and density, are all largely subjective. No, no, I could never serve as a judge. I preferred evidence. Hard facts. The science of deduction. Though I suppose a sleuth never *can* get away from judgment. To ascertain what is and is not evidence, to identify and interpret a clue, to construct a criminal profile: these are judgment calls. When you really think about it, we make judgments all the time. To bike or to walk? Judgment call. To read or to go to the pool, where I would be mockingly called Miss Margarine by Will Warner? Another judgment. We are all judges, I thought, and congratulated myself on the thought.

Canned Foods and Vegetables was up ahead past the Flowers section, which gave off its own heady perfume. I made my way slowly through the exhibits, looking for Mrs. Stillwater's flowers. As I toured the rows of glass vases, I noticed something very strange. In nearly every category, there was a flower that far surpassed the others: whether in size, extravagance, vividness of color, or all of the above. It was as though, for each category, someone had produced a superspecimen. Take, for example, the chrysanthemums. The most common hues among them were lavender and white, a few pale orange, some pink. All rather lush. But one stood out above the rest: a nearly neon, white-green bloom that was twice the size of the others in both height and petal span. And on the next table stood an astounding rose that boasted obscenely red petals, jurassic in size and thickness. Both flowers, I learned through reading, had been submitted by our very own Mrs. Adrienne Stillwater, as had the other superspecimens. Well! Apparently our humble science teacher had been hiding a brilliant green thumb. I suspected her talents went far beyond middle-school education. What else might she have been keeping from us?

Last came the potted plants, and I identified Mrs. Stillwater's exhibit at once. Her begonias burst from the pot with vigor and bounce, bright and cheerful and a little bit arrogant too, as though they knew very well they had won. The petals seemed pleasantly velvety and I compulsively shot out my hand. Like velour. Remarkable. In the soil, a shock of blue caught my eye. I hovered over it, wishing I'd thought to pack a magnifying glass; a sleuth should always be prepared. There, in the dirt, was what appeared to be a fragment of a butterfly wing. And not just any butterfly. I felt sure it bore the distinctive markings of the blue morpho, a rare exotic butterfly—and one of the four stolen species.

CHAPTER 2

"Hi, Ms. Stern," I said. "I'm looking for Angie."

Angie's mother stood before a metal shelving unit with a clipboard in one hand and a jar of pickles in the other. "Oh, hello, Margaret. She's around here somewhere. This one has a rusty lid," she added to herself. "I think I'll have to disqualify it." She consulted her clipboard and made a note.

Angie popped up behind a pyramid of canned beets. "Hi, Margaret! Mom, can I take a break? Janet's pageant is starting soon." Her thick hair was in a loose ponytail with strands framing her face, and her expression was cheerful as always. You'd never know she was dealing with the devastation of her parents' divorce.

Angie Stern lives three cul-de-sacs away, and we've been best friends since third grade. We even look alike. We're both tall and stocky, with brown hair that falls past our shoulders. But I suppose such similarities are superficial, really. I'm pale and soft where Angie is tan and muscly. Angie loves sports and running around, while I'm more of an indoor person. I prefer reading and writing and thinking a lot, though I have sometimes pretended to like sports so I can spend more time with Angie.

Ms. Stern nodded absentmindedly. "Be back by six, all right? I'll need your help with the judges." She lifted another jar. "And this one has a name on it. Sorry, *Betty*, but you're going to have to be disqualified."

I wondered if talking to herself was a habit formed in the wake of her marriage falling apart. Angie had broken the news to us in July (see GCSA #3: Angie's Bug Secret), and I still had a hard time believing it. The Sterns always seemed like one big, happy, perfect family. Angie is one of five kids: she has two older brothers, Luke and John; an adopted sister, Grace, who was born in Korea; and a younger brother, Matty, the baby of the family. Angie's parents are very Christian and believe in strong family values, which seems to be shorthand for rules like no short-shorts or *Aladdin*. But apparently that didn't mean they had to take their marriage vows seriously. It was a bit hypocritical, if you asked me. At least the separation seemed cordial.

She gave her mom a quick side hug and joined me at the front of Canned Foods.

"You'll never believe it," I told her. "I think I've found a clue."

When I showed her the butterfly wing in Mrs. Stillwater's begonias, Angie's mouth formed an O. "The blue morpho."

"I thought so too!" I said excitedly. There was really no mistaking its distinctive color and markings. "But what would Mrs. Stillwater want with it? Or the other butterflies?"

"I don't know," Angie said. "But she fits the profile. She's smart and may have a scientific or business interest in butterflies."

"She does know a lot about organisms. Hard to say, but I bet she's good with a net."

"Do you think she's trying to breed them?"

"That's one possibility." In our research we'd learned how highly valued rare butterflies could be. They were sometimes stolen or illegally bred for jewelry, medicinal purposes, or wall decorations. That's why there were federal regulations to prevent certain species from living outside their natural habitats or approved exhibitions, such as the show at the Chesterfield Botanical Gardens.

As hard as I tried, I couldn't imagine Mrs. Stillwater stealing butterflies for such purposes. Then again, there was a lot I didn't know about her. I was stumped. "Let's keep thinking. We'd better get to the pageant. Jina's probably wondering where we are."

If indeed Mrs. Stillwater had stolen the specimens, what could she be up to? I didn't know. But I was determined to find out.

"Helloooo." Jina nudged me. "Now's the time to clap."

"Sorry." I was doing my best to pay attention to the onstage proceedings, but I was preoccupied by our new evidence. I put my hands together as Janet stepped onto the stage and began buzzing around in her "fun-wear" outfit, a homemade and surprisingly fashionable bumblebee costume. A surprising choice, though I knew goldenrod was Janet's favorite color. I guess she was "bee-ing" creative (ha!).

"I came up with this concept," Jina whispered proudly. "I thought it would support what she says about conservation in the interview part." Conservation? Right. I had never known Janet to express any interest in environmental issues and in fact could recall numerous occasions when I had seen her toss perfectly recyclable soda cans in the trash. Wisely I said nothing. My role here was as supportive friend.

Bumblebees, of course, are another important pollinator, and I couldn't help but turn my thoughts back to the case. If Mrs. Stillwater were our culprit, did her theft have something to do with pollination? Why would exotic butterflies like the blue morpho produce such flamboyant flowers? Were their pollination capabilities more effective than native butterflies such as the monarch? Mrs. Stillwater's flowers were verging on mutant in their extravagance; it was as though they were on steroids.

And then there was the matter of Mrs. Stillwater's glimmering skin and the startling bulbousness of her eyes as they blinked behind her glasses. I would keep those details to myself, I decided. It was possible I was suffering from heatstroke. I would suggest Angie or Jina speak to Mrs. Stillwater at school this week, see if they noticed anything different about her. I clapped politely for Janet, wishing the pageant would end so we could strategize.

Gretchen's name was called next. She slunk onstage in

a dark trench coat, her blond waves loose under a fedora. Holding what looked like an actual magnifying glass, she pretended to examine the stage curtain and floor. I frowned and exchanged glances with Angie and Jina, unsure what to make of her girl-detective shtick. Was Gretchen McGann making fun of us?

I hoped not, but I didn't know her well enough to be sure.

What I knew: Gretchen had moved to Chesterfield from DC a few months ago; she'd met Jina and Janet at the pool and they'd become fast friends. Her mother had died when Gretchen was a child, and her father was raising her solo. A busy business executive, Mr. McGann treated Gretchen like an adult who could take care of herself. And she could, for the most part. She seemed very independent. Gretchen lived one neighborhood away and was over at the Castles' pretty much all the time. Somehow she managed to be friends with both Jina and Janet, and she often helped them watch Darryl, the twins' younger brother, who has special needs.

I also knew that Janet thought our club was stupid, but of course she would: it meant Jina was no longer at her beck and call (see GCSA #2: Jina's Double Trouble). But despite Janet's exaggerated eye rolls and annoyed sighs, Gretchen had always seemed interested in hearing what GCSA was up to. Maybe this whole time she'd been gathering information in order to mock us publicly.

Whoa. Rein it in, Margaret. Obviously Gretchen McGann wasn't mocking us. Hers was an earnest fun-wear performance. I was being paranoid.

But if she wasn't making fun of us, what *was* she doing?

Onstage, Gretchen pretended to locate something behind an amp. She presented the object to the audience: a knife! We watched as she stabbed herself theatrically (don't worry:

the knife was fake, a prop), then shrugged off the trench coat to reveal a slinky red dress. Propping up one foot on top of the amp, she lifted the skirt of her dress over one knee and tucked the knife into a holster buckled around her thigh. She straightened and waltzed across stage, stopping midstride to light a pretend-cigarette. Then the song and the skit were over.

"Wow," Angie enthused, applauding animatedly. "That was incredible."

Jina clapped grudgingly. "Pretty good. Janet's was better."

I kept my opinions to myself. Gretchen's fun-wear routine was certainly adventurous and, as such, would not do her any favors in the competition. I eyed the three judges, whose disapproving frowns confirmed my assessment.

Next, the contestants paraded across the stage in modest evening wear, featuring shoulder ruffles and brocaded torsos. In their pastel hues, they looked not unlike flowers, especially Janet, who, in an off-the-shoulder lavender dress, could easily have been a chrysanthemum. But not a super-chrysanthemum. Gretchen stepped out in the same red dress, the trench coat slung over her shoulder. Wow. Gretchen McGann was cool. And she looked, well, hot. If I can say that. I don't know if I can.

Neither of them won. A boring fifth grader named Trisha Church took the tiara and waved boringly. I almost yawned. Janet came off the stage scowling.

"You moved up a spot," said Mrs. Castle soothingly as Mr. Castle filled Janet's arms with a giant bouquet.

"I should have been first," Janet grumbled.

"You were robbed," said Jina. "Again."

"I made my own bumblebee costume! I bedazzled it myself!" Mrs. Castle shushed her, and Janet lowered her voice. "She was a *princess*. Like, the most obvious fun-wear ever."

"You were terrific," I added sincerely. "You were so much more fun to watch than that Trisha girl." Janet stared at me blankly. "And prettier," I added.

"I know!" Janet said, glowering.

"So were you," I said to Gretchen before I could stop myself. I blushed. But it was true. Janet and Gretchen were both much more interesting in their looks and more original in their concepts than boring old Trisha Church. If that's not what the judges were looking for, well, they had bad criteria.

Gretchen smiled. "Did you like the detective look?"

I searched for the best description. "It was very . . . innovative. And theatrical."

"I'm a big fan of noir," she said, "but the genre is so sexist, so I thought, wouldn't it be cool to be, like, both the detective and the femme fatale at once?"

"Cool," I said coolly, annoyed that I hadn't figured out the underlying concept myself. "I love that idea."

"Thanks. It was a lot of fun to pull off."

"You made sleuthing look hot," Angie said approvingly.

"Detective work isn't hot," I said sharply, though I didn't disagree with Angie's comment. "It's serious. We ought to know." I didn't mean to be rude, but I wanted Gretchen to respect what we did. Real detectives had nothing to do with either hard-boiled toughs or sultry sirens. We weren't tropes. We were bona fide gumshoes, legit private eyes, true girl detectives with active investigations.

"I know." Gretchen bit her lower lip. "And I have a ton of admiration for the work you do in GCSA. I was actually wondering . . ." She trailed off as her dad jogged up, sweating through his dress shirt. He had obviously come straight from work. "Did I miss it?" he said breathlessly. "Did I miss the whole thing? Did you win? Where's your tiara? You look beautiful. I'm so proud."

Speaking of active investigations: "We have to tell Jina what we found," I whispered to Angie. We made eye contact with Jina until she got the hint and came over.

"No way," she said after we explained about the flowers and the butterfly wing. "Show me."

We turned to go. "Wait," I said. "I know what we need." I tapped Gretchen's shoulder. Her dad was striking up a conversation with Mr. Castle.

"Do you think we could borrow your magnifying glass?"

"Sure." Gretchen fished it out of the pocket of her folded-up trench coat. "GCSA business, I presume?" She winked as she handed over the prop. "Think I could tag along?" She beamed her smile like a weapon.

Angie grinned with what seemed like excitement. Jina shrugged affably.

I surveyed the situation.

Did Gretchen McGann want to join our club? Did Angie and Jina *want* Gretchen McGann to join our club?

What did I want? As president and head detective, I was protective of the club and reasonably concerned about the threat of outsiders. It was true that Gretchen *seemed* all right—creative, forward-thinking, and invested in mysteries—but she was still that: an outsider, about whom we knew little. And—a terrible fear crept up and whispered softly, slitheringly in my ear—Gretchen was cool. What if she was *too cool* and my friends decided they liked her more than they liked me? What if they all banded together to push me— a stickler for rules, responsibility, and research ("the three R's," I called them)—out? The prospect was unstomachable.

Yet, as I played out the possibilities, I also found myself wondering what the group might be like joined by Gretchen's fresh energies. I held the magnifying glass to my eye and scrutinized her, an act that I knew would seem playful but that I meant very seriously. Under the fierceness of my gaze, Gretchen's sure smile wobbled and I saw it—there, then not there: the uncertainty, the hope, the clot of lipstick on her lower teeth. She was a girl between worlds like the rest of us. And, I supposed, inviting her to look at one piece of evidence did not have to mean inviting her into the club. I pocketed the magnifying glass. "Fine by me," I decided. "Come on."

CHAPTER 3

"I hereby call this meeting of Girls Can Solve Anything to order." I rapped the edge of Gretchen's magnifying glass on Angie's desk with ceremony, silencing my friends' excited chatter. It was our usual meeting day and time, Tuesday at 5:30 p.m., but the energy was more vibrant that day: in part because Gretchen was joining us as a trial member, in part because we were exhilarated from our first day back at school. Seventh grade promised to be a good year. No more sixth-grade cluelessness: in this middle year of middle school, we knew the ropes well enough without needing to know everything. We were comfortable. And we had an exciting lead on an active case.

But I'm getting ahead of myself. As I've mentioned, GCSA was my idea, but it was a bad idea at first. What I mean is, the original idea was terrible, lousy, though it seemed like a great one at the time. Eventually we figured that out and revised it into something brilliant.

It all started months ago, at the end of sixth grade. I was lounging on the futon in the sunroom with our cat Egor curled against my calves, reading the next volume in my favorite series, The Baby-Sitters Club. Lately I had been spending more and more of my afternoons in this position. I would plow through my pile of library books, occasionally reading aloud to Egor. This was all very well and good, but I was beginning to miss my friends, who were surely at the pool . . . again. The pool, the pool . . . I disliked it. I had spent countless summers at the Chesterfield Community Pool and what had they given me? Earclogs and sunburns. Discomfort when I could have been reading. I knew exactly what I was missing, and I didn't miss it at all: The sun searing my shoulders through my T-shirt as Angie and Jina baked and bronzed, luxuriating. The hard plastic slats of the beach chair biting into my skin. If I tried to pass the time with a book the pages would blaze white and dizzying, unreadable. To cool off, I'd suck in my gut and rearrange the drape of my giant T-shirt before heading toward the deep end, and plunging in and out of sight before Will Warner could call me Miss Margarine, which I guess was supposed to remind me I'm fat, although margarine is actually *lower* in fat than butter is. That's the whole point of margarine. But as I was saying: Then back to the beach chair, the sun . . .

No more! I'd much rather stay home.

So that's where I was, eating up several books a day. And while I did value my alone time, I was starting to get a bit lonesome. Was this my future? Me, myself, and my rich imagination? I wanted to be in a club, I thought. A Baby-Sitters Club. And then I sat upright in the futon and thought, Why not? I called Angie, and then I called Jina.

Neither were home, of course, being together at the pool. When they called me back later, I pitched my idea. They were in.

And so the Shady Bluff Baby-Sitters Club was born.

I had it all figured out. We would follow the original BSC's example with minor tweaks. We'd make flyers, meet at Angie's house (her family has two phone lines) to take calls once a week, on Tuesdays from 5:30 p.m. to 6:30 p.m. (the BSC's three meetings a week were excessive, I thought). We would keep a club notebook for calendars, meeting notes, and job reports. We would make some real money and become closer than ever by eating snacks, trading tips, and laughing a lot.

It would have worked well except for one small detail: I'm a lousy babysitter. I was only in it for the club.

The SBBSC didn't last long. My very first client, Mrs. Morgan, turned out to be harboring a terrible secret. I knew at once that something was strange from the children's dreary drowsiness. Jacob and Harriet, ages five and six, moved around like joyless zombies, which I admit to at first appreciating, as it did make my job rather easy. But as the evening wore on, I began to have misgivings. The master bedroom was locked (I was snooping), and a hall closet was filled with hanging crucifixes. Mrs. Morgan had instructed me to douse the children's food with a murky elixir that I quickly surmised was a drug. Then there was the dog, Bob, an old cocker spaniel with strange, undoglike qualities. His whining sounded almost human. As I was measuring out the elixir for the children's stew, he jumped up and knocked the spoon from my hand. Okay, Bob. I got a new spoon. He backed up, focused intently, and jerked his head to the left. The elixir went flying at the wall. Later, when I grabbed my bike to leave, I looked up and saw, in the window of the locked bedroom, the shadow of a woman.

I consulted with Jina and Angie. We did some research into the Morgans, came up with a working theory, and broke in that very same night. It turned out Mrs. Morgan had been keeping her adult daughter Sadie locked in the master bedroom while taking charge of Sadie's two children. A sad story: Sadie had grown up with telekinetic powers but had learned to repress them through prayer (or at least *act* like she had). She left home in her late teens, had premarital sex (bad), then got pregnant (the worst). As soon as it became clear that the children had "gifts," her cowardly boyfriend abandoned her. Sadie returned home, where her mother separated her from her children and drugged them all, with the aim of dulling their powers. It worked until Sadie stopped eating, thereby avoiding being drugged, so she could teach herself how to astrally project into Bob, through whom she could keep an eye on the children. It was through Bob that she had attempted to communicate with me. Well, thanks to our interventions, Sadie is now reunited with her children and Mrs. Morgan is safely behind bars.

Angie, Jina, and I decided we enjoyed detective work—certainly much more than babysitting. We disbanded the Shady Bluff Baby-Sitters Club. In its stead, Girls Can Solve Anything was born.

We'd solved three cases so far and were already becoming known and respected around the neighborhood. But The Case of the Stolen Specimens had confounded us. Until now . . .

I shared my findings first. I had poked my head into Mrs. Stillwater's sixth-grade science classroom before lunch and found nothing incriminating. "Hi, hello?" It was empty, a relief. If she showed up unexpectedly, I would tell her I wanted to congratulate her on her flowers. She had won every contest she entered.

Keeping one eye on the door, I conducted a search of the lab cabinets. The shelves of beakers and pipettes, goggles and neatly folded lab coats were just as I remembered them. Nothing out of the ordinary. The storage room was unlocked, and on the shelves I found the usual. A familiar Styrofoam solar-system mobile, all tangled up. The photosynthesis poster Mrs. Stillwater had taped to the board for our Plants and Cells unit. Markers and construction paper. No evidence of butterflies or superflowers as far as I could tell. But I did detect a notebook on the counter, open to pages with numbers and equations and—I leaned in to see—a detailed drawing of an odd-looking butterfly . . . person. Hmm. Highly peculiar.

I was about to make a pencil rubbing of the drawing when I heard whistling. Shoot. I couldn't very well hide out here until she left again: that could take hours, and I needed to eat my lunch. I cleared my throat and announced myself.

"So I congratulated her on her plants and we had a nice chat," I told my friends. "She mentioned her greenhouse and told me I ought to stop by and see it sometime." Her mouth had twitched when she said that, and I wondered if she regretted the invitation. "I don't *think* she was suspicious."

"A greenhouse . . ." Gretchen said. "She must be using it as a private lab for some kind of illegal experiment. We have to check it out."

But Gretchen was getting ahead of us. GCSA meetings followed a set agenda, and we hadn't yet reached the brainstorming stage.

"Angie?" I prompted, ignoring Gretchen, who would learn.

"Success!" She pulled out a piece of paper. "I've got the address right here." Angie was an office aide and had looked up Mrs. Stillwater's home address in the school database.

"Nice," Jina cheered. "Go Angie."

"That's in my neighborhood," Gretchen said. "I think." She opened a baggie of tiny carrots and passed them around. Gretchen had cut out sweets in solidarity with Janet ahead of the pageant, and she had turned up her nose at the bag of Christmas-colored M&Ms I'd brought. Already, I fretted, the culture of our club was shifting. Angie and Jina both took carrots politely. I passed.

"Let's review the facts," I suggested, for everyone's benefit as much as for Gretchen's—we mustn't forget any details. Angie, Jina, and I traded off to outline the case: On the twentieth of July, eight butterflies and four cocoons had gone missing, presumed stolen, from the Philip-Morris Conservatory at the Chesterfield County Botanical Gardens. The stolen specimens represented four rare species in both cocoon and adult stages: the great purple hairstreak (*Atlides halesus*), the red-bordered pixie (*Melanis pixe*), the question mark (*Polygonia interrogationis*), and the giant blue morpho (*Morpho didius*). Since many other rare butterflies had been left untouched, we suspected something linked the stolen species—some shared quality we had yet to uncover.

"Let's look through our notes again," Jina said, and spread our file on the floor. For the past month we had been compiling Internet and library research on the stolen species, printing out or making copies of whatever we found.

"Hmm," Gretchen said, poring over our notes. "Could it have something to do with how they pollinate?"

"Possibly," I said, thinking of Mrs. Stillwater's flowers.

"Or it could be related to color. These all have bright

splashes of color on their wings," she said. "Or the contrast between the upper and lower wing patterns. Do all butterflies have that?"

"Yep," Jina answered. "We did some research and most butterflies do. The topside is usually a lot prettier. The underside is kind of like camouflage, for when a butterfly is at rest."

"Oh," said Gretchen. "Maybe they were just the only butterflies she could catch."

Of course we had already considered these possibilities, but it was good to have fresh eyes, and Gretchen was asking the right questions. I was pleased with her contributions.

"So what next?" Angie asked.

"We break into her greenhouse," Gretchen said. "Right?"

"Bingo. But we'll need to do a stakeout first," I said. "Get a sense of her comings and goings. Gather evidence. Build a case against her. We need to be sure." The others nodded. "Who's free tomorrow?"

Jina had to watch Darryl. Angie was having dinner at her dad's. That left Gretchen and me. We'd never spent time alone before, and the idea made me queasy. She flashed me a dazzling smile. I gulped.

CHAPTER 4

Mrs. Stillwater lived three cul-de-sacs behind Gretchen in a beige home with vinyl siding. Her prize-winning begonias and chrysanthemums were displayed prominently in her front yard. Parked in the driveway: a Dodge van, presumably hers. We were in luck, as next door was an unfinished house, the perfect spot for a stakeout. We left our bikes in the open garage and strolled inside, just two twelve-year-old girls exploring a half-finished home. "Careful," I cautioned Gretchen. "Don't step on any nails." The last time I'd visited a construction site, I'd caught one in my arch (see GCSA #2: Jina's Double Trouble).

The stairs had no railing but were firm beneath our feet. We climbed to the second floor, where we found a suitable window frame with a perfect view of not just Mrs. Stillwater's side door and van—we would be able to see when she left—but also the large greenhouse in the backyard.

We knelt, exchanging shy grins. But as we settled down to wait the evening out, that same nervousness crept up on me again. Gretchen and I would have a lot of time to pass. Alone. Together.

"It's too bad Angie and Jina aren't here," she said, as if reading my mind. I wondered if she was disappointed it was me she was with, not them.

"Yeah," I said. "Too bad." I racked my brain for an interesting remark, but I was tongue-tied, officially. My *too bad* hung in the air, insipid and cloying. Then my stomach spoke for me. I hadn't had my afternoon snack.

"Hungry?" Gretchen said. "I have Nutri-Grains." She rummaged around in her purple backpack and pulled out two strawberry cereal bars.

We sat there a long while, staring dully out the window and listening to each other's mastications. Her chewing was spittier than mine. My swallows were louder. We made eye contact and dropped it, three times. Finally we both blurted out inquiries at once.

"Why butterflies?"

"Why cocoons?"

"Butterflies are fascinating creatures," Gretchen recited, answering her own question, "because during the chrysalis phase, all of their insides break down into a molten sludge made up of imaginal cells, which can turn into any new cell. Then they reconstitute themselves and make a whole new body. It's a miraculous transformation."

"You're a walking encyclopedia." I laughed, then, embarrassed by my corniness, abruptly looked away. But what she said only further confirmed my hunch about our suspect.

At the creaking of a door outside, we snapped to attention. There she was, Mrs. Stillwater, in frumpy shorts somehow both baggy and too tight at the waist. What was that in her hand? I pulled out my mini-binoculars. It was a key! Which she used to unlock the greenhouse door. When she opened it, out flew an unusually large butterfly with flashing blue wings—"The blue morpho," I breathed. It seemed to fly right into my binocular lenses. I dropped them and fell back with a clatter. Holding my breath, I resumed position. Mrs. Stillwater had stilled and appeared to be listening. Not for long. Quickly she grabbed a large net hanging by the door and swung it in a wide, efficient circle to capture the slow-moving fugitive. (Skilled with a net: check.) Through the half-open door, I could see whole rows of superflowers, and a few monster butterflies drifting through the air.

Mrs. Stillwater drew the morpho inside and shut the door. Through the opaque greenhouse walls, I could see her shadow bend down and then—disappear. "Possible trapdoor," I observed and passed Gretchen the binoculars. She nodded pensively. I checked my watch: 4:30 p.m.

When she emerged from the greenhouse at 4:52, Mrs. Stillwater was trembling and twitching. Very odd. She peered around her, looking every which way, before locking the greenhouse and slipping in through the side door of her home.

"Has Mrs. Stillwater always looked like . . . that?" Gretchen whispered.

"Like what?"

"It's just . . . her eyes. They seem awfully big, don't they?"

"I noticed that at school. No, something's different about her."

"It's like they're bulging out of her face. Almost like an insect," Gretchen mused. "Like a . . . a . . ."

We exchanged an excited glance. " . . . butterfly!" we finished simultaneously, and let it sink in, our sleuth minds whirring away.

"She must be conducting some sort of experiment," Gretchen said. "To . . . become a butterfly herself?"

"You may be right. But why?"

"Maybe she wants to learn how to fly," Gretchen said, but I could tell she wasn't convinced.

"No, that doesn't seem right," I said. "Let's keep thinking."

To be honest, I had already figured it out. Mrs. Stillwater had stolen the specimens in order to experiment with their DNA. My own research, conducted earlier that afternoon at the new library with the help of Mr. Dillinger, revealed our humble Mrs. Stillwater's impressive PhD in bioengineering. I learned that her former research team had been nominated for a major scientific award, but by that point she had already left research to teach. In a profile for the local newspaper, she claimed that her lab—in fact, the entire field of bioengineering—was sexist.

I was dubious. I thought maybe she was just fat, which *can* make a remarkable difference in how people treat you.

It was all coming together. The superflowers were a happy accident, I believed, and the actual experiment far more complex and horrifying. I suspected Mrs. Stillwater was orchestrating this criminal operation in order to manufacture a new body. I suspected she was conducting research to understand how cocoons transformed into butterflies ... so that she could use their technology to transform herself. The idea took my breath away. I envied Mrs. Stillwater's scientific ingenuity. I would have given anything to cocoon myself up and be refashioned as—well, I didn't know what exactly. But people don't just walk around remaking their bodies. There are laws. She was breaking them.

Eventually we left. There was nothing to do now but confront her, for which we'd need GCSA in full force.

"Great job tonight, Gretchen," I said at the end of her driveway.

"Thanks! You too." She leaned toward me to give me a high ten.

But it wasn't a regular high ten. She bent her fingers over mine. It was like we were holding hands but at eye level. A curious position. And I felt, in my stomach, the flutterings of what felt, uncomfortably, like butterflies.

CHAPTER 5

The next day we met at Gretchen's house at dusk. We had changed into our stealth outfits (dark clothing, soft-soled sneakers, hair tucked into ball caps) and clipped on our customized GCSA fanny packs, each with a penlight and its own special tools: invisible ink kit and emergency flare (Angie); disposable camera and measuring tape (Jina); binoculars, face mask, clothesline, and pocketknife (me). Since Gretchen didn't have a fanny pack, I stored her magnifying glass in mine.

Night had settled. It was time. We rode our bikes silently in single file to Mrs. Stillwater's cul-de-sac, where we dropped them in the ditch of the next-door lot. Then we skulked toward her house and into the backyard, keeping to the grass to avoid the alerting crunch of driveway gravel.

The greenhouse door was closed, but the light inside was on. I peeked through the foggy plastic and caught no movement. No hulking Mrs. Stillwater–like shapes. Nothing. Angie jiggled the doorknob. Locked.

I cupped my ear against the wall and heard faint music. Classical. "Yep. She's in there," I whispered. "Probably underground." If indeed there was a trapdoor.

Angie removed the two bobby pins she kept tucked under her ponytail at all times. She had learned to pick locks after spending a few weekends at her dad's new home, an old farmhouse with doors that seemed to lock of their own accord. At first we'd thought it was the wind, but our investigation revealed the house to be haunted by the ghost of a forgotten farmwife who was attempting to herd Angie to secret passages leading to her skeleton (see GCSA #3: Angie's Bug Secret). That's where all the bugs were coming from (not the skeleton; the secret passages). Angie hates bugs.

While Angie worried the lock, I held my ear to the door and listened for sounds of movement. Nothing. A faint ripple of diabolical laughter.

And we were in.

A giant butterfly floated toward us, big as my head. "The great purple hairstreak," I said softly. I counted two dozen butterflies drifting from flower to flower—several times more than had been reported stolen.

"Ew," Angie breathed. "I can't do this."

"You can," I urged, surprised to learn that her bugphobia extended to butterflies, arguably the least buggy of bugs. "Girls can do anything." Angie gritted her teeth and gave a determined jerk of the head. "But if you need to leave, we understand."

We heard a malicious snort from below us. "You're mine, you pathetic grub. Mine!" Yes, there it was, the trapdoor, beside a lattice of creeping roses. Open.

"She's gone nuts," Jina observed.

"Start taking photos," I whispered. "We'll need evidence." Jina pulled out her disposable camera and went to work capturing every square inch of the greenhouse.

I approached the trapdoor, motioning for Angie and Gretchen to follow. We descended into what appeared to be a sophisticated and well-funded lab. On one counter I observed a set of petri dishes and syringes. A shiny, imposing microscope on another, next to a whirring centrifuge. Syringes and bloody scalpels. Caterpillars pinned to trays for dissection. An aquarium that seemed to be some sort of incubator for giant pupating cocoons. A closer look revealed the cocoons to be wetly pulsating. Taped to the walls were diagrams of the same unsettling butterfly person I had seen in the notebook. We glanced at one another with horror. What sort of evil genius was this?

And there she was: Mrs. Stillwater. Humming on a stool with her back to us, with one hand she was wrestling an enormous butterfly. With the other she brandished a fat syringe that she was attempting to plunge into the butterfly's thorax.

"Mrs. Adrienne Stillwater!" I shouted.

She shrieked and let go of the insect. It flapped toward us, its abdomen grotesquely furry. A wing brushed Angie's face. "Yaaah!" She flung her hands around her head and raced up the steps, leaving Gretchen and me alone to confront the treacherous teacher.

"What the— Where did you girls come from?"

"We know what you're up to," Gretchen accused.

"And we know why," I added. "You're combining human and butterfly DNA to develop your own metamorphic technology. You want to change your whole body."

"Very impressive, girls," Mrs. Stillwater said, standing up. Her tongue slipped out, long and thin and black. No longer a tongue but a proboscis, I realized, shuddering. "You've found me out. Now what are you going to do about it?" Her experiment was well underway. Her neck and upper arms had taken on a husk-like texture, and her eyes had traveled toward her cheeks, where they bulged out alarmingly.

Gretchen and I held our ground. "You should be ashamed, Mrs. Stillwater," I said.

"Of what?" She leered at us. "Of finally taking control of my life after years of passively waiting?" Around her unloosed proboscis, she lisped. "Of actually doing original science instead of teaching *earthworm dissection* to ungrateful nitwits year after year?" She reeled in her new tongue and swirled it awkwardly around the inside of her mouth, which clearly did not have the space for it.

"I was grateful!" I protested, hurt. "I loved your class."

Mrs. Stillwater's expression softened. "Really?"

I nodded vehemently. It was true. "I learned so much. And I really enjoyed myself." I'm not sure I was convincing given the circumstances. But she seemed to be listening.

"I'm new," Gretchen chimed in, "but I've heard a ton about how amazing your class was. How amazing you are. I wish I could have taken it. I love science. And scientific experiments. This one is ingenious."

She was very compelling. Mrs. Stillwater's bulbous eyes moistened. I gave Gretchen an appreciative nod. We had successfully disarmed our perp. Now it was time to get down to business.

"Why do you want a new body, Mrs. Stillwater?" I demanded.

"Well, Margaret." She slumped on her stool and looked me over critically. "Wouldn't you?"

I reddened. I suspected she was calling me fat. "Answer the question."

Antenna nubs wiggled on her forehead. "Here's a better question. What's wrong with using science to get one?"

"What's wrong with it?" I echoed. "You're becoming a bug."

"Scientific progress succeeds through trial and error. Have I taught you nothing?"

"This isn't science. It's fantasy."

"Ah-ah-ah." She clicked softly and shook her head. "You're smarter than this." She sloped her thick body toward me, expressing a smell like decaying lettuce. I stepped back and bumped into Gretchen, who steadied me with two hands.

"We all use technology to alter our bodies, Margaret." Mrs. Stillwater seemed to have slipped back into teacher mode. "Why should bioengineered metamorphosis be any different?"

My mind raced. "Because you're a thief. You're a pathological criminal and you need to be put behind bars."

"Margaret," Gretchen breathed into my ear. "Don't you think you're being a bit harsh?"

I glanced at her, mystified. How could she defend Mrs. Stillwater?

"She needs help. Not punishment."

I didn't understand. "She's a criminal, Gretchen."

Mrs. Stillwater reared up before us. "And a mastermind. A criminal mastermind. Take that!" She flicked her proboscis at me. Spittle flew from the wet whip. I jumped back, narrowly avoiding the slap. "And that!" She wound it back up and flicked again. I fell against Gretchen and we tumbled to the floor.

"Mrs. Stillwater!" Gretchen scolded, sitting up. "We're just girls. Are you actually resorting to violence?"

"Hrrrmph." But she retracted her weapon.

Then Jina scrambled down the steps. "We took pictures."

"What? No!" Mrs. Stillwater shouted, her volume fading to a whimper. She shook her head, and her pupils went walleyed. She shook it again and they righted themselves. She seemed to be having realizations. "Blast!" She brought a fist down on a petri dish and smashed it. Then slumped. "I give up," she whispered finally, defeated. "This has all been a foolish mistake." She touched her huskified shoulder and sighed. "I'm rotting from the outside in . . ." She straightened. "But you never know until you try. That's what science is. Experimentation. Controls, variables . . . visionary thinking. . ." She trailed off, then coughed. The decaying-lettuce smell grew stronger. "But I must accept that my experiment failed." She nodded in resignation. "I'll reverse the process and return the specimens. Just, please, whatever you do, don't tell Principal Royle."

"The principal?" I sputtered. "Try the chief of police!"

Gretchen put an arm around me. "Margaret, can't we let this one go? Seriously, look at her."

I looked. What I saw was a monster, a freak, a threat to humanity. My sympathies remained unroused. Yet strangely

I found that, more than anything else, I wanted Gretchen McGann to like me. Like, *really* like me. I nodded helplessly. "Okay."

"We won't tell anyone," Gretchen promised Mrs. Stillwater. "Let us help."

Mrs. Stillwater sniffled.

Gretchen squeezed my hand and I started to feel more of those . . . butterflies. Disconcerting and highly inappropriate. I pulled my hand away.

Then I felt a strange mass alight on my head. The question mark had landed. "Get it off me, get it off me!" I screeched. Jina came at me with a net.

"I'll have a chocolate shake." My usual.

"Fries, please." Our server left and Gretchen smiled at me from across the sticky table. "I wonder what's keeping Jina and Angie?"

We were meeting at Ward's, the local malt shop, to debrief. I grinned. I knew something she didn't. "They'll be here." I racked my brain for something interesting to say. "So. What do you think was the best moment in The Case of the Stolen Specimens?"

She pursed her lips. I suspected she thought this was part of her trial. "All of it," she said finally.

I laughed. "I still can't believe the size of those butterflies! What do you think she'll do with them?"

"Good question. No clue." Gretchen paused. "I wonder how she's doing."

I groaned. "Who cares? I still think she ought to be punished."

"I think she has been," Gretchen said. "She's probably been punished for a long time."

I was considering that notion when the door squawked open. "Sorry we're late," Jina said.

Angie followed, beaming. "We brought you something." She handed Gretchen a black fanny pack with the letters GCSA monogrammed in stealth black lettering. She and Jina had filled it with a penlight, a fingerprinting kit, and evidence bags, leaving one pocket free for Gretchen's magnifying lens.

"Welcome to the club!" Jina said.

Gretchen stared down at the kit. When she didn't reply immediately, I froze, wondering if we'd done something wrong. Finally she looked up, blinking back tears. "This is amazing. Thank you."

Jina slid into the booth next to her and gave her a warm side hug. Angie and I grinned at each other. Jina extended a hand over the table, and I placed mine on hers. Angie smacked mine playfully ("Ow!" I laughed) and Gretchen added hers to the top of the pile. "One . . . two . . . three . . ." we cheered. "Girls Can Solve Anything!"

OutKast's "ATLiens" blurts on as the car shudders back to life. Only hours ago, she had been testing out this mixtape made for Eisha, listening through and listing revision notes in her head. *Choose a different Tricky song; cut the second Tori.* She had been eager to see Eisha, who wasn't at school yesterday, hadn't yet heard Margaret's pressing updates. And she had been excited to finish this mix, themed on the topic of friendship. Arriving between Missy Elliott ft. Aaliyah's "Best Friends" and Queen's "You're My Best Friend," OutKast's "ATLiens" is among the more subtle inclusions, being not *about* best friendship per se, but rather *exemplifying* it—Big Boi and Andre 3000 having been BFFs since high school. Margaret's goal was to communicate her joy at how close she and Eisha are becoming now that they're not just school friends but also coworkers at the Coffee Beanery at the mall.

Margaret sits for a while, letting the engine warm up. Her shift is now over. How wrong she had been.

Let's recap. This morning Margaret rolls up to the counter, waves, smiles, the regular. *We missed you yesterday.* "We" meaning Margaret and Davina. *We wrote you, like, five million notes.* Eisha gives her a weak *what's up.* Margaret returns it, with sincere and literal intentions. Eisha looks tired, upset;

offers no real response. *No, really*, Margaret persists. *What's up?* Eisha shrugs, withholds. So Margaret keeps prattling. *I guess I'll give you the report now. It'll make my notes obsolete*, she says with a shrug, *but whatever. So. I'm finally IM'ing with Stephen.* She pauses, anticipating Eisha's gushing response. *Great!* Eisha chirps, unconvincingly. Margaret goes on: *I know it might not seem like a big deal, but it is, actually. It's major. A big step. Now we know he knows who I am.* Margaret clocks in, waiting for Eisha to congratulate her, to wink, to pump her for info. No such luck. *Cool*, Eisha says, and spins around to start a new pot, back turned, the end. Fine, she must be in some mood. At which point Margaret ties on her apron and asks, generously, if Eisha needs a break, at which point Eisha removes, rudely, her apron, stalks off, only to return twenty-five minutes later (ten minutes over: bad) with their manager Jamal and a giant Orange Julius, which has a million empty calories (bad), which, okay, it's not like Eisha, who burns energy so fast she's supposed to lie down after eating, needs to care, but does she need to rub it in Margaret's face? No. No, she does not. That's mean.

Even Jamal could feel the ice. *Why're you being so cold?* he said. *Let me guess. You're fighting over a guy. You're fighting over me. Am I right? I'm right. I knew it.* Eisha frisbeed a coffee lid at him. *Shut up.* Margaret smirked in solidarity but Eisha ignored her, faux-fencing with Jamal using the tiny red straws, very mature, as Margaret filled up on coffee, chatted uncomfortably with customers, and obsessively cleaned the countertops when she wasn't peeing in the cramped store bathroom. Now she's edgy and short of breath, her stomach bloated and hollow and mewling like a confused cat.

She had been excited to share OutKast with Eisha, who listens mostly to mainstream hip hop and probably doesn't know about them since, being from the South, they're off the grid of East Coast/West Coast rivalries. As such, they have more room to be weird, to spread out. In fact (she had imagined writing this out in what would have been extensive liner notes), OutKast were booed when they won Best New Artist at the 1995 Source Awards. *The South got something to say*, Andre 3000 boldly proclaimed in response, and "ATLiens" says it: raising its southern freak flag high before blasting off into outer space. The song is a study in tension, southern heat balanced against alien coolness, tightly wound flows relaxing into drawls or the reverse. And while it's true that both Big Boi and Dre can be very funny, it's also true that their comedy is a response to feeling left out. Under the snickers, the song hovers between melancholy and slow-burning rage. "ATLiens" is a song about being *made* an alien: the alienation it describes is an active process done *to* you, not some internal existential crisis. Big Boi and Dre are expressing what it feels like to be on the outside—of hip hop, of white America, of the whole human race. Margaret, ex-detective, can at least partially relate, and she had thought Eisha, second-generation Indian American from Queens, might too.

Oh well. Never mind.

She switches to the radio. No more mysteries, no more investigations. Margaret has learned her lesson. Whatever Eisha's problem is, Margaret won't be sleuthing it out of her. Eisha can use her words. Until then, no mixtape for Eisha.

She puts the car in reverse and checks the rearview mirror but doesn't *really* check it, absorbed as she is in this upset, this problem she can't understand. Her stomach blanches and she regrets, a teeny bit, not taking up Jamal's offer to get her a slice from Sbarro, but no, she's on a diet, she had said, definitely *not* something she'd normally say in front of

Eisha, around whom she's just not hungry, never hungry, and he said, *Girl, you don't need to be dieting,* to which she said *Yes, I do,* to which he said *Nuh-uh* to which she said *Ye-huh* to which he said *Nuh-uh* to which she said *Ye-huh* to which he said *I'm getting you a slice* when Eisha cut in with *Don't bother, she doesn't eat,* at which point her body rattled with heated confusion, to which she responded by gulping more coffee and escaping to the bathroom for the fifth time.

Fuck Eisha. Eisha sucks. Margaret pounds the gas and reverses.

Crunch.

She reparks the car and quakes, waiting, waiting. Maybe it was nothing. The sound had been small. A minor impact. And it wasn't her fault. Her white lights had been on. She had been signaling! She peeks into her rearview mirror. A gray-faced man is climbing out of a Jeep and shaking his head at his front fender, then he's glaring at her through the windows. "Any day now," he yells, palms up. She jerks her gaze away.

The next thing, she knows, is to step out of the car and review the damage, which will be real. The corner of her trunk has collapsed where it hit the Jeep's fender; the metal has come close to scraping the wheel. Then there's the terse conversation, where she'll trade information with the other driver while he unambiguously judges her dumb. After that she'll steer home, slowly and contritely, her ugly blunder broadcast to the world. At home, her father will grumble and groan, then grudgingly follow her to the body shop. Then for days—days!—she'll have to take the bus to school or catch rides from Angie and Davina, which means no driving time, no control, no release. Days. Ugh. Why. Eisha's fault. Margaret shrinks into the driver's seat, delaying as long as she can.

I can't believe you let Richie smoke in your mom's van," Margaret says, nudging Davina's *Boys for Pele* disc into the thin slot as Davina accelerates out of Richie's paved driveway.

"I know!" Davina laughs. "If she says anything I'll just tell her I . . . bought a lot of incense?"

Richie had offered them the joint, but neither she nor Davina took it. Smoking marijuana is a crime but—Richie Trufano had some hippie cool factor that made it seem okay, normal, even. It helped that she asked if she could smoke right after inviting them to a party. Which was cool.

"Maybe she won't notice," Margaret says. "Let's roll down the windows." She presses the button on her door and leans into the fresh air. She had been grateful for Richie's chatter; she's drained after another long school day, followed by two hours at the field site in Amelia County. The forestry department will be executing a controlled burn next week, and Margaret and her team of advanced junior scientists have been specially chosen to conduct research tracking regrowth over time. They're focusing on insects as a marker of ecological health: if more species are represented after the fire than before, they'll have solid evidence of the efficacy of planned burns to renew an ecosystem. Each session they choose a representative sector of the field and divide it into four squares, one for each of them. In hers, Margaret counted eight spiders, five beetles, twenty-one ants, and twelve grasshoppers. She sketched their likenesses for identification purposes later—Richie had the group's one field guide—and tried not to pass out. She misses her car, which is still in the shop, but—maybe it's good she's not driving.

"Richie's party sounds fun," Margaret says, but the words get swallowed by the wind as Davina merges onto 288 and accelerates.

"What?" Davina shouts. She's in a periwinkle boatneck and bootcut jeans, her thick curls clawed together at the nape of her neck. No makeup—she'd rather have those extra few minutes of sleep. Margaret's in a flowery, formfitting top, see-through with rippled edges, over a white tank. Her modestly flared jeans trumpet out over her old gym shoes, which she changed into for fieldwork. This morning she neutralized her problem spots with sticky green concealer under CoverGirl foundation, compressed powder, and blush. Hours later, her problem spots have risen like supple nipples ringed in green crust.

It's Thursday, 4:10 p.m. They pass stretches of dying grass and the occasional cluster of young, slender-trunked trees.

Davina skips ahead to their favorite song. "Ready?" She rolls the volume up.

Margaret grins. With echoing bells and dizzying harpsichord, "Caught a Lite Sneeze" sounds like a magnificent light storm, its winds stirring up shrieking birds, churning waves, a chorus of angels. Over this supernatural atmosphere Amos's voice soars, lofty and searching as she despairs over some dude—but Davina and Margaret can barely hear her under their scream-shouting. *do you think this is about standing in the middle of an electrical storm as a metaphor for love?*

Margaret had asked TheVoice23 when it first came out. *i thought it was about catching a cold*, he typed back. *jk.* Some fans suspect the "lite sneeze" may refer to an orgasm or, more specifically, ejaculation—no way. Margaret objects. She thinks it means that attraction to boys is infectious. You catch it, like a sneeze, which is why the speaker needs the help of other girls to stop the cycle and get out. Like most of the album, "Caught a Lite Sneeze" was recorded in a church and it does sound very church-like, vast and echoey. A kind of prayer. A prayer to girls. Boys show up one final time *in dresses*: A funny line. Ironic.

It was Davina who introduced her to Tori Amos, long ago on the bus their freshman year. *You have to listen to this*, Davina said, sliding her headphones over Margaret's ears. *It'll change your life.* And it did.

The car phone lights up as Davina exits the highway. "Will you get that?" Davina says, clicking the sound off. "It's my mom. If she asks, we dropped off Eish at the library."

"Uh, sure." Margaret gives her a questioning look and lifts the sleek receiver uncertainly. She's never seen Davina use it, had assumed car-phone technology was bogus.

"Margaret, is that you? Where are you girls?"

"Hi, Mrs. Gupta. We just got off 288."

"Ah, good, good. Is Eisha with you?"

"Eisha? Oh, we just dropped her off at the library."

"Ah." She pauses. Margaret gives Davina panicked eyes. "Okay, I'll let her mother know. Why don't you join us for dinner? I'm making biryani, ah, you know. You like it."

Margaret hesitates. Mrs. Gupta would load up her plate and tell her, *Eat, eat*, and she'd have to, to be polite. She'd want to, is the real problem. The food would be too good. "I don't think so," she says. Only recently has she won the right

55

to make her own dinner, after going vegetarian. *Fine. Eat what you want,* her mom shrugged, exasperated. *I'm not cooking two separate meals.* She will stick with her Lean Cuisine as planned.

"Are you sure? We have rice pudding."

"Ma!" Davina interjects.

"That sounds delicious but I should get home. Thanks, though."

She hangs up. "What's going on with Eisha?"

Davina makes her uncomfortable chipmunk face. "What has she told you?"

Margaret shrugs. "She's just been really weird lately."

"Weird how?"

"Just— She seems mad at me. But I don't know why."

Davina gives Margaret a nervous glance. "Have you asked her?"

Margaret reddens. In fact, she has asked her repeatedly. There are only so many times a person can write *what's up* in her notes and not be rewarded a response. Besides, when have they talked about anything beyond school, boys, music? That isn't part of their friendship, though apparently it's part of Eisha and Davina's. But they can be intimate in ways she can't—touchy-feely—and that's fine, they can be girls. Angie too. Stroking hair, plucking stray lashes, hugging with boob contact. Margaret can't. Knows better than to try. She's reminded of the big mess with Gretchen; whatever it was, she still doesn't get it.

They sit in silence a moment, passing Ward's, where she spent so many afternoons with her fellow GCSA members, enjoying milkshakes or soft serve with magic shell, their customary treats after solving a case. For an instant she's sure she sees Jina and Gretchen in their usual window booth, splitting an order of fries. Nope. Some other girls, middle school girls. Margaret lifts her thermos, takes a sip of cold tea.

Davina sighs, relenting. "Eisha is . . . dealing with stuff. Her mom can get pretty psycho sometimes. She stays with us when things gets too tense."

So it isn't about her, she thinks with relief. Psycho how? she wonders. She's met Eisha's mom a few times and she seems totally normal. Younger and thinner than most moms. Distant, sad. But normal. No evidence of maladjustment or violent impulses.

People are not what they seem, she reminds herself. Then again, if you pay attention, you can usually intuit what they're hiding. There was a time when she could look at a person and determine, from the tiny stray hairs on the tops of their earlobes and the frequency with which they checked their digital watch, that they had just had a trim and were on their way to deliver an important speech within which they had embedded a dangerous subliminal message that would compel the whole audience to remove their clothing (see GCSA #36: Margaret's First Perm). She and her team of Angie, Jina, and Gretchen used to be able to solve, well, anything.

No more. Margaret has killed her inner detective.

"Poor Eish," Margaret says.

"I know," Davina says. "And my mom is good friends with her mom. So it's a whole big deal. Very complicated." She sighs, turns onto Branders Bridge Road.

"Wow." Margaret absorbs this information. "But why is she mad at me?"

Davina looks caught. "What makes you think she's mad at you?"

"She barely acknowledges my presence."

"Maybe"—Davina's voice gets really high—"she thinks you've been . . . I don't know . . . maybe a teensy bit self-involved? But I don't know. You should talk to Eisha."

Margaret takes this in silently, stung. She had expected Davina to dismiss her question, to tell her it's nothing, she's done nothing wrong. Now she's *self-involved*? What does that even mean? She's the one who's been thoughtfully sending the usual battery of notes and getting zilch in return. She thinks back to the last few she crammed into Eisha's locker. Documentation of what Eisha missed during debate— Stephen Colson's pointers on speed-reading, how hot his shaggy hair looked. Has she been overusing the word *hot*? But for so long she wasn't using it at all! What else . . . She reported her quiz grades (A+, A, A+), made fun of Carolyn Rand, Eisha's adversary in Spanish. A lot of nothing, which is nothing unusual. Margaret is miffed. She's expended so much energy constructing her current self, it's bizarre to have it backfire in this way.

Davina shrugs, clearly uncomfortable. So? Margaret's uncomfortable too. She thought she'd been doing a good job. She sighs. Her head hurts. *Self-involved.*

"Okay, whatever. I'm guessing she's not at the library."

"Doubtful."

"So where is she?"

"Well." Davina shrinks into the seat. "Probably Jamal's."

"What? Our Jamal? Manager Jamal?"

"Yeah." Davina is sheepish.

"Oh. Wow. Gosh. That's news." She sits with this information, shaken. Trembling. A mess. Her astonishment swirls into sympathy swirls into hurt swirls into apology for being *self-involved* swirls into resentment at being called that—*self-involved*—when it wasn't like anyone was asking *her*, Margaret, "Hey, what's the problem, what's actually really going on in your life," for example, do her friends know she is dealing with her first online breakup or her brother's grief at the death of Cory, how awful her parents are for understanding nothing, how they don't care what she thinks or feels, how no one does. Do they know she is constantly at the mercy of her stomach and guts, that their noises threaten to humiliate her at any quiet moment? *That's called borborygmus*, Aaron Feldman told her matter-of-factly after a particularly loud burbling. *It refers to the sounds of digestion.* Do they know she pissed herself during field hockey last week? Do they know she fucking fainted? Try putting that in a note. *Get this: Last week I peed in my shorts during field hockey practice and collapsed in the locker room bathroom. Ha!* No. Notes between friends were supposed to be fun.

She had been lobbing the ball back and forth to Sarah Kelso, whose hairline was sweating, whose mouthguard shuddered around the shoulder strap of her sports bra. Margaret liked watching her move. She was just so *at ease*. In the locker room, she strutted around in her underwear, repeatedly pointing at the small pimples spread across her chest. *These aren't zits*, she insisted. *It's a rash.* What would it be like, Margaret wondered, was always wondering, to move through the world and be comfortable? She couldn't imagine. She walked around heavy and swollen, a ball of wet bread. Practice was nearly over, mercifully: she had to pee, bad. But Beth Smelley and Adriana Cellini were goofing off, balancing their sticks on their chins, and Coach kept them all late with more laps. Her bloated bladder sloshed with each stride. She was on the last lap when the first dribble dribbed down her leg. A trickle light enough to ignore until it steadied to a stream. She didn't know what to do so she pretended nothing had happened, kept running, piss streaming down her legs. Are you there, Margaret? What's your problem? She'd lost control. She was furious with herself, furious at everything, this insistent beating in her head. At church some flubby man leering at her when she shuffled down the aisle. Gross. At the family barbecue, her uncle giving her a once-over and saying she's *looking good*. Her smiling, saying thanks. But she was . . . mad. Impossibly, unspeakably angry. And at what. She didn't know. In the locker room she stopped short and listened to her own ragged breathing. She was shaking, seeing spots, crackling stars in her periphery. Her shorts and shin guards were soaked. She was sitting on the toilet when Beth and Adriana came in. *What does that even mean?* Adriana was saying. *To have a weight problem.* They must have seen her running, observed her thighs wobbling under clingy wet shorts that got sucked into her crotch with each step. *Like, just lose weight*, Adriana continued. *Problem solved. Yeah*, Beth said. *If I were fat I would kill myself.* She laughed, a light, easy titter. Margaret's heart pounded. She stared critically at her thighs, the red spots from bad shaving. She picked one off, then another, then stood up. And collapsed.

She came around shortly after. She had fallen hard on the toilet seat, twisting it sideways. Her cheek against the wall, planted on top of Wite-Out graffiti: *Rachel Creeley is CREEPLEY & LEZZLEY / shoud be her name.* The second line had been added in different handwriting. She brushed the flakes off, rubbed her neck. Pulled herself up and out of the stall, changing as quickly as she could. The other girls had left or were in the showers, steaming up the room. She was fine, fine, she would have assured anyone who asked. No one did. She flicked open a Diet Coke and chugged.

"You okay?" Davina asks. They're nearly to Margaret's neighborhood.

"Just, um . . . digesting." She lets out a shaky breath. "It's a lot . . ." She trails off, not ready to think about it. "And, uh, how about you? How are *you* doing? Anything I should, you know, anything I should know?"

Davina snorts. "Me? No. What you see is what you get. Just your average above-average Indian girl trying to get into premed." She pauses. Glances at Margaret. "And you? Anything going on with you?"

Margaret smiles uneasily. There's the entrance to Shady Bluff, the dark wooden sign, sharp hedges snapping up at it. "Nope. Just trying to make it through high school." She searches for a subject change, remembers the party. She and Davina are in the magnet program and live farther out. They rarely get invited to Hillside parties. Richie is in that narrow slice of the Venn diagram where the groups overlap. So is Stephen. Who will probably be there.

"Do you want to go to Richie's party?" she asks.

"I can't. Fred will be home and we're having people over that night, remember? You're coming, right? It'll be family mostly—which means you! Eisha will be there. And her mom." Davina sighs, apparently stressed just thinking about it.

"I don't know yet. I'll try." Margaret is tempted to say yes. She usually jumps at these invitations: she enjoys soaking up the Guptas' happy glow and knows they'd be glad to see her. And she could be there for Eisha. Make up for being *self-involved*. She should say yes. But there's the food thing. Davina's family always has too much of it. Anyway, she should take the opportunity to have face time with Stephen outside of school, which is so confining. Her plan has been working. Their IM conversations are getting longer and more involved every night; yesterday they even smiled at each other in the hall. Hmm. She has eight days. If she loses two more pounds, she'll go to the party. If not, she'll join the Guptas. She's not sure which one is the punishment.

M orning, ladies." Angie's boyfriend Chad pops his head between the two front seats. In the passenger's seat, Margaret twists toward him and recoils at a whiff of his morning breath.

It's a gray day, dark and raining. The front wipers swing back and forth. Angie's car is overwarm, heat blasting, mildew smell. Propped against the door Margaret's umbrella drips onto her Airwalks.

"You have a ride home, right?" Angie asks Margaret. "I've got a game." Angie's in her slippery Hillside Hoppers jersey, her braided pigtails woven through with green ribbons.

"My mom's picking me up early," Margaret says. "Doctor's appointment."

Chad buckles in and Angie reverses the car.

Angie is the only GCSA member Margaret has really seen since the club's demise: they're both in Hillside's magnet program, twenty miles from Shady Bluff. While Margaret has become generic, a smart kid among smart kids, Angie has jocked out, now a triple threat, a star: on the basketball court, on the soccer field, around the track. That's how she met Chad, another jock, who's part of the regular school. Now Angie drinks (bad), smokes (bad), and *has sex* (the worst). The class clown, Chad's a big bear: heavy, and no one cares, since he's been deemed funny.

Jina attends their district school. For a while Margaret would see her around, walking her dog at dusk, sometimes with her twin, Janet. At first they waved; then they didn't. Then, she guesses, Jina adopted a new dog-walking route.

As for Gretchen, she attends an all-girls Catholic school outside of Richmond, where she wears a uniform and prays a lot, though she isn't Catholic. Margaret has run into her a few times, most recently last month when their field hockey teams faced off on Hillside's home field. Margaret and Gretchen glared grimly at each other, gritting through their mouthguards, before Gretchen seized the ball in a flash of purple plaid.

Giving Margaret a ride this morning is an easy generosity on Angie's part. It's been a favorite refrain of Margaret's mother—*Why not carpool with Angie? Save some gas?* They have conflicting schedules, Margaret has explained, which is occasionally true. But with her car back in the shop, she'd asked Angie to pick her up. Margaret is excited, actually. She has updates. She'd given Angie the brief version last night, over the phone: the party, key moments with Stephen— *WHAT!* Certainly more satisfying than Eisha's nonplussed response. On the way to Chad's, she'd filled in the details, carried along by Angie's theatrical gasps. She left out the embarrassing parts.

"So, heard you got some action, Marge." Chad's leaning forward, gripping her seat back.

"Don't call me that," she replies. She shoots a worried glance at Angie. Did Stephen say something to Chad? The thought horrifies her.

Angie grimaces. "Was I not supposed to say anything? Sorry."

"First base? Second? Is Stevie a good kisser? I've wondered."

"Chad," Angie scolds. "Hush."

"I'm genuinely curious. What happened?"

"Nothing," Margaret says shortly. "MYOFB."

"Ooh," Chad taunts. "She said '*F.*' I'm telling."

Margaret ignores him. What happened was Richie's party. What happened was she had followed the plan. Lose two pounds, go to party. At party, initiate conversation with Stephen Colson. It didn't have to be a good conversation. She just needed contact. Action. Progress. Keep things moving. There he was at the snack table, snatching the last of the pretzel shards from the bowl. Alone. *Hey. Great job at the debate tournament*, she pushed out. He was chewing, so couldn't say thanks. She barreled ahead as he swallowed. *I like your Away messages.* Maybe he would think she was drunk. She wasn't. But he laughed. Easy. *Thanks. I like yours too. And you know what? I like our IM conversations even better.* She gleamed. It was happening. The plan had worked. Then he said he was starving and pointed at the ransacked table, just a few hunks of pizza crust left. *Want to peace out and go for some nosh?*

She followed his Camry out of Richie's neighborhood and down the highway to Archie's, where she spat her food into her napkin when he wasn't looking. *You eat*, he said, watching her gingerly bite into a fry. *Most girls don't.* She raised an eyebrow. *I'm not most girls.* That's what she should have said, in a light, flirty voice; acting. Instead she smiled stupidly, her napkin, the evidence, agitating in her periphery. He then revealed astonishing information. *Laura didn't*, he told her, referring to his ex-girlfriend, whose mysterious absence last year would have made the perfect case—maybe Laura had been teleported to another dimension, she had found herself speculating, or more probably, like Melanie Flowers, picked up by some creep. But there were no news reports; Laura had simply and quietly gone away. Without the empty desk in

Latin to remind her where a sweet-faced girl with distinctive lettering used to sit, Margaret had since forgotten about her. *Eat, I mean . . . She had to get treatment. That's why we broke up.*

He took a bite of his burger, pink juice sluicing out from the back end. She lifted her napkin to brush her lips while extracting partially eaten potato. She was swallowing about a third of what she was putting in her mouth. *What do you mean?* she prompted. He chewed with a faraway look. *I'm not supposed to say but . . . I trust you.* He peered at her with soft brown eyes. *And I'm drunk. Don't tell anyone, okay?* She promised. *She had to get treatment. She's anorexic. I mean. She didn't say that word but that's the word.* She stared at her fries, thoughtful, scheming, needing to know more without seeming overly, suspiciously interested. *That's terrible.* He nodded. *She was at a center in Richmond for a while. Now this fancy place up in Maryland.* She munched a fry slowly, trying to delay its inevitable dissolution. *That must have been hard*, she said sympathetically, spraying a few spitty potato bits onto the table. She covered her mouth. *Yeah, it was shitty. But I mean, there's nothing I can do.* His face had grown heavy, closed. Margaret realized the conversation had turned unfun and she needed to turn it back. *Did you hear Alanis Morrissette had to get her stomach pumped and they found a pint of semen in it? True story.* Yikes. His lips twitched. *No way.* He put his burger down, gulped some water. *I bet you anything Richie and Justin Yager are boning right now.* She scrunched her eyebrows. *Isn't he recovering from surgery? He shouldn't be—* She stopped herself. *Cool. Sounds fun.* She smiled without showing her teeth. *Yeah it does*, he said, smirking hard at her. Uh-oh. Has her plan worked too well? *I have an idea*, he said in a teasing voice. *Something else we could be doing with our mouths.* He waggled his eyebrows. Before she could respond, he was sliding into her booth. *Right?* he said. *This is cool?* She nodded uncomfortably and forced down the half-chewed food packed in her cheeks. Recalling the teen-magazine instructions, Margaret parted her lips slightly and braced herself for contact. A distorted, needy mouth came at her and then there it was, a tongue, thickly bobbing at hers. She slid back, pressed up where the bench met the wall, and stared past his head at the fluorescent ceiling lights, the glare making the scene appear as unreal as it felt. Then his hands were groping her hips, and tiny bolts of lightning were jabbing all over her. Her stomach lurched. Alarmed, she jerked away, knocking her head against the wall of the booth. *Uh*, he said, laughing, pulling back a moment. Relax, she told herself. You're participating. You're doing a great job. Her guts creaked. Oh no. This afternoon's laxatives. Her eyes got wet, wild with panic. Abruptly she slunk down from under him, crawling under the table and out the other side. In the women's bathroom she unleashed one bout of noxious, painful diarrhea, then another. Hurry up, she told herself, heart racing. Please, no one come in here. No one did. Her face was hot when she returned. *That was weird*, he said. *I know*, she said. She should not have eaten those french fries. *Sorry. Um. Should we get the check?*

"Hyello," Chad says. "Earth to Margaret. What happened to your car?"

Margaret shakes her head. It was too dumb. This time she backed up straight into a lamppost. Luckily Stephen had already pulled away and didn't see or, if he did, didn't stop.

"Fine," Chad says. "We'll call this one 'The Mystery of the Makeout That Didn't Make Out.'"

"Um . . . whatever." Margaret glances distrustfully at Angie. What has she told Chad about their club? Have Angie and Chad made Margaret the butt of their private joke? That would be unfair. Angie had been just as into it as Margaret had been, had solved plenty of cases on her own (see GCSA #7: Angie and the Slippery Salamander, for starters).

"*Chad.*" Angie reaches back to bat the bill of his baseball cap. "Stop talking."

His grin is obnoxious. "Call me Josh. I'm just joshing." He pauses a moment. "Have y'all taken the health exam?"

"Yeah," Margaret says to the air in front of her. "It's not bad. Just remember nothing is as effective as abstinence." Angie shoots her a dark look. "What?" Margaret goes on, oblivious. "There are, like, five versions of the same question." She needs to return Davina's note, that reminds her, which was written on the back of Davina's half-completed worksheet.

CONTRACEPTION
how well will it protect; cost, availability, safety, side effects
    1) use it properly
    2) may not work, but protects somewhat
    3) w/ abst. you can't get pregnant

MATURE RELATIONSHIPS
    1) communicate well
    2) abstinence/mutual monogamy (till marriage)
    3) commitment
    4) respect each other's values & views
    5) love each other
    6) support each other
    7) trust
    8) learn from each other

MARGARET!
Hello, I'm recycling my family life notes, so don't think
I'm trying to give you any hints/anything— Yeah sure
Margaret, I've heard about you!

"Ah yes, we know all about that, don't we, Ange."

Angie laughs. "*Chad.*"

"*Ange*," Chad mimics. Is this communicating well: saying each other's names in italics of varying degrees? Margaret sighs. She absolutely does *not* want to hear anything about their sex life. Chad pokes Angie's tricep as they turn onto the main road. "Want to swap spit before first period?"

Angie giggles. "*Cha-ad*," she whines back, inadvertently mimicking herself. "Let's see how much time there is."

"Come on. What girl could say no to such a gallant proposition?"

Margaret groans inwardly and slumps in her seat. For breakfast she ate a slice of toast, no butter. Coffee, no milk. She glares out the window. Nothing to see. The window's a rain-stained blur and the sky's heavy, hovering; her head aches from the pressure of it. She searches the outside, the beyond, but the longer she looks, the more opaque the window becomes. It's Chad's morning breath, she thinks, it's polluting their air and making her nauseous. She opens the window a chunk.

"You're letting the rain in," Angie says. She clicks the window shut and presses the defroster button. Some of the fog begins to clear.

Margaret and the Mystery of the Missing Body

CHAPTER 1

People are not who they seem; in my ongoing career as a girl detective I have learned this again and again. Whether bumblingly or with shrewd calculation, people go about their lives with any number of secret selves knocking around inside them, private layers vibrating deep within—in some cases, just past the surface of the skin. Sometimes I imagine that with the right kind of binoculars you could see just about anything, including the inner workings of your closest friends.

It was 5:32 p.m. and Gretchen was late. Again. She'd been late to our last three meetings. This was very unlike Gretchen, though I guess it was *becoming* like Gretchen. And it was extremely annoying. What was worse, she responded to my inquiries with insulting vagueness. I didn't know what was going on, but I was determined to get to the bottom of it. I always do.

Along with Gretchen, the other members of Girls Can Solve Anything are Angie Stern, Jina Castle, and me— Margaret Worms. Angie, Jina, and I founded GCSA, a detective club for girl sleuths, the summer before seventh grade; Gretchen joined us not long after. In a year and a half, we've solved almost fifty cases. We've rescued drugged children from the hands of their devious grandmother (see

GCSA #1: Margaret's Bad Idea); confronted the vengeful spirits of Confederate soldiers (see #8: Angie and the Ghosts of Hollywood Cemetery); and ensured that confused dinosaurs did not return to Shady Bluff (see #11: Jina and the Prehistoric Portal). We've negotiated with aliens from the Planet X (see #14: Gretchen and the Beep from Outer Space); and returned a lot of stolen pets (see #7: Angie and the Slippery Salamander and #23: Angie and the Case of the Furless Ferret, for starters). In the process, we've teased one another and laughed a lot. Now we're in eighth grade, and thirteen years old. No longer girls, yet not really women. A challenging time.

The digital clock flipped to 5:33. Now Gretchen was *more* late, and I alone seemed to care. Jina and Angie were preoccupied with exchanging intel pertaining to their crushes and the upcoming dance. I was frustrated. We had active cases: Mrs. Strudebaker's stolen camera; Harry Sousa's missing and potentially dangerous python; the mysterious lights seen by Francesca Decrecenzo over Shady Bluff last week. Not to mention the disappearance of Melanie Flowers: our investigations in that case had dragged to an embarrassing halt.

With so much club business to attend to, we had no time to waste on the likes of Jake Miller. But waste it we were. He had sat next to Angie in math, and she felt sure this was evidence he liked her. "He said *hey*."

"*Hey?*" I repeated, disbelieving.

"Yeah. *Hey*. Like this." She slumped down and gave me a curt nod. "Hey."

"Hey. Great." I cut my gaze pointedly to the clock. 5:33.

"Yep. He likes you," said Jina. "He never sits up front." She popped a banana chip into her mouth and crunched.

Angie glowed. I didn't want to be a naysayer, but what kind of evidence was that?

Angie Stern is my oldest and geographically closest friend. We both moved to Shady Bluff in third grade and have been best friends ever since. She's just three cul-de-sacs away and we even look a bit alike—or we used to, before Angie cut her long curtain-like hair into shoulder-length layers. It looks fine, I guess. Mine still drapes halfway down my back—when it's not in a ponytail, which is most of the time. Angie is athletic and loves to be outside, whereas I'm more of an indoor person. I would much rather be reading and writing than running in circles.

"I've got less than two weeks," Angie said, referring to the upcoming dance. "Maybe I should send him a note."

"You might have to," agreed Jina. "Sounds like he needs a nudge." Jina was the club's authority on boys. Her twin sister, Janet, exchanged them like clothes.

Jina Castle is my second-oldest and second–geographically closest friend. She's studious like me, but we look nothing alike: for one thing, I'm white and she's African American; she's also very slender and elegant (I'm neither). She and Janet are both gorgeous, though they're very different personality-wise. Janet can be awfully shallow, while Jina is wise about everything (except Janet, who can easily manipulate her twin to get what she wants). Like me, Jina thinks boys and fashion are trivial distractions at best. Or so I thought, until she told me she'd asked Garrett Vaughan to the dance. I, gobsmacked, suspected Janet's influence. Unfortunately he said yes, and now Jina needed to go shopping.

I wanted to be excited for her, and for Angie, who was purportedly making progress with Jake. But the whole thing was so tiresome. The dance, the dance: It was all anyone wanted to talk about. Who was going with whom, and what were they wearing. I guess the whole school had grown tired of talking about Melanie Flowers, an eighth grader at our rival school who had been missing since November. To be honest, so had we. None of us had known Melanie, and the scene of the crime was outside our usual Shady Bluff jurisdiction. That didn't stop us from examining the evidence, but we'd hit dead end after dead end; at this point, all we could do was speculate. Angie theorized that Melanie had been kidnapped by the family friend who "forgot" to pick her up at Skateland. Jina suspected Melanie was dead, killed by a random stranger. Gretchen thought she'd probably just run away. I didn't know what to think. Maybe she was a witch or a vampire pretending to be a thirteen-year-old girl, and had vanished to avoid her discovery. Maybe she was controlled by alien parasites. You never knew.

"Sorry I'm late." Gretchen flew in, her dirty-blond hair streaming behind her. "I just passed by the weirdest thing on the sidewalk. It looked like a brain. Well." She laughed. "I guess we've seen weirder things."

It was 5:36 but I grinned, my annoyance evaporating. Was Gretchen referring to giants, sorcerers, mutant bugs? Ghosts, time travelers, werewolves? Telekinetic or invisible pets? Probably all of the above, and she was right. Shady Bluff was overrun with weirdness.

Gretchen McGann moved here almost two years ago, and she has quickly become one of my favorite people. Mrs. McGann died when Gretchen was just a child, so it's just been Gretchen and her father, a workaholic business exec who grants her a lot of freedom. She's very independent and more mature than the rest of us, as well as a talented performer who has won the lead in practically every school play since she moved here. She was also switched at birth, as we recently discovered after a blood drive at school revealed she did not have the blood type she thought she did (see GCSA #42: The Truth about Gretchen).

I lifted the club magnifying glass, our unofficial gavel. I was about to call the meeting to order, but apparently the more urgent matter was whether Gretchen had a date to the dance.

Gretchen yawned, something she was doing more and more, I'd noticed. "Nope. Do you?"

"Angie's working on Jake Miller," Jina answered.

Angie blushed. "Jina's going with Garrett Vaughan."

"Oooh," Gretchen said with playful exaggeration. "He's cute. Margaret, what about you?"

I futilely lowered the lens. Of course I didn't have a date, they knew very well, because I, Margaret Worms, did not "date." I had more important things to do than develop crushes on unworthy young men. Anyway, the more I heard about the dance, the less I wanted to go. It's not like I'd never been to a dance before, but something about this one was different. You know how when All Skate turns to Couples Skate and you have to hold hands with a boy or get off the rink? That's bearable because it only lasts a few minutes. Eighth grade was starting to feel like Couples Skate all the time. Was this what the future looked like? Couples galore?

Thoughts of Skateland brought me back to the case of Melanie Flowers. The roller-skating rink was the scene of the crime—assuming there was one. Melanie was last seen on Skateland's front steps, alone on a Friday night. Wherever she was now, I hoped she was all right. And I hoped we would uncover a new lead soon.

"Can we talk about club business now?"

"You *have* to go!" Angie protested. "It's our last middle school dance."

I was about to hurl our club notebook at the floor when we heard a thump on Angie's bedroom door.

"Sounds like we have a client." Jina jumped up to get it. "Huh. Isn't that strange?" She'd opened the door to discover: there was nobody there.

Just as she was about to close it, we heard a squeaky voice say, "Down here! Down here!" We looked down and sure enough, there was our client. But you won't believe what kind of client it was. Guess. Guess what kind of client. I'll give you a hint. It wasn't a full person. Are you guessing? Okay, fine, I'll tell you . . . It was a brain. A pink, wet brain that was drooling all over the green carpet.

We gasped in shock—all of us but Gretchen, who had encountered the brain on her way. "Hello!" I said. "Welcome to Girls Can Solve Anything. Please come in. How may we help you?"

The brain inched forward and squeaked "thank you." It took a long time for her to move inside enough for us to close the door, but finally she did.

"What brings you to our office?" I asked brusquely.

The brain sighed. "Well, girls, it may sound strange, but you're probably expecting that from my . . . lack of physique." She let out a crazed giggle. "I seem to have lost my body. Can you help me find it?"

Angie, Jina, Gretchen, and I exchanged glances. We'd never handled something like this before.

The brain, whose name was Frieda Normandy, told us she'd woken up that morning without her body. Her body was gone, vanished. It had been there when she went to bed, but when she woke up, it was missing.

After she left, we talked among ourselves. "Do you think she's for real?" Angie asked suspiciously. "Who loses their body?"

Jina shrugged gamely. "She's obviously missing something."

I wouldn't mind it if my body went missing, I thought, then paused to think that through. If we all went around in just our brains, sooner or later we'd be calling our brains too fat, too gray, too slimy . . . which obviously wouldn't solve anything.

"Shall we . . . er . . . brainstorm?" Jina said, waggling her eyebrows.

Gretchen groaned.

"Or maybe a . . . uh . . . mindmap is in order," Jina quipped, snorting.

We all had to laugh. "Okay, seriously," I said. "How could Ms. Normandy have lost her body?"

Angie opened a box of Ring Dings and passed them around. Jina and I each grabbed one; Gretchen kept working on her banana chips. We munched and thought, munched and thought. Snacks are important for thinking.

Finally I clapped my hands. "Ideas?"

Angie suggested it was a hoax. Ms. Normandy was remote-controlled by one of her brothers. Jina agreed, though expanded the circle of suspects to our school's science club. It was clear they weren't taking Ms. Normandy's situation very seriously.

Gretchen gave a great yawn and attempted to speak through it, with mixed effects. She rubbed her eyes. "Sorry."

She smiled sleepily. "This could be a case of the supernatural. Maybe Ms. Normandy needs us to find her body so her spirit can rest."

"Interesting idea," I said, though it was clearly half-baked. But I wanted Gretchen to feel supported. Her crime-solving streak had become shaky lately, unreliable; in our ongoing investigation into Harry's missing snake, she had botched our stakeout by falling asleep and missing my signal, in addition to misplacing valuable evidence.

I was concerned. For weeks now, Gretchen had been showing up to school and club meetings with dark circles under her eyes, her smiles drowsy, her yawns relentless. She'd missed homework assignments; her sleuthing was distracted at best. But when I asked her point-blank what was going on, she was evasive. "Oh, nothing. Everything's fine. Did you write down our Latin homework?" I had. I shared it with her. But I knew there was something more, something she wasn't telling me.

Picking up on my skepticism, she tried another tack. "Or maybe it has something to do with Melanie Flowers."

"Why do you say that?" Jina asked, sitting up sharply.

"What if Melanie didn't disappear?" Gretchen continued. "What if her body was stolen, and she's in hiding? I mean, just her brain. Like Ms. Normandy."

"A serial body snatcher," Angie said. "Cool."

Jina pursed her lips, dubious.

This new theory was certainly the most plausible so far. "We've got two missing bodies," I considered. "It does seem possible they could be connected. But let's keep our minds open. And, sleuths," I added, "I think this could be a big case." By which I meant: Get *with* it. No more distractions. I think they caught my drift. I tapped the magnifying lens ceremoniously. "Meeting adjourned. Meet here tomorrow. Four p.m." I glanced at Gretchen. "Sharp."

CHAPTER 2

Our client lived two cul-de-sacs from Angie's, so we met there and walked over together. (Gretchen was, predictably, late—by twelve minutes.) I had done some private investigating beforehand and believed I knew what was going on, but didn't want to leap to any conclusions until we had visited Ms. Normandy's house.

On our way we passed the Hawkins family, whose vandalized home we had investigated just last month (see GCSA #47: Angie and the Mystery of the Melted Mailbox). The light dusting of pyrotechnic glitter left behind by the perp became our primary clue in his nabbing.

Ms. Normandy lived in a two-story house with vinyl siding, one of many such homes in our neighborhood. A beat-up two-door sedan was parked in the gravel driveway. Ms. Normandy must not have kids, I surmised, or she would drive a station wagon or van.

Gretchen rang the doorbell, and we heard Ms. Normandy squeak, "It's open!" We let ourselves in. The brain had arranged herself delicately on an armchair in the living room.

I noticed several photographs lining the wall. They featured the same woman, who I assumed was our client—before her body had gone "missing"—posing with various other people.

"Is this you, Ms. Normandy?" I asked, pointing to a photo

of the woman embracing a tall, handsome man with salt-and-pepper hair.

"Yes, that's me with my first husband, Peter."

In the photos, her likeness ranged from an unusually thin, attractive young woman to a noticeably obese middle-aged woman with stringy hair and splotchy skin.

"Tell me, Ms. Normandy," I said. "Do you live alone?"

"Yes, ever since Bill divorced me. He's my second husband."

"Why did he divorce you, Ms. Normandy?" Angie asked.

"He claimed to no longer find me attractive."

"Were you attractive, Ms. Normandy?" I asked. She certainly didn't look it from the more recent photographs.

"What kind of a question is that?" she squeaked at an even higher pitch.

I raised my eyebrows. A bit touchy, I thought. A bit defensive. A bit . . . nervous. "May we take a look around?" I asked.

"Go right ahead."

I had just gotten started examining the windows in Ms. Normandy's bedroom when Gretchen cried out from downstairs.

"Margaret! Jina! Come quick! I think we've found a clue!"

Jina and I raced downstairs. It was a clue, all right. The window had been smashed and the door busted open. Greasy fingerprints spotted both.

"She must have noticed this," Jina whispered. "Why didn't she say anything?"

"Because this is a setup," I answered smoothly. "Friends, we're being used."

"What do you mean?" Angie asked.

"I don't have it all figured out just yet," I said, "but I have a feeling Ms. Normandy is hiding something."

"I can't believe this." Gretchen groaned as she patted her waist, where her fanny pack should have been. "I forgot my pack. No fingerprint kit. Sorry."

I frowned, frustrated. But there was no use dwelling upon it. "We'll have to come back tomorrow. Let's see how she responds to this 'clue.'"

We marched into the living room. "Ms. Normandy—" I started.

She was quivering with excitement. "Did you find something?" she squeaked eagerly, shrilly, her words drilling into my ears.

"Did you notice the smashed window?" Gretchen took charge, clearly trying to make up for her failings.

"What? No. Show me." Ms. Normandy slid down from her perch, and we went through the whole rigmarole. Jina rolled her eyes and shook her head, as annoyed as I was. It was insulting. Ms. Normandy clearly thought we were silly, easily fooled girls. Make-believe detectives. Hacks. She was in for a surprise.

On our way home I mentioned the body-insurance policy Ms. Normandy had recently purchased.

"That explains it," Jina said drily.

"Explains what?" Angie asked.

Jina put the pieces together. "Ms. Normandy must have taken out an insurance policy on her body, then made it look like her body was stolen so she could collect the money."

I nodded grimly. "Then tried to get us 'stupid girls'"—I scare-quoted—"to confirm the lie. Her body's likely being destroyed by an accomplice as we speak."

"But why?" pressed Angie.

"I would guess that she wants to use the money to purchase a new, better body," Jina said.

"People can do that?" asked Gretchen.

"Money can buy anything," Jina said. She adjusted her glasses with authority.

We were coming up on Angie's house. "Speaking of shopping," Angie said, nudging Jina. "Have you bought a dress?"

"Let's review the facts," I said quickly, loudly, as though Angie hadn't rudely changed the subject to the dance. "So, Melanie Flowers. What do we think? Is there a connection?" I thought not, but since it'd been brought up earlier, I wanted to rule it out.

"Melanie's body *could* be the new body Ms. Normandy is going to swap into," Jina considered. "But if she adopted the body of Melanie Flowers, everyone would know she'd stolen it."

"Not if she showed up *as* Melanie," Gretchen reasoned. "Melanie coming back after having been gone. Maybe that's her goal. Not just to get a new body, but a new life and personality and family and future."

"I don't know," Jina said. "That would require a whole criminal team. A hit man, underground doctors, all that. And if she really wanted to do it right, she'd have to have profiled Melanie beforehand to know what her life is like."

"Not if she claimed to have amnesia," Gretchen pointed out.

"And why Melanie?" Jina continued. "What would be the connection? Of course we should investigate the possibility, but I just don't think Ms. Normandy's the type. Especially when you take into account how crude her fake 'evidence' was."

I nodded along.

"She may be shady," Jina added, "but she's no evil mastermind."

"We can't know though," Gretchen said. "Don't forget Mrs. Stillwater."

I smiled at her, stirred by the memory of that case, the case that had brought us together. Privately I agreed with Jina. But I didn't want to leave Gretchen out in the cold. "We have seen some pretty elaborate criminal operations," I offered in her defense.

Gretchen nodded. "How much do we know about Ms. Normandy, after all? It's kind of hard to read a brain."

"Yes, but . . ." Jina frowned. "It just doesn't make sense. The timing's not right. Melanie's been missing for months."

"Angie," I said. "What do you think?"

Angie pursed her lips, thinking. "I think we need more information."

"Which we could have," I proposed, "if we conducted a more thorough search of Ms. Normandy's home."

"I'm still skeptical," said Jina. "But there's no harm in looking around."

"Exactly. And whatever the case, we need those fingerprints."

Gretchen grimaced. "Sorry about that. I can go back tomorrow."

"I have soccer," said Angie quickly.

"I have Darryl," said Jina, referring to her younger brother, whom she often watched after school.

"I'm free," I offered. "I'll go with you."

"Great." Gretchen's grin swelled into another yawn.

CHAPTER 3

"You've got your kit this time, right?" I checked Gretchen's waist as we set off for Ms. Normandy's.

Gretchen forced a smile. "Yep. I'm not *that* incompetent." She was in a prickly mood.

"You *have* been tired a lot lately . . ." I ventured again. "Is something going on?"

"Nope. All good," she said shortly.

My enthusiasm for our private time deflated. Maybe I should have let it go, but something seemed suspicious about Gretchen's chronic fatigue. After Melanie's disappearance, Gretchen's historically laissez-faire father instituted a strict 9 p.m. curfew and 10 p.m. bedtime—his parenting decisions increasingly influenced by Ms. Stern, Angie's overbearing mother, whom he had begun seeing romantically (which meant Angie and Gretchen might become stepsisters!). Gretchen ought to have been getting plenty of sleep. I considered the possibilities. Perhaps she was struggling from insomnia. We were all under a lot of pressure to decide which high school to go to—our district school or one of the magnet programs. Maybe she was simply staying up on the sly, finishing homework, rehearsing her lines, or reading a good book. Yet I couldn't discount the sneaking suspicion that there was something more going on . . . But what? I didn't know, because she didn't want me to know. It hurt my feelings. I was merely trying to be a good friend.

We walked quietly, my blue Keds in step with her soft gray ankle boots.

Gretchen cleared her throat. "So I wanted to talk to you about . . ." She paused for what seemed like a long time.

"What?" I prompted, sure she was about to divulge something big.

"It's nothing. Never mind."

"No, tell me. What is it?"

She sighed. "Okay, fine. So." She paused again. "Would you want to go to the dance together?"

"What?" This was not what I expected to hear. If I sounded totally clueless, I was.

"I mean, since neither of us have dates, maybe we could go together." Her gaze was shy.

"Oh, like last year." But last year we'd gone as a group.

"Well," Gretchen seemed flustered. She looked ahead. "Sort of. Not exactly." I waited for her to say more, but she didn't. My stomach twisted.

"I'm not sure what you mean," I said slowly, carefully. Did she want to go as friends or as— No way. Was *that* what was keeping her up at night? "Do you mean . . ." I couldn't get the words out. My butterflies fluttered furiously. No. She was just doing what best friends did. She had picked up on my dismay about the dance and was asking me out of generosity or pity or both. "I mean . . ." I couldn't finish my sentence.

"Never mind," she said glumly. "Forget I said anything."

I stared at the pavement. The silence was suffocating. Whatever she meant by the invitation, I had missed my chance to say yes. Yes, I thought, yes. I would love to go to the dance with you. But I couldn't say this out loud. One couldn't be too careful about suppressing one's feelings. I was reminded of the painful loss of my friend Lavender Bean in the fifth grade. She had been my first best friend, before Angie, before Jina, before Gretchen. I loved Lavender with a sweetness and purity—a naivete—I hadn't allowed myself since. Lavender taught me how to tie thread to my hair and make knotted wraps. She introduced me to Lip Smackers, to charm bracelets, to the Trauma-rama section of *Seventeen* magazine, which we chortled over in our tree fort after school. Because I was grateful to Lavender for these moments, this knowledge, our bliss, I wrote her a thank-you letter, as I'd been taught, which grew into a thorough cataloguing of all the great many things I appreciated about her, including her *funny laugh, which jolts my heart with jolly joy*. The next morning in class, I passed her the note, too thick for any of the more complicated folding patterns I thanked her for teaching me inside it. I trusted her to overlook the crude, basic rectangle pattern with one tab tucked into the corner, because I was sure the note would cement our best friendship.

Things did not go as planned. As I watched Lavender read over the first page, her smile became strained. As she turned to the next page and flipped too quickly through the four that followed, her smile went out completely. I clawed my nails into my thighs as she balled it all up, not bothering to reconstruct its shape.

Then Ms. Decair was hovering over Lavender's desk with her arm out, palm up. And then Ms. Decair was clearing her throat and reading in public my most private feelings.

Thank you, Lavender, for giving me the rest of your pizza that one time. It made my mouth burst with flavor. To think, I was putting my saliva where your saliva had been. To think, we were so connected. Ms. Decair grinned, her upper lip stretched tight over Chiclet teeth. "That's very sweet, girls, but class is not the time for trading notes."

Lavender flushed deeply. Her attentions toward me cooled, then tapered off entirely.

I had since deduced I wasn't supposed to tell my friends

what they meant to me, or thank them for how their hair smelled like their name. These were criminal acts. Though other girls treated one another with tenderness and appreciation, I understood it was somehow suspicious when I did. Someone like Gretchen could ask me to the dance without being suspected of anything. Of being—weird. Whether her motivations were friendly or—something else, she would be seen as kind and generous, choosing friends over boys. But someone like me couldn't reciprocate. I knew this intuitively without understanding why.

Fine. I would forget it. I changed the subject. "Mrs. Strudebaker found her camera. It wasn't stolen after all. It was in the doghouse."

"Oh. Cool."

The suffocating silence resumed.

Ms. Normandy's house came into view. "I think we should look for a freezer," I said, thinking she might warm up again if I supported her theory. "Maybe Ms. Normandy is keeping Melanie's body inside it."

"Whatever." Gretchen yawned so big she had to stop midstride to finish it. "I'm exhausted," she said. I knew better than to ask why. I was getting exhausted too.

We did not find the body of Melanie Flowers in a freezer in Ms. Normandy's basement. We did not find anything but an impatient and simple criminal mind. Brain, if you want to be literal-minded. Okay. Literal-brained.

The walk home was painful and interminable. I wanted to shrink into a walnut and die.

At home, I thought and thought. What was Gretchen hiding? I waited until ten o'clock at night. Then I snuck out to investigate.

CHAPTER 4

The air was cold, mild for February but chilly enough to support a ski mask and gloves, which happens to be my spy outfit (plus a heavy sweatshirt over a long-sleeved tee, jeans, obviously, and my soft-soled Keds). Crouched in the bushes in the cloak of night, I lit up the face of my digital watch: 11:43 p.m. Her bedroom light had been on since 11:16, well past her 10 p.m. bedtime.

A moment later, a vehicle turned into the cul-de-sac, its headlights flicking off as it approached. Suspicious. The vehicle (low-riding sports car, older model, color indeterminate in the dark) parked at the curb between this house and the next, intending, I deduced, to be unseen, unobtrusive—like me. I ducked down farther into the hydrangeas.

Gretchen's light went off, and her first-floor window slid open from the inside. She seated herself on the ledge and swung her legs around, careful not to snag her hose on the zippers of her combat boots. She hopped down. From a bordering hedge, she dragged out a cinder block and positioned it under the window. Using it as a stepstool, she pulled the window mostly shut, then returned the cinder block to its spot.

She was wearing a red dress, I saw, a familiar red dress. Where had I seen it? Combing my memory I recalled it with a hat, a specific hat . . . a fedora. That's right! She'd worn it during her pageant skit, under the trenchcoat, when she had transformed from detective to femme fatale. Fitting, I thought. That seemed to be exactly what was going on here.

I disapproved. The dress sat too low on her chest, and the oversized blazer she wore over it (likely her dad's) was too thin for the weather. She looked like an adult and she was going to freeze. Whatever she was up to, I didn't like it, and I almost sprang from my hiding place to say so. I didn't. Instead I watched, sympathetically shivering, as she tiptoed up the driveway, blazer flapping in the cold air. Approaching the car, she effected confidence, shoulders broad, hips rolling. The passenger door of the car opened (who was the driver? a dark shadow . . . a man . . .) and she tucked herself inside. She shut the door softly, and the car pulled away.

When the car was out of sight, I dragged out the cinder block and hoisted myself up to the window ledge, scampering up the siding as softly as I could. Oof. I dropped inside, panting heavily.

With my compact but powerful penlight I swept the room, illuminating her princess canopy bed, her wall of collaged photos, her prominently displayed poster of Scully and Mulder from *The X-Files*. In the corner I caught movement, a dim figure, and gasped. But it was just me, spotlighting myself in her full-length mirror. A fright. I continued my sweep, eyeing her sponge-painted vanity, her white dresser. Wait. I floated the beam back. Conspicuous on the top of her dresser—I stepped toward it, stunned—lay the complexly knotted friendship bracelet I'd made for her last year, chopped clear through the middle. Of course she knew that a friendship bracelet was meant never to be removed. It was meant to last, through showers and baths, thick and thin, accumulating time and grime, until it fell off, meeting its natural end. I fingered my own rigid and decaying bracelet, the colors muted and gray. Hers must not have suited her adult look.

Symbolic. Don't you think?

I did another sweep, of her bookshelf, her desk, her closet. I was searching for clues, any clues, to Gretchen's secret life.

A journal or diary, perhaps. A shoebox of personal memorabilia. I felt under the mattress. Nothing.

Footfalls in the hallway. Thinking fast, I hopped onto her bed and slid under the covers. "Honey?" Mr. McGann said. "Lights out." I clicked off the penlight and listened to his retreating steps.

As I sat up, my hand brushed against an unexpectedly hard edge under the pillow. Something was tucked into the pillowcase. I pulled it out. Bingo. A sleek purple journal— with no lock her diary was practically begging for me to open it. So I did. I sat on the rug and read. And it all came out.

People are not who they seem.

And Gretchen McGann was not the friend I thought she was.

CHAPTER 5

The next day Jake Miller asked Angie to the dance in third period. At lunch, Angie gave us the details. He smoothed his hair twice and stammered six times. His breath smelled like cherry Life Savers. He asked for her number but he didn't have a pen so she gave him hers and he sucked on the cap while he wrote. He returned it, wet. Yes, Angie was a skilled detective, trained in the art of observation. I just wished she would go back to using her skills for more important things, like club business. I smiled weakly and focused on my lunch.

"Margaret," Jina turned to me. "What about Richard Gibbs?"

"What about him?" I was president of our school's Latin club, and Richard Gibbs was VP. Together we had organized the liveliest Saturnalia in the history of our school.

"You should go to the dance together."

"Right," I said.

"Look," Jina nodded at the air behind me, "he's checking you out right now."

"He's probably just staring into space."

"I don't think so."

I turned to look. Richard Gibbs waved shyly. I swiveled back, horrified.

Gretchen sat down with a tray of two tacos, and my heart beat at my chest. She looked terrible. She hadn't slept at all. I wondered if she had any inkling I'd been in her room last night. Probably not. I suspected she was too wrapped up in her secret boyfriend Will Warner to notice anything else.

That's right. *That* Will Warner. The high school sophomore who had cruelly nicknamed me Miss Margarine, depriving me of fun pool times with my friends. The grade-A jerk who was always saying mean things about girls. If he thought they were hot, he'd elbow other boys and make gross comments. If he thought they were not, he'd elbow other boys and make gross comments. We all hated Will Warner. Or ought to.

"What would you say if he asked you?" Jina persisted, still fixated on Richard Gibbs. "Would you say yes?"

"I don't know!" I sputtered. I wished she would leave it alone.

Angie pressed. "Do you have another date we don't know about?"

I slurped my Diet Coke loudly, too annoyed for words.

"Don't you *want* to go to the dance?" inquired Jina.

"You *have* to go," whined Angie. "You're my best friend!"

I glared at my bologna-and-cheese sandwich, which I was eating in small, measured bites.

"You're just nervous."

"But Richard is so *nice*."

Finally I put down my sandwich. "I'm not going."

Angie and Jina looked at each other in shrugging defeat. They'd tried. Angie turned to Gretchen. "Have you decided? Are you going?"

"I guess not," she said, glancing meaningfully at me. "I don't have anyone to go with."

If her "glance" was designed to make me feel guilty, it backfired royally because it made me hopping mad. I had deduced from reading her diary that she hadn't *really* wanted to go to the dance with me. Mr. McGann would never have let her go to the dance with her secret high school boyfriend, so her big scheme, I guessed, was to go with boring, available Margaret under the pretense of being a good friend. I couldn't stand the lies anymore. "What about your new boyfriend?" I said.

"My new boyfriend?" Gretchen gave me a surprised look.

"You know. Your secret boyfriend. Will Warner."

Her mouth fell open in dismay.

Jina squinted. "*Sophomore* Will Warner?"

"Tell them, Gretchen."

"Tell them what?" She let her eyes rove around the table, ready to deny everything.

"Oh, I don't know. Try the fact that you've been seeing Will Warner behind our backs for months."

She met my gaze then. "Have you been following me?"

"Is it true?" Jina cut in.

"He's kind of a jerk," Angie said cautiously.

"Yeah," said Jina. "He was a jerk to Janet." He had called her things like *slut* and *easy* and some other things I didn't understand. He was a jerk to me, too, I wanted to add, but I didn't. If they were oblivious then, they'd be oblivious now.

"He's not a jerk. And we're not— It's complicated," Gretchen said. She spun to me. "You *have* been following me."

I hesitated. "Not exactly."

"You snuck into my house, didn't you?" She was livid. "You snuck into my room! I knew something was different."

"I was investigating," I said, unapologetic. "There were mysteries to solve, and I solved them."

Mysteries that involved *me*. No, Gretchen had not wanted to go to the dance with me as—anything. She wanted to go with me as a lie. *I asked Margaret about the dance*, she told her diary, *but she got all weird and uncomfortable*. Not true! Not true! I was just confused and . . . she was weird and uncomfortable too! *I knew it was a stupid idea as soon as I said it. I guess it's just as well. She's one of my best friends and all but she's* really *immature. I can't imagine her dancing with me without making a big joke out of everything*. To which I must respond: correct. That's because the dance *is* a big joke, and I would much rather be out sleuthing. *I honestly feel sorry for her. I just hope one day she figures it out*. Yes, thank you. I'm figuring it out right now. *It's too bad I can't bring Will. We'd scandalize everyone and have such a blast. Like Will says . . . we're so much bigger than this boring town. Four more years till college. I don't know if I can stand it*.

Okay. I stared at the page, confused and angry. Her diary was more feelings than events and there was a lot left out. Other things were transcribed into some code. If I had more time, I would be able to decipher it. But I didn't. She could have arrived home any moment.

But I did stumble upon one other shocking revelation, buried in a long, anxious passage dated the day after Melanie's disappearance.

"Tell them about Skateland," I challenged Gretchen. "Where was Will when Melanie went missing?"

Jina and Angie gave me incredulous looks. "You're kidding," Angie said. "What?"

"Where was he, Gretchen? Do you know?"

Gretchen's mouth was tight, her face pale with rage. Jina and Angie looked at each other, then at me. They waited for me to explain. "It's possible Will had something to do with Melanie's disappearance," I said. "He was conveniently MIA for a long chunk of the night."

"You were there?" Angie swerved to Gretchen, shocked.

"That's right," I said when Gretchen said nothing. "She may have been the last to see Melanie on the steps of Skateland, not long before she disappeared. And Will was nowhere to be found." According to Gretchen's diary entry, Skateland was closing down for the night when Gretchen went outside to look for Will and ran into Melanie sitting alone on the steps. As they were locking up, one of the employees let Gretchen back inside to find her friend, and when she came out again, Melanie was gone and Will was waiting for her in his car. After that, the diary entry had devolved into frantic, self-pitying *it could have been me*s.

"How do you know all this?" Jina asked slowly.

"She snuck into my room," Gretchen said slowly, "and read my diary." Her voice was low and shaking. "That's how."

"Whoa. What?" Angie said. She shook her head in disbelief. Jina glowered at me.

Who cared how I knew. The point was that Gretchen had withheld key information. All these months of dead ends, Gretchen had kept these pesky, *incriminating* details about Will to herself. "Tell them, Gretchen. Where was Will? Do you even know?"

We waited. Storm clouds gathered in her face. Finally she spoke, with steely calm. "It is none of your fucking business."

Angie's jaw dropped.

I blinked, recovering. "I think it is our business. It's actually the definition of our business, given that it's pertinent to our—"

"Okay," Jina said. "That's enough."

"I'm with Margaret on this," Angie stepped in. "This is huge."

We waited for Gretchen's response.

"Fine," Gretchen said, glowering. "Will was in the bathroom. Blowing the DJ. Are you happy now?"

That wasn't in the diary. Wait. Will Warner was— "Yeah, right." I didn't believe her. It had to be another lie designed to cover for Will. She was a gifted actor, after all. Or maybe Gretchen wasn't lying, or didn't know she was. Maybe Will was the liar. Whatever the case, his whereabouts would need to be investigated.

Gretchen grabbed her tray and left, shoulders squared, strands from her messy, tired low ponytail floating behind her.

Jina packed up her things and followed her.

I turned to Angie triumphantly. "I knew she was keeping secrets. I just needed to know why."

Angie looked troubled. "You may have gone too far," she said carefully. "I, um, I have to use the bathroom." And she followed Gretchen too.

I had solved the mystery of Gretchen's incessant yawns. Why weren't my friends grateful? And what about Melanie Flowers? Did this new information mean nothing to them? A girl was missing—a girl *like us*—and we had a new lead.

Why weren't we following it? I slumped in my seat, confused and a little annoyed.

Gretchen and I avoided each other the rest of the day. It wasn't hard. We had only one class together: band. Gretchen sat in front as first flute, and I, first bassoon, behind her to the right. I kept watch, observing her sharp huffs all period long while channeling my anger and insult into my instrument, striking the reed with my tongue ever forcefully until my bellowing caught Mr. Conway's attention. "Less bassoon!" he yelled, holding a finger to his lips. "Pianissimo. Not you, saxophones. Keep it up."

Meanwhile Richard Gibbs popped up at every turn. He lingered after band class. He lingered after Latin. I shielded myself behind classmates and scurried off as fast as I could. But at the end of the day, there he was again, strategically planted in front of my locker.

"Hey, Margaret!" he said with shaky enthusiasm.

I reversed course.

"Margaret— Hey, Margaret—" he called after me, following me uncertainly.

I jerked around. "No."

"Oh." He let out a breath. "Okay," he muttered, his cheeks glowing with embarrassment. He shrank away.

Gretchen wasn't on the bus that afternoon. She must have gotten a ride home with Will Warner, I thought, scornful. "Blowing the DJ." Ha. Did she think I was stupid? No *way* Will Warner was—that. And if he was, why was Gretchen hanging out with him? I was sure it was all part of an elaborate cover-up. Will had to be involved in Melanie's disappearance—I didn't know how, but I would find out— and Gretchen, our dear, *deceptive* friend Gretchen, was his unwitting alibi. Angie and Jina were quiet. When I brought up my theory, they gave me long looks. Jina put on her head-phones and turned the volume up loud. Angie left our spot to sit with Jake Miller. Finally I started my homework. No use wasting time. I would get home and I would follow this new lead myself.

CHAPTER 6

Tuesday, 5:34 p.m. Jina and Gretchen were late but I held out hope. In the long history of GCSA, neither had missed a meeting. I turned to a fresh page in our club notebook, wrote down the day's date, and waited. Angie sat cross-legged on the rug. She passed me a tray of Oreos. I declined.

Melanie Flowers had been found, finally, last night. According to morning news reports, her decomposing body was discovered buried shallowly in the front yard of a man who worked at the McDonald's near Skateland. He was arrested on charges of sexual assault and murder. Case closed.

School was a gloom. The news spread quickly, and a pall crept in by second period. Though few of us had known Mela-nie, it felt as though we had come to know her these past months, with her crooked smile plastered all over town. The report of her death was unnerving, and everyone was upset. Still, when Betsy Kitchell started weeping in algebra—Ms. Smith had unwisely used the word "kill" while leading us through an equation—it seemed a bit much.

I had already cleared Will Warner of suspicion. The DJ that night, a Mitch "DJ Lucky" Lombart, would not say exactly in what capacity, but admitted to having been with Will during the twenty-minute time frame in which Melanie was last seen. I'd been trying to share this info with Gretchen, but she hung up each time I called.

The phone rang and Angie answered. Jina wasn't coming, she reported. She had to watch Darryl. It was an excuse, we knew. And we understood without saying it that Gretchen wouldn't be joining us either. At least Jina had the decency to call.

I rapped the meeting to order. Maybe it was silly with just me and Angie, but it was routine. "First order of business," I said. "We need new clients. It may be time to expand out of Shady Bluff."

Angie sighed. "Margaret . . ."

"What?"

"Have you talked to Gretchen?"

I sighed impatiently. "I've called her twelve times. She hangs up."

"Maybe you could try writing a letter."

"Angie, this is club time."

"Margaret," she said softly. "Do we have a club anymore?"

"We have open cases."

Angie pursed her lips and examined her split ends, her thinking pose. "You might have to solve them on your own. I've been thinking . . . I really ought to focus on school and sports for a while."

That was a lie. What she really wanted to focus on was Jake Miller. Ugh. I was trembling. I excused myself to use the bathroom. Some internal levy was about to break and I needed to summon reinforcements.

Pressing my hands against the cool bathroom counter I breathed deep, steadying myself. It's okay, I told myself. You'll be your own sleuth. You'll organize another club. You'll be fine. I looked up in search of the reassurance of my own gaze. But my image in the glass was a blur, some pinkish-gray blob, unrecognizable and alarming. Must be my contacts, I thought. I blinked. I was crying.

Deep breaths. Stop it. I washed my face, dabbed it dry with a fluffy hand towel. When I rejoined her, Angie gave me the most insultingly sympathetic look. I scowled back and sat down in my spot.

The phone rang. I lifted the receiver and heard a familiar squeak.

"Any updates on my case?"

"Ms. Normandy," I said sharply. In truth, I'd forgotten all about her. I composed myself. This was business. "As you know very well, your body isn't missing. You arranged to have it stolen so you could collect insurance money. You are the criminal and we will be alerting the authorities to your crime. Goodbye." I hung up.

"Another case closed," Angie said with forced cheerfulness. "One less open case to worry about."

"Fewer," I corrected. "One *fewer* open case to worry about." My eyes were starting to sting.

Angie and I met up once more, but I could tell she was just being nice. I sent a few rounds of notes to Gretchen and Jina, apologizing in a professional and businesslike tone and inviting them back to the club. They didn't respond.

We were done. Girls Can Solve Anything was over. Maybe it was time. For one thing, we were no longer girls. We were teenagers.

And I had come to an uncomfortable conclusion. I, Margaret Worms, head detective, did not understand a thing.

If adolescence is a passageway, a twilight zone or liminal space, it's also the time when, like thick blobs of gummy dough, we get poured into shape and rise. It's a plastic time, a time of self-discovery and growth, and in some cases tremendous creativity. Teenagehood is that stage when you get to become who you are, or who you can be. Ah, there's the rub: How can you be who you are when— Margaret doesn't know how to finish this question.

Dear Davina, dear Eisha, dear Angie—

She's back in her own car now, new dents hammered out, back fender replaced. She's heading home on the back roads, and she is composing pretend letters in her head. *Sorry I was so moody today. Sorry I'm such a lump. But get this! Remember how I said I was at the doctor last week? Well I was. But it wasn't for my annual physical like I said. It was for—*

She flips the station to Q94. Then B103. Then 106.5, where it lands on the a cappella opening to "Bohemian Rhapsody," which reminds her of Angie, Jina, and Gretchen. She's not supposed to be thinking of them. But she leaves it.

Dear Angie, dear Jina, dear Gretchen— Margaret should have been Freddie in their music video years ago. Not Angie. Angie doesn't have pathos this big, enough to fill up a six-minute rock opera. *Do you remember?* It was the first time

Gretchen joined them for one of Angie's slumber parties; she had just joined the club. They made friendship bracelets while watching *Wayne's World*, then, inspired, remade the video to "Bohemian Rhapsody." God, how old were they? Eleven? Twelve? Seventh grade. *It's my house and my video camera*, Angie insisted, in a plaintive voice Margaret recognized from elementary school. *I get to be Freddie!* So Angie was in the center, flanked by Jina and Gretchen with Margaret hovering on top, trying to leave space between their bodies, trying not to be weird. Even then she'd looked weird to herself on video, but they all did when they watched it, dark pits for eyes, the details of their faces blotted out in the blast of their flashlights. Weird. Wrong. Whatever. They didn't make it far their first take because, at the second or third *Mama*, Ms. Stern yelled up, *What, Angie, what?* And they collapsed into a giggle fit that revived itself several times.

I miss you. I hope you're doing great. I'm fine. I guess.

"Bohemian Rhapsody" is structured like a trial, she realizes now. It begins with the criminal's confession and proceeds to his prosecution and defense, and finally delivers his judgment. Though he claims to need no sympathy, this poor boy is sympathetic: born into a context that has not adequately supported him, he has killed a man for reasons we haven't been made privy to but would maybe understand.

As well, we learn, he is sick and he is tired, stuck in a body that is aching all the time. And so he must leave.

Dear Eisha, dear Davina, The truth is, there's so much I haven't told you and I don't know where to start—

After Margaret fainted in church on Sunday, her mother made her go to the family doctor. Margaret objected: the fainting was over before it began. She wobbled, fell back on the pew. After a moment of disorientation, she jolted upright. Humiliating. Not the fainting—that was tragic, romantic, impressive—but the long string of silent gas she released before she sank.

The checkup was humiliating too. *The solution is simple*, Dr. Ashton told her mother, not bothering to speak to her, Margaret, the patient. *She needs to eat more.* The adults talked around her; she hadn't said a thing.

Dear Davina, dear Eisha, I don't know what to say. It's . . . embarrassing, to be honest.

She passes a Wendy's. She wants a Frosty. No—she can't. She won't. She will not succumb. Not again.

Even as she objected to the appointment, Margaret had harbored a thin hope that Dr. Ashton would see how bad she is and send her to a clinic like Laura Graber. Nope. He flicked up her eyelids and looked at her nail beds, prescribed iron pills, and sent her on her way. She's not bad enough. Yet.

Last night she binged at home, as punishment. A punishment demanding its own punishment. She stole food from the kitchen under cover of night. And she ate it. Wildly, desperately, disgustingly. She left traces in absence: What was there—leftover macaroni and cheese, half a jar of peanut butter—isn't there anymore. Including a fresh pan of chocolate chip blondies. It's a whole routine. Margaret doesn't eat dessert when her family does, declining proudly. Instead she sneaks little slivers of brownies, of blondies, of cake, whatever's on offer, there's always something, while making her next-day lunch, slicing inward, at a slant, hardly noticeable. Last month her mother caught her in the act. *Just eat a whole square*, she said, watching from the doorway. *It won't kill you.* Margaret grinned sheepishly, put the knife down.

Last night started with the usual slivers. Then she couldn't stop. Sliver here, sliver there, shaking, shaking. She can't remember the rest. By the time she heard her brother's truck rolling in on the gravel, there was just one hunk of blondie left. Hurriedly she cleaned up and slunk back to bed. After she was sure Brian was asleep, snoring lightly, she crept into the bathroom. Blech.

You know, her mother had reflected, driving Margaret home after the doctor's appointment, *I've dieted all my life, and it never works. I've always been chunky. It's just how we're made.* Margaret snorted at the changed tune. The old one was *Think how pretty you'd be if you just lost some weight.* Margaret had been, oh, seven or eight, sucking in her gut like a goof, pretending to be a bodybuilder. That was just around the time Dr. Ashton put Margaret on her first diet, saying she was *in danger of becoming obese.*

Her vision goes blurry, then settles, blurry, then settles.

A chorus of falsetto voices swoops in, entreating the judge to spare the boy his life in faux Italian. Margaret notes the abruptness of this tonal swerve from tragedy to comedy, the startling abruptness of all the song's many transitions—and yet it achieves cohesion.

Blech.

Dear Eisha, dear Davina, I just need to get this—

Her seat belt cuts into her gut, which is still somewhat distended. Uncomfortable. She unclasps it, slips out from under its hold.

She drives past Munchy, who munches. She slows down, waves. Way to go, Munchy. She's a bad pony too. A loud honk blasts behind her. She's slowed to a creep in the middle of the road. Oops. Bye, Munchy.

Dear Jina, dear Gretchen, I miss you, I miss you, everything's wrong—

Her knuckles are white on the steering wheel. She should

head home. She has calculus problems, science chapters, a bassoon to honk and her throat is burning, her stomach is seriously eating itself though *why why* when she devoured so much blech last night, and she should call Eisha, who's been absent two days now, she should check with Davina, ask what's up. What's up? What's up? Stop.

Unfortunately she wants to do none of this. She wants to keep driving, stay in suspension, kill time. Another reason the nation should convert to renewable energy, the topic of this year's policy debate. So girls like her can drive the days away. She'll add that to her and Eisha's evidence box, impress Stephen, fuck Stephen, who cares.

Her vision beats red, darkens at the corners. She's got this terrible pulsing migraine—what she imagines a hangover must be, from too much sugar, too much everything all at once. *Mama! Oo-oo-oo-ooh.*

It won't kill you, her mother had said about the blondies. But maybe it would. Something is wrong with her. Something is very wrong. What is it. Some other mystery. She'll solve it on her own.

There are no more mysteries. No more friends. No more love interests. Only problems, problems, problems. What's her problem? The problem is Margaret. She's the problem.

She needs a Frosty. That's the problem.

She turns out of the neighborhood, heading toward the Wendy's on the other end of the county, where no one she knows might see her. The song cranking up to that vengeful guitar solo, she's at the sharp turn where Cory died, Frosty Frosty Frosty, she vibrates in anticipation, the guilty thrill. She twists back, they should replace those dead flowers, how morbid, how sad, and speeds up again, seeing a dark Lexus encroaching on her. *So you think you can love me and leave me to*— She glances in the rearview mirror and abruptly stops singing, it can't be, it can't be, it's Gretchen with her perfect hair and skin and makeup, singing along to something, coolly, absently, perfectly, maybe this very same song. Margaret reaches up and adjusts the mirror, Gretchen mustn't see her, her mission is bad, undercover, she'll know. Now her range of vision's off and disorienting. It's not Gretchen at all. It's no one. When she glances up she sees herself, the thick planes of her cheeks. She should be skinnier after all this work. Her face should be more gaunt. The mirror blinks. Dark edges crackle in her periphery. Her wheels are running off the road and she's hitting gravel, shit, she's swerving left too fast, too hard, overcorrecting, and the steering column is locking, the dark edges are creeping inward and blotting the field. The last thing she sees is the tree, its thick and unmoving trunk, the gnarled bark, the bloom of the airbag. The black.

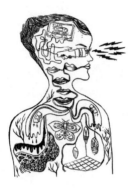

*P*eople ask, *How did you get in here? What they really want to know is:* How do they get in here themselves? You can't acknowledge the real question. And it's rare that you admit the real answer, because the truth is: *it's easy.*

And it is easy to slip into a parallel universe. There are so many of them: worlds of the insane, the criminal, the dying; art. These worlds exist alongside this world and resemble it, but are not in it.

Thank god. Without these other worlds, we would have no way of surviving this one.

One girl among you had to eat through a tube. She had a hole in her stomach she liked to show off. It connected her insides to her tube. She purged so much she ruptured her esophagus. Eventually she decided it would be easier to bypass the mouth and throat.

Her name was Suze. She had a single room, which meant her parents paid double and she got to thinking she owned the place. Your first night you made the mistake of sitting on "her" couch during social hour. She fumed until you caught her meaning and scooted.

This was her third time at the center, she told you when her fumes had worn off. She'd been to three other programs too. Her voice was boastful; she'd won.

The next day you learned she had a reserved spot in line: last.

"No one's allowed to stare at her butt," Natalie explained while you waited for weigh-in. "She goes ballistic."

You turned to test this information, but there she was, hostilely facing you, flannel shirt wrapped around her waist.

"You have a pimple," said Natalie. "You've been picking it." Her face was lumpy with acne scars. "You've been picking at yourself," she went on.

You focused on peeling your banana, the evenest peels.

"Got a boyfriend? Mine's Charlie." She sighed dreamily. "Charlie Flickers. He's big and muscly, but lean. He's a football player." She squirmed as if overcome by the joy of it. "He's coming next Visiting Day. You'll meet him."

"Cool."

You would never meet Charlie Flickers. Natalie left two days later, when her insurance coverage ran out. They made you eat cupcakes at the party for her release.

Perhaps it's unclear how you got here.

It was easy. You went for a drive. A long drive. You drifted, suspended, in loops. You put on some music. You drove and drove. You kept driving.

You glanced at the mirror.

You crashed.

The last thing you remember is the front hood folding in on itself, a Diet Coke can, crushed. Then you, your body, kept going.

You left the hospital with a cracked rib and some stitches at your temple. You were lucky. Your vitals were bad but not bad enough, so when you got out, you got worse. You did your research and found the center online. *At the Briarwood Residential Treatment Center, we believe that girls and young women are highly intuitive, sensitive, and* blah blah blah.

Your mother pored over the printout with a dubious frown.

But she called. She made arrangements before your father could object to the cost. Insurance would cover most but not all of it, for a while.

You had two days until check-in. Two days to lose as much as you could. If they judged you not thin enough, you would not have been able to bear the mortification. If they didn't admit you, you'd die.

During intake, you exaggerated how little you ate, how much you exercised. You needed to compete with your image of the other girls. You were sure they exercised twice as much, ate next to nothing.

You weren't exaggerating. You were sick, you were sick, you were sick.

"Have you ever experienced sexual assault?"

"No."

"Physical abuse?"

"No."

"Suicidal thoughts?"

Your armpits grew damp. What was your problem? Nothing was wrong. Nothing bad had ever happened to you. Girls were supposed to lose weight.

"No."

But you got in. You made it. You won.

"All right, then." The nurse closed the folder and appraised you. "We're very glad you're here."

ETIOLOGY

You are (pick one):
    on a perilous journey from which we can learn much when
        you return
    starving for attention
    dying to be thin
    faking it to fit in
    ill, and must be isolated from society and treated with (pick
        one)
        food
        yoga
        art
        community
    sane in an insane world
    superficial
    vain
    suffering from suburban American overabundance
    saving the environment
    a feminist
    a white girl
    a girl
    a girl, interrupted
    a copycat
    just following directions

out of control
overcontrolling
testing the limits of your body
starving away your feminine parts
trying too hard at being a girl
covering over the real problem
grrr

The parking lot, the lobby, the front desk. The bright lights and black vinyl chairs, the sliding doors and the squat shrubs they looked out on. The crowded nursing station and its clean plastic smells. The lounge, where nothing much ever happened.

The cracked leather couches, big and cushy, engulfing. You loved them; they made you feel small. The Jenga blocks wedged between cushions. The boxy TV up high and bolted to the wall. The big floor pillow, its tassels you clung to like a raft.

Around the corner, a corridor connected to small rooms used for therapy and team meetings. Muffled voices, the occasional laugh. Frosted windows that fuzzed the scenes inside. Around the next corner, the art room and the utility closet, where you hid among brooms during personal time. Giggling, complaining. Comparing the width of your wrists.

Then a hallway leading to a shorter hallway leading to your room.

The twin beds pushed to opposite sides, your desks hugging the wall between them. On her desk, a journal and pens. Two abstract watercolors pasted to the hutch, their edges curling, their angry, swirling colors suggesting storms of ugly feelings. One black, one red.

Nurse Irene, apologetic that first day. "I've just got to take a look in your bag."

You dropped it on the bed and wandered into the bathroom. Score. Unlike most of the residential centers you'd found online, this one offered en suite bathrooms. "You start with basic privileges," Nurse Irene explained during intake. "But they can be taken away." If staff discovered patients purging, cutting, or smoking, for example, the bathrooms would be locked and you'd have to be supervised. Other privileges could be earned: day passes, weekend passes, Internet time. The center operated on trust. They trusted you to make good choices, which meant they presented the good choices to you and it was your choice whether to choose them. If you didn't, there would be consequences. You nodded; you understood. The center's policies corresponded with your worldview. Crime means punishment. You are all the same in the eyes of the law.

In the center of it all, the cafeteria.

Big round tables, heavy plastic chairs. Broad metal tray rack. Overstuffed clipboards dangling from the thick central column.

It was always so cold.

Eating was trying. You sat with Natalie, Jess, Evie.

Those trays. Massive gray slabs that hung past the table. They were passed out pre-loaded, so much food you were shocked. You had hoped to ease in.

The clinking of utensils, the dull scrape of a bowl. You took your cues from the others. Natalie stared straight ahead and chewed methodically, jaw working with metronomic consistency. Evie dipped her fork in applesauce dubiously. Jess, the youngest at only thirteen, smashed down her veggie burger and cut it into small cubes.

You took a careful bite of your wrap.

"Jess," Nurse Irene said. "You're just wasting time."

Jess muttered and continued cutting, expressing with each huffy slice her open contempt for the world. Or maybe she was simply a mouth breather.

"Twenty minutes," said Irene.

One turkey-and-swiss wrap, one yogurt cup, an apple, a salad, one Chips Ahoy! cookie, crisp and perfectly round. If you didn't entirely finish an item, only half its caloric value counted, even if you *almost* entirely finished it.

Later, a cheese stick and granola bar.

After that (you had filled out a menu during intake), pasta and broccoli with cheese, a roll, milk.

Then a banana and a second cup of yogurt.

All of it timed. All of it supervised and recorded. You could do this, you told yourself. You might even like it. It could be a relief: to give up and eat, to let the center take over for a few days. You would sail ahead on autopilot, just do what you're told. No bargaining. No punishing. No rewarding. No bingeing. No restricting.

None. The realization hit hard. This is what it will look like. Every meal. The pace of your eating slowed.

"I'm bisexual," Natalie said out of nowhere.

"Awesome," said Evie. She sipped down the rest of her juice. "I'm straight, I think. But girls are really pretty. Does that mean I'm bisexual? Sorry. It's all very confusing."

Now that no one was watching, Jess stabbed two columns of her burger with her fork tines. She brought them to her mouth like a secret.

"No food rituals," Irene reminded her, but it was perfunctory. She just wanted Jess to eat.

"How do you know you're bisexual?" Evie asked Natalie. "Have you kissed a girl?"

"Of course I have. I had a girlfriend last year."

Evie seemed impressed. "What about guys? You've gone out with them too?"

"I've done lots of stuff. More than Carrie." Natalie's eyes gloated. "My boyfriend Charlie's coming on Visiting Day."

She wasn't the first to mention Carrie, another resident, conspicuously absent. You'd ask about her later, you thought. Right now, the food was too much.

"I haven't done anything," Evie said sadly. "I'm not what boys like."

"Why not? You're so pretty."

Evie gave her a shy smile and looked like she was about to respond, but Natalie cut in. "Margaret," she said. "What have you done?"

You shrugged uncomfortably and let your gaze rest on Jess's fork.

She turned to you, venomous. "Stop watching."

"I wasn't."

"You were!"

"Jess," warned Irene. "You can talk after you finish."

Jess pushed her tray away, glaring at you. "I'm done."

Irene assessed what was left. "That's two Boosts for later. Are you sure?"

Jess folded her arms over her chest. "I hate you," she growled.

Irene sighed. "Ten minutes."

Dr. Grunch was the one who was feared: she was large and broad-chested, penetrating and severe. Dr. Holly was the nice one, the pushover; slim, quiet, a listener. Her glasses were always sliding down her nose. She leaned toward you and beamed, transmitting an energy like *like*.

Over the course of your sessions, you observed Dr. Holly's

unswerving fixation on family as the root of your eating disorder. "They don't sustain you," she offered. "They don't provide the emotional or intellectual nourishment you need to thrive. So you've been unable to nourish yourself." She paused, waited. "How does it feel to hear that?"

Family, family, family. What did it mean that Dr. Holly was so obsessed with them? Did Dr. Holly have awful parents? A terrible brother? Had her family driven her to stop eating too?

You didn't think so. You felt reasonably sure, from her thinness and kindness, that Dr. Holly had enjoyed an easy life. Oh, you know: there was a lot you weren't seeing. Still, you couldn't help but imagine her in a sensible one-piece at the beach, propped up in a chaise longue and absorbed in a frivolous read.

She seemed to believe that writing could solve anything. At the end of each session, she gave you exercises to write letters home, letters that would never get sent. Some days she asked you to write angry rants; others, to imagine things from different perspectives. Dr. Holly felt these assignments would help you identify buried feelings and understand their origins, that they'd help you take control over your story.

What story? Nothing bad had ever happened to you. You had no real problems. That was the problem. You barely existed at all.

To facilitate a feeling of closeness, the chairs and sofas in the dayroom were arranged in a circle. The furniture was comfortable but made obscene noises when you moved.

Dr. Holly sat in the therapist chair and began with an icebreaker. The stand-up/sit-down was your favorite.

"Stand up if you're having a good hair day," she would

start, and stand, fluffing her Rachel layers. "Stay standing. Stand up if you've had a good hair day in the past week." She continued—"past month . . . past two months . . . past year"—until everyone was standing.

Then she'd pick a new topic: favorite color or sport, something benign, simple. The other girls groaned but you loved it. It gave you exercise. It made you feel seen.

"Stand up if you like *Dawson's Creek*."

Nope.

"Stand up if you like *The X-Files*."

Yep.

"Stand up if you like *Buffy*."

Were half stands allowed?

The sad boy in the corner, Ian, didn't like anything. He slumped with his arms crossed over the x-ed out eyes on his Nirvana shirt, his favorite: he wore it most days, the druggy happy face in harsh contrast to his perpetual unsmilingness.

"Stand up if you think this is dumb," Dr. Holly said to him pointedly.

Ian rolled his eyes and shifted uncomfortably. His thighs and butt spilled over the edges of the hard plastic chair he had chosen. He was among the biggest ones there and the only boy, though with his dark straggly hair and black nail polish he sometimes looked like a girl. Grudgingly he stood and collapsed again, resuming his cross-armed pose.

Then it was time for group share and support. *I so relate. I have the same problem, but for me it's like . . . worse.*

You were not impressed with the other girls' problems. There was Suze's butt, aforementioned. *I feel like I'm walking around with spotlights on both cheeks.* There was Jess's perfect sister. *I just want to beat her at something. So I'm beating her at this.* Evie worried she'd never be as skinny as her mom.

Vietnamese girls are supposed to be tiny. I'm big. Everyone says so. And you: your brother got all the attention. Wah. That wasn't the problem, you knew, but it was the easiest to say. You weren't impressed with your problems either. Yet every time you spoke you had a gross little catch in your voice. *I'm tired of it. I'm ready to change.* You bowed your head. You were acting. *That's why I'm here. To change.*

"You're in the right place," Natalie offered clumsily. "You can do it. I believe in you."

"Yeah." Jess stifled a yawn. "I believe in you too."

Dear Mom and Dad,

Here goes. You suck, you're fat, and I hate you. I hate you when you chew with your mouths open. I hate you when you chew with your mouths closed. I hate you when you make loud bathroom noises. I hate you when your clothes fold into your pudge. I hate you when you come home with doughnuts. I hate you, I hate you, I hate you. These are some things you can change.

Now I'm supposed to see things from your perspective. Your perspective is bullshit. Fuck you.

Love,
Margaret

Your head ached. That first long day was a blur, out of focus and hard to watch. During social time, you sat quietly on one of the two couches, your sleeves over your hands.

"Carrie self-sabotaged," Natalie informed you. Her blood pressure dropped too low. She had spent last night and today in the hospital. Now she was on her way back. "She's your roommate," Natalie said, widening her eyes significantly.

You squinted out the front windows as a van rolled up.

"Here we go," Natalie muttered.

Nurse Irene opened the front door and Nurse Hannah led a frail girl in by the hand. "I'm fine, I've got it," the girl snapped, dark waves clinging to her pale skull. She entered shakily. "What's all this?" She was pleased by her reception, the lot of you staring openly. She dipped her head, curtsied.

Nurse Irene jabbed a finger at her and said she was in for it.

Her lips curled. "Aw, Irene. I missed you too."

When your eyes met, your heart thumped dangerously. Her wide, smirking mouth. Her frank gaze boring into you, through you. Power. Intensity. Zap.

"What's your story?" Carrie zigzagged through the room as she unpacked the small duffel bag brought back from the hospital.

"Anorexic?" She paused outside the bathroom and studied your body. You shrank in response. "Bulimic? Both? Over-eater?" She scrutinized your thighs and stomach.

"Both," you blurted, mainly to stop her guessing. Her stare a punch. "'Eating disorder not otherwise specified.' That's what they wrote down."

"Ah yes, the bullshit diagnosis."

You froze, heat rising to your cheeks. You were sick, really sick, you wanted to explain. You collapsed in the bathroom. You had to take iron supplements!

"That's what they say when the categories don't fit. We're all EDNOS, for the most part."

"Oh. You're EDNOS too?" The word felt funny in your mouth.

"Yup. I like to use all the tools at my disposal." She sat

down on the other bed and you compared your thighs against hers. Some people you look at and know: they've never been fat. You scooted to the edge of the mattress.

"But what's your story? I'll go first."

Carrie had grown up with a single mother who was a dieting fanatic. New craze every month, she told you. Like your mom except hers was serious; you beat back jealous pangs. South Beach. Atkins. The no-sugar cleanse. Every new diet pill released on the market. Carrie had been made to try all of them. "Finally I just stopped eating," she said nonchalantly. That made her mother nuts.

She hopped off the bed and lifted the mattress. She stuck a hand in and rummaged around, finally pulling out a strip of laxatives. She tore one off and offered it to you.

You looked at her questioningly. "That's against the rules."

"Oh, I'm sorry." She raised an eyebrow. "Are you *that* kind of girl?"

You hesitated, then took it. Why not. Dinner still stuck in your gut. You watched her pop hers out and swallow it, then did the same. The pattern in place. She'd lead, you'd follow.

"This is my third treatment center," she went on. "They're all just holding pens. No one actually gets better. Most of us don't want to." Her previous roommate had left two days ago, eight pounds under goal weight. Her insurance had run out.

When it was your turn to share, you spoke haltingly. You didn't want her to know you'd been fat. You were already bigger than she was. "I've always dieted, I guess. It just got easier and easier. Like an addiction. My mom's always dieting too, like yours. But she never lasts long. She cheats." You reddened, embarrassed for your mom. And for yourself, for the binges, which you leave unmentioned. "Anyway. Now I'm here." You heaved a melodramatic sigh and wished you'd said something more interesting.

Carrie wrestled her legs into a complicated pretzel on her bed. She tapped her thumbs against her knees. She seemed to fidget constantly. "So it's your first time," she guessed. "What do you think?"

You shrugged. "Dr. Holly seems nice."

"Yeah, she's a softie but she doesn't know shit. Is writing really going to save our lives?" She rolled her eyes, and you blushed again. You had wanted to say the right thing. Around her you felt queasy and electrified, some uncomfortable thrum rising inside you. Like the fluttering you'd felt around Gretchen, but this was stronger and more cruel, sharper, a panic.

"But you can get her to do anything," Carrie continued. "That's the trick. If you show her you have some will to get better, she'll give you whatever you want."

"Like what?"

"Privileges." Carrie's eyes lit up. "Internet. Day passes. More phone time. Exercise time. You'll learn. Everything's a game. You have to pass the levels."

LEVEL ONE

You are eating lunch with Carrie, Evie, and Jess. For today's meal you have chosen a veggie burger with cheese on a wheat bun, broccoli with one butter packet, an apple, an oatmeal cookie, and apple juice.

Jess sips her juice, eyeing the spread before her. Evie delicately dips into her chicken noodle soup while supplying the table with a friendly ramble about her newest collage, in progress in the arts-and-crafts room. Carrie takes large, showy bites of her veggie wrap. You work through your burger with diligence and impatience, until Carrie catches your eye.

You

— ignore her. If it means following the rules, you *are* that kind of girl. Rules get made for good reasons.

— grab your throat *subtly*. Pretend you are choking *subtly*. Don't oversell it. Be believable.

You gag quietly, swallow your breath. Nurse Hannah jerks to attention, prepared to administer the Heimlich though you can tell she would rather not move. You cough and hack and nearly barf up your food, pretense teetering into reality. Gasping, you lean back.

"I'm okay." You make your voice feeble and faint. Cough once more.

Hannah swoops her eyes over the table, perturbed but uncertain. She sighs and checks her watch. "Fifteen minutes."

Later Carrie will show off the cookie she yanked from her tray. She'll give you a high five and an approving grin.

You have passed this level.

LEVEL TWO

Eating disorders supposedly come in two basic varieties: excess and restraint.

The predominant quality of the excessive form is anarchy. *Making yourself sick, purging, yakking, scarf and barf, self-induced vomiting, engaging in bulimic symptoms. Barf is an upheaval, born of our hangover from imbibing too much Western Civ. Hierarchies jumble in the thrill, in the imperatives of purge. The Barf is not so much anti-logocentric, anti-dichotomy, as outside the whole fucking system.*

The predominant quality of the restrictive form is discipline. *Starving, restricting, fasting, compulsive exercising, engaging in anorexic symptoms.* Whittling down the self into a perfect system. Nothing in, nothing out. The sickest version of ableism there is.

Neither of these systems adequately describes your contradictory and improvisational performance.

It's fat-free everything, diet pills with black coffee, then sliding through three drive-throughs and bingeing in your car. It's celebrating your birthday with the most meager slice of homemade chocolate-marble birthday cake you can get away with, then getting up in the middle of the night to shave off slivers from the tray. When your miniscule shavings accrete into noticeability, you decide you need punishment and pack in the rest with mean swoops, comforted by the certainty that no one will dare confront you. Comforted, then resentful.

It's remembering nothing about your summer away at Latin camp, nothing about the movie you just watched or the book you just read, beyond the estimated number of calories you consumed before, during, after.

It's flaking on Mother's Day, avoiding Davina's family party, forgetting Angie's track meet and Eisha's big choir concert, all while convinced they don't love you, they've never cared, you don't matter until you drop more weight.

It's having nothing to live for but losing.

Carrie is making you over. You breathe in her plumeria scent. You've placed your headphones sideways on the counter, the best you can do with no boombox. Trapped in the tiny speakers, Fiona Apple sounds tinny and small. Carrie adores her too. "Doesn't everyone?" she had said, and you chose to ignore the snark. You're so alike, you've decided. You're going to be best friends.

She massages leave-in conditioner into your roots, then scrunches. Your head becomes heavy and romantic, thick with smells. As she slides cool liquid onto the planes of your cheeks, you worry over the hugeness of your face. She dabs at it with a sponge to blend the foundation, and you think of your mother, the disc of powder she uses to muffle her shine. Do you miss home? Not yet.

"Now that I've applied foundation," Carrie is saying, narrating her actions like an instructional video, "I'll use some concealer to cover up these small blemishes I'm seeing."

You cringe, mortified by your small blemishes. "First I'll use the green concealer." She holds it up for you to see. "It cancels out the redness."

She seems to assume you have never used makeup, that you haven't been incorporating *Seventeen*'s monthly makeup tips into your routine for years. Are you that bad at it, have you been failing all along? But you don't mind. Her easy chatter soothes you, and someone like you can always benefit from learning more tricks, especially from someone like her. Carrie is more glamorous, more daring and dramatic with her colors, her swoops, her lines, than you are. Already you can feel yourself spreading out and defining yourself against her, even as you want to become her. How close can you get? You've taken to showering after her to absorb the skin molecules she's released into the air.

She grips your chin. "Look down. Now I'm applying the regular concealer on top of the green, red-canceling concealer." An array of wands and brushes sprawls across the bathroom counter. Premium stuff: Clinique, Bobbi Brown, MAC. It must have cost a fortune.

"Do you ever get mad about it?" you venture. "Makeup, I mean."

"Mad?" She flutters her fingers over the counter until she finds the liquid eyeliner she wants. "Like 'fuck the beauty industry' kind of mad?"

"Yeah. I mean, it gets so expensive." You're thinking of your own collection, much of it barely used. None of it's quite right so you just keep buying more. "And, like, guys don't have to spend their money on it like we do."

"Hmm." Carrie pushes her lips to one side, considering her work. From her arsenal she plucks out a different eyeliner, this one by Bobbi Brown. "Not really. I mean, obviously it sucks that the world is sexist and we have to pay for, like, tampons and birth control and abortions when a guy can buy a condom for a fucking dollar. But makeup is like . . . different? It makes me feel good." She unscrews the cap.

"That's true." You backpedal. "Me too."

"And I stole a lot of these," she says. "Look at me." Her gaze rests above your eyes. She looks thoughtful, removed. "You're smart," she tells you. "You can tell by your eyes." She waves her hand over her tools again. "So I'll accentuate your lids, your lashes. Make them pop." She's back to the instructional monologue. "I like to start at the middle of the lid and spread it out both ways. First inward, then outward." She falls into a contemplative silence as she lines your eyes. The wand's flicks are cold on your lids.

"No," she says. "I'm not *mad* about makeup." Repeated, your words sound foolish, young; you want them back. "It's art," she says decisively. "Just like what we're doing with our bodies. That's what these people get wrong." She begins filling in your left brow. "They think we don't know what we're doing. We know exactly what we're doing."

Some idea or understanding hovers into view. "Right. It's like everyone is telling us to be thin all the time, and then when we are, we're wrong. We're psycho. We're sick."

"That's what's so infuriating. Go like this." She wraps her lips over her teeth. "Being thin is the best thing we have. Why would we want to lose that?"

A rush of warmth. She called you thin. "Sometimes I think I only want to get skinny to punish them," you say. "Like, hey, look. Isn't this what you wanted? This nothing girl?" You redden. "But I'm not that skinny yet."

"Exactly." Carrie runs a smear of chalky-tasting lipstick along your lips. "I don't want to get fur, though. No more talking." She puts the finishing touches on your lips. "There. Look at you." She leans back to assess from farther away. She holds up a hand mirror and smiles.

Your face looms large and garish, too strongly defined. "Hmm." You wrinkle your nose, and the stiff makeup cracks. "My face smells like chemicals."

"I only get the good stuff."

"You look fancy," Nurse Irene says when you walk into the cafeteria together.

"See?" Carrie nudges you. You flush with pleasure, though you still feel too visible, too solid, too much.

Irene looks like Melissa Etheridge, if Melissa Etheridge were a volleyball player with short hair. What you mean is she looks like Ellen DeGeneres, if Ellen DeGeneres looked like Melissa Etheridge, and both were taller and heavier. What you mean is she moves through the center with a bigness about her, a jaunty ease that's unfamiliar and curious.

"You think she's hot," Carrie whispers as you hover over the snack table.

"I do not," you protest. You blink rapidly at the accusation.

"Do too. You want to bone Nurse Irene. Admit it."

You collect your granola bar and cheese stick and aim for a steady voice. "Sounds like you do."

"Maybe I do." She gives Irene a toothy, mischievous grin. Irene raises a questioning eyebrow. She has a soft spot for Carrie, unlike the rest of staff, who are convinced Carrie's a monster and spend the days waiting for her to prove them right. *It's because I'm borderline*, Carrie told you once, matter-of-factly. *Borderlines are impulsive risk-takers. We can't be trusted.*

I trust you, you said, then looked down, embarrassed.

"Y'all are both lesbos," says Suze, behind you.

Carrie wraps an arm around your shoulder and kisses your temple wetly. You stiffen, shrink. She's just joking around, you assure yourself and shake her off with nervous laughter. She can do that because she's a girl. You, on the other hand—bite into the granola bar.

Jess considers her banana. "I don't ever want to have sex."

Hiding out in the utility closet during free time, you line up your forearms and wrists to compare. Her fingers end where yours begin. Restlessly Carrie arranges her body so she's kicking up the wall. She twists her limbs every which way. "You look like Fiona Apple in that video," you say approvingly.

She grins, shadowy in the dark. "Did you know there's a ghost here?" she says.

"In the closet?"

"No, dummy. In Briarwood. Some sad lady."

"Cool," you say, unsure how to respond. It's the first you've heard of it. "Have you seen her?"

"No, but Evie swears she saw her last night. She told me all about it," she says smugly. "She was really freaked out." Carrie's grin feels like a taunt. When did she and Evie get so friendly? Last you'd heard, Evie was an overeager eater who didn't need to be here. "Her name is Nell," Carrie says. "The ghost of Briarwood." Her laughter sounds derisive. "Apparently Evie's not the only one who's seen her. The others are all gone."

"Gone?"

"Not gone as in 'dead.' Gone as in they've left Briarwood."

"Oh." You can relax. "Do you believe in ghosts?"

"I don't know," she says with indifference. "Do you?"

"I used to but not anymore." That was another time, you think. You were another Margaret.

"I guess to me 'believe' is probably the wrong word. I mean, obviously they exist. How could they not? But to *believe* in them means, like, something else."

"Yeah," you say. "Totally." You can't say anything right. Your guts are going to squelch. You shift in place. "What were you like as a kid?" you ask her. You want her to return the question.

"I was a brat. A little scamp. I knew how to get what I wanted, and I did. How about you? You were a nerd, I bet."

You chuckle nervously. It's your opportunity to tell her everything. "I was a detective," you start. "I was part of a club. We solved mysteries—including paranormal ones. So yeah. Ghosts."

She doesn't comment. You go on, tentatively. "It all started with . . ." You tell her about your babysitting job with the Morgans. The drugged children. The locked room. Sadie and her telekinetic powers. Carrie traces shadows along the wall. You can tell she's not listening, so you pick up the pace, jump over key details. "So Sadie stopped eating," you explain. Carrie snaps to attention. "And she got her powers back."

"Exactly," she nods vigorously. "That's it. That's what we're doing."

"Right. Yeah. Wait, what?"

"I wonder if we have them right now." She twists into a cross-legged position, knees touching yours.

"Have what?"

"Powers. Hold my hands." She grips your hands tight; you feel her bones. "Maybe we can float."

"Uh . . ." You're breathing shallowly. "I'm not telekinetic. Sorry to break it to you."

"Who knows what the power of two can do. Wait, wait." She lets go of your palms and adjusts them so the tips of her fingers lie lightly on yours. "Like in that levitation game," she says. "Ready?" Carrie whispers. "One . . . two . . . lift."

Carrie's torso lurches up then drops. You haven't moved. "You weren't trying," she accuses.

"Sorry. I wasn't ready." You take a deep breath, steady yourself. This is stupid, you think. You feel dull, heavy, more liable to sink than float. But you'll pretend.

You close your eyes like Sadie did when she was summoning strength, and concentrate on accessing whatever energy you can find. Nothing. You move your arms forward as if pushing energy out through your fingers and into Carrie.

"Ready?" Carrie whispers.

You nod. "Now."

Carrie flips her palms down to squeeze your hands and you could swear there's some sort of surge. You can almost feel yourself rising. You let out a small moan and lose focus. Maybe Carrie does too.

Breaking into nervous giggles, you let go of her hands.

Carrie composes herself. "Again," she says, chin lifted slightly, a challenge. She sits tall with her palms up. You clasp them. You stare at her frame, her slight, lanky body, doing your best to hide the creepy feelings pulsing through you. You gather all of your eye energy and direct it around Carrie, wrapping her body up in it. She focuses intently on you, drawing a supportive frame around your body. You're too heavy, you worry. Even if the powers were real, it wouldn't work. You're about to say so when you feel your body heat up in Carrie's energy field. There's a boost, a whoosh. You're floating. You kick your feet out and meet only air. But you're still on the ground. What's happening. You're starting to feel light-headed. Little black crawlies creep into your vision.

Carrie gleams at you, her pupils magnetic. It's as though

you fall into a groove then, a pocket of air that draws you both inward. Before you know what's happening, you're holding each other's shoulders, leaning in, leaning in, and Carrie is kissing you. Her mouth tastes rubbery and . . . hungry. It tastes hungry. You're hungry too.

Too intense, too intense.

You jerk back. "Whoa," you say.

"You took that seriously," Carrie squeals, snickering. "You totally took that seriously."

"No, I didn't. I was just—" You stop short. You can't breathe. Everything has changed and you don't know how.

"You did too—admit it." She punches your shoulder, a mean punch. She's still laughing. She's laughing at you.

It wasn't serious. It was a joke. Carrie was joking and if you don't get out of here, you'll die. "Come on," you manage to croak. "We can't be late for lunch." You punch the door open and crash into the hallway, not bothering to wait for her to follow.

Dear Davina, dear Angie, dear Eisha,

Friends. You may be wondering where I have been. Guess what. It's a secret. I'm away at eating disorder camp.

Don't act so surprised. You've seen me eating tea for lunch. You know about my frequent bathroom trips. What do you think I do in there? Use your imagination. And have you ever said anything? Checked in? Accused me of having a problem? No. You just go on about school, and boys, and crushes. Here's another secret. I don't give a shit about any of it. Ha!

Dear friends, I am learning from this exercise that I may have angry feelings toward you. But don't worry. It's not like we ever say anything real. My roommate here is named Carrie and we talk about real stuff all the time. We talk about empowerment and escape. We talk about gaming the system. We have so much to talk about. Right now we are talking resistance. Last night we stayed up for hours going over everything. We're formulating a plan. We're going to hide food, manipulate weigh-in, sneak out, have fun. Soon we'll bring in other girls. We're building a revolution. That's the last secret I'm going to tell you. We're sick of everyone telling us we should love our bodies. We don't and we shouldn't have to.

My doctor's all right. Her name's Dr. Holly, and she is smart and kind. I like her, but Carrie says she's soft compared to the Grunch, who only takes special cases. Carrie's a special case. She's the worst one here. I want to be a special case too.

LYLAS,
Your friend,
Margaret

J ess is in, you report to Carrie in the bathroom mirror, where most of your talking takes place now. It's as though the kiss didn't happen. Neither of you has mentioned it; you've been so focused on the plan. The goal of the plan is to gain privileges without gaining weight. The goal is to band together. The goal is to take over Briarwood, to win the right to maintain. You've got it all figured out; the time has come to execute.

You approached Jess during social hour, asked if she wanted to play Jenga. She agreed, pleased. Her favorite game. You waited for Irene to float over to the other side of the room, then gave Jess the rough outline of the plan.

"What I'm saying is," you murmured, poking a loose block. "We could work together."

Her eyes went narrow. "How?"

You sighed, annoyed. She didn't seem to be getting it. You poked the block until it was pullable, extracted and placed it on top. "We could help each other out. With food and stuff. It's all about distractions."

Jess's expression didn't budge. With steely patience she tapped one Jenga block, then another, competitive as ever. She settled on a block that was wedged in firm, a challenge. She tapped and tugged, thinking.

"Snack," called Irene.

"We just ate," Jess groaned and yanked the block out clean. "Okay. I'll try it. Count me in."

Carrie grins at the news, froth bubbles shooting out of her mouth. She spits.

"I should get Internet privileges soon," you continue, pushing an OXY pad around on your face, skin tingling. "We can start a LiveJournal, build a following."

"Jesus, how much do you weigh now?"

For a moment you say nothing, hurt. You expected appreciation. Celebration. A high five. "You should be gaining too," you reply. "Just enough until we can drop again. That was the plan."

Carrie blinks at the mirror and you regret your comment. "I just— I know. I am." Her eyes connect with yours, expressing something dark and malignant you choose to ignore. "I will. Um . . ." She waits.

This is it, you think. She's going to bring up the kiss. She's going to tell you she loves you and you'll get to say it back—*if* you don't stumble all over yourself. Don't stumble over yourself. "Yeah?" It's all you can squawk out.

She swivels her head to look directly at you. You do the same, fearful, hopeful.

"What?" you manage. You almost can't breathe.

"Could you, like, leave?"

She's using the pained saccharine voice that means she thinks you're dumb. You can't compute. You stand there dumbly.

"Hello?" She waves her hand in your face. "I need the fucking bathroom."

"Right. Sorry. Duh." You search for a compliment to

135

redeem yourself. "That bra looks really good on you," you say. Then freeze. "Sorry. I wasn't serious."

Carrie looks at you funny. "Okay, weirdo. Now get out."

"So what are your ambitions? What do you want to be?" Dr. Holly leans forward and appraises you with interest. You wonder, as always, how much of this interest is feigned.

Your response is obvious, canned. Something about college, a career as a lawyer or maybe judge. This is a new line of questioning from her. Usually she focuses on your parents, all the ways they hurt you. Who cares? The whole point is to get out from under them.

"Why? What draws you to these careers?"

You shrug. You've given the right answer. What more is there to say?

She reaches further. "I'm trying to get to know you better, your interests and passions. Are there any issues that interest you?"

"Issues?"

"Social or political, for example."

You search. What would Carrie say? "Helping the hungry," you supply with a sarcastic bite.

"That's something!" She actually claps. "Do you think about this a lot?"

You didn't expect to be taken seriously. Or is she calling your bluff? You slouch down on the couch. "Not really."

"What *do* you think about?"

You rack your brain but can't produce the right response. "Nothing," you say, and feel like you've failed.

"I doubt that. What were you thinking about just now?"

Nothing. For today's midmorning snack you chose a chocolate chip granola bar and a cheese stick with apple juice.

You ate the granola bar first, jaw working hard, washed it down with the juice. The faster you ate it, the more time you would have with your cheese stick. Your goal was to peel it slowly, methodically, produce a thin, unbroken strand with each pull. If you were at home, you would throw away any broken strands. Here that would count as not finishing and you would be made to choke down a Boost. So you established a new rule. If you break a strand you have to take a bite of the whole stick. In this way you could punish yourself and still finish.

Before that, your standard breakfast: cinnamon-raisin bagel with one half cup of scrambled eggs, globules of slime that slid down your throat. The bagel you consumed in measured, meticulous bites, moving in concentric circles, first clockwise, then counterclockwise, until Jess burst into tears and you pocketed the rest.

A glass of orange juice. A glass of water.

"Well," you start, then stop. Dr. Holly lets the moment stretch until you give in. "Okay. Food. Yeah. I guess that's what I'm usually thinking about." She can have it. You aren't going to confess to the other things: Carrie. What she says (*we're* going to develop our powers; *we're* going to take over the world) and doesn't say (her feelings toward you are . . . what?); what she eats (for snack, an apple with peanut butter; for breakfast, granola with yogurt and juice) and doesn't (today's cookie, one half of yesterday's bagel). She's wrapped up in each meal, with you, watching you. You want to impress her, want to compete. Earn her approval, her pride, her devious grin. You're coconspirators, in on it together. Her secrets are yours.

She's supposed to be gaining but she's hoarding more and more. Sneaky. And she's getting away with it, because of the stones. You're starting to worry. If she collapses again, she'll get kicked out. Then you'll be alone.

Dr. Holly pounces. "Good. It's important to be able to admit that." Resentment pulses through you. Food food food. Family family family. It's like the real problems don't matter. Like how hard it is, these feelings. How much easier it is, when your world is small.

"Your assignment for tomorrow is to devote mental energy to something besides food. Your goals, for example. Your ambitions." She makes a note on her pad. "In a place like this, there is a danger that the eating disorder will be reinforced. You're being asked to pay close attention to calorie counts and explore your relationship to food intensively. We expect this to be illuminating and therapeutic, but for some it gives their disorder more control than ever. That's where we get patients leaving and getting worse and having to come back again. I don't want you to fall into that trap."

She hands you a worksheet with two prompts. "Your first exercise for tonight is to journal about something other than calories and food, for at least ten minutes. Second, envision yourself five years into the future, then ten. What do you look like? Who will you be? Journal about that for ten minutes too.

"Now. You've been eating very well. How are you feeling about it?"

She doesn't know about the food you aren't eating, from half of one to two items per day. "Fine, I guess."

"Fine? It's wonderful! I want you to be very proud of yourself, Margaret. I'm very proud of you."

You grin shyly. It doesn't matter if the praise is misguided; you swerve to absorb it like a plant to sunlight.

Back in your room, journaling, fixing your mind beyond calories and food. You envision the anorexic revolution that you and Carrie have been dreaming up, the plot still fuzzy in your mind. What will it look like? How will it work? You'll band together: all of the sick girls, first in Briarwood, then all over the world. You and Carrie will be the leaders. You'll stand up on the tables at lunch and shout:

HUNGER STRIIIIKE
THIS IS UNJUST
THIS IS A PRISON
LET US UNITE
AND FORM AN ARMY

Then you'll float, hovering above them all, showing them what it is to be powerful, the worst-best, the best-worst. And below you, the others will cheer. They'll salute, rise up. You'll take over Briarwood. Spread communiqués to all the other girls in all the other treatment centers. Then beyond. There are so many of you, learning to fly, to thunder, to destroy. You will make your power known, push back against this disordered, disordering world. You will do it with strategy, and totally organized. You are the Thin-as-Knives, the Girls with the Least Cake.

DIETS ARE RIOTS
LET US TAKE OVER THE CLINIC
LET US TAKE OVER THE WORLD

Then all of you, all of the sick girls, will raise your skinny wrists to the heavens and—
What? You don't know. You're stuck.
You turn the page.

In five years I'll be . . .

In ten years I want to be . . .

You sound like a fucking kid. The problem is you look into the future and can't see anything at all.

You break off the exercise. In the bathroom you look in the mirror to see what you see. Solid shoulders. Stubborn breasts. *How can it be that all your life you will drag this body like a fetter imposed on your spirit?* Stop. Maybe you're the fetter; your body's dragging you. Surely it deserves more than you give it.

There's the door slamming. Carrie's back. She deserves more too. One day she'll realize you're nothing, nobody, a fat phony with a biscuit face.

You take a minute. Swallow the lump in your throat, fake a smile. You join her. "So? What did the Grunch say?"

"Booyah. I get Internet tomorrow."

"Awesome. Finally!"

"They all say you're a good influence on me," she says. "Did you know you're therapist's pet? Brownnoser," she says through a fake cough. "I'm working on our manifesto right now. I'm going to post it to my homepage and leave the link on my Away message."

That wasn't the plan, you think. "Won't you get in trouble?" you say. "You can't just leave your IM account open like that."

"Right. Shit. Okay. I'll send it to Jill and Abby and ask them to get it out there."

Jill and Abby? They're not part of the plan either.

"My Rosemont friends," Carrie says. "Oh my god. They're going to freak."

You hover. "Can I read it?"

"No, no." She shoos you off. "It's not done yet."

You hesitate. If the kiss hadn't happened, maybe you'd linger here, be playful, try to catch glimpses over one shoulder, then the other. No. You shrink away.

Carrie closes her notebook, clears her throat. "So, here's today's million-dollar question. Ready?" She pauses for drama. "Is Irene or is Irene not . . . a massive homosexual?"

You freeze, unsure of the right response. "I don't know. Why?"

"Whatever. Never mind. She's just so touchy-feely all the time. Suze thinks she's into me."

Suze? Carrie hates Suze. She's watching you closely. Change the subject. "Did you hear Jess has to leave? Her insurance ran out."

Carrie rolls onto her back. "Too bad. I'll miss her mouth breathing."

You shoot her a reproving glance, so easy to play the good one. "Let's hope she'll be okay."

"What?" Carrie says, defensive. "She never really looked that sick."

You wonder what Carrie thinks of you.

"Not like us," she adds, laughing. "We look terrible."

Irene has brought a few of you out for a short walk behind the center, a Level Two privilege hard-won. It's Jess's last day, and it's a pleasant day for February, brisk and sunny, a breeze lifting up the dead-leaf smell. You lean into it and the blood rises in your cheeks. Ahead is the bridge, which traverses a shallow decorative pond.

You're a strange and sorry group. Irene leading you all in blue scrubs and Timberlands. Carrie's wasp waist tiny beside your broad hips. Hopped-up Jess alongside sluggish, uncomfortable Ian. Shoulders round and hunched, hair plastered down on either side of his head, Ian looks like a reluctant musk ox. You consider sharing this observation with Carrie, who would appreciate its cruelty. Don't. You'll regret it.

Together the five of you spread along the bridge, forming an uneven line. You lean against the wooden railing and stare into the pond, which is dead inside, smooth stones in stagnant water. Carrie's right. These are palm-sized, perfect. But Ian isn't in on it. He could ruin everything. Carrie nudges you in the side.

You

— jerk your head toward Ian, who might snitch. It's not worth the risk.

— tap Jess and shout *race you to the tree* as planned.
You break into a sprint, heading to the giant oak tree some hundred yards off. You haven't run in ages and your muscles are thrilled. Buoyed by nervous energy, you're sprightly and light. Still, Jess, a runner in real life, passes you quickly. You don't mind. That's part of the plan too.

"Slow down," Irene calls, trotting after you. "No running," she tries again. "Do you want to go back to Level One?"

You slow and let Jess beat you. She has nothing to lose. You walk after her, winded, panting, and find a raised root to stumble into. You drop to your hands and knees.

Irene crouches down beside you and pulls you up by your elbow. "Ups-a-daisy. We okay here?"

You position yourself so Irene can't face you without her back to the others. Ian watches blankly as Carrie pockets stones, unwittingly walling her off from sight. He turns and stares at you with an unreadable expression. Crap. He better not be a tattle or—what? What will you do about it?

Irene is waiting. "Just embarrassed," you say, and dust yourself off. "Hey, Irene," you go on, stretching the diversion but you don't know what to say. "Some of us have been wondering. Are you a—" You can't say "homo," it won't come out. "Are you a, like, feminist or something?"

"Am I a feminist or something?" she echoes, chuckling. "And why, may I ask, do you want to know?"

You shrug, embarrassed. "Oh, just . . . Some of the girls are saying you are."

"Yeah," says Jess, cheeks flushed, breathless, lightly jogging up behind you. "Are you?"

Irene lets out a full-throated laugh. "Kiddos, we're all feminists here. Even the Grunch." She puts a hand over her mouth. "You did *not* hear me call Dr. Grunch the Grunch." She gives Jess a side hug. Behind her, Carrie throws you the all clear.

"That means we're on your side," Irene says. "We want to see you grow into your power. Would you do that for us?" She winks, checks her watch. "All right, everyone. In you go."

LEVEL THREE

"I feel so fat today," Carrie says. Cross-legged on your bed, you're journaling about group therapy. Dr. Holly made everyone do the exercise where you outline what you think your body looks like, then she traces your figure against a giant sheet of crinkly paper to see the difference; when you step away you're supposed to be surprised by how normal you are. You hoped your outline would be magically straight and thin. Nope. You were a lumpy gingerbread man, all wrong. Carrie's outline was right. Still she wrung her hands, performing. Now when she rolls onto her back and pulls up her shirt, you try not to look but you look. Her stomach like rolled-out dough, soft, taut. She sucks in her abs and watches her belt buckle hover over the concavity.

"You're not fat," you say automatically. "You're the skinniest one here."

"Whatever. Look." She manages to push a thin roll of tummy fat together.

"Stop," you say, and return to writing. Your letters loom large and distorted. "Everything seems fat today. It's, like, humid or something."

Carrie smiles sourly. "The walls do seem to have put on weight."

"This pillow is definitely fat. All flab. Water weight."

She lets out a laugh, and you smile down at your journal. Carrie rolls to her side. "Hey. Come here." She pats the side of her bed. Clumsily you lie down beside her, on your back so your stomach caves in. You're aware of the flimsy mattress sinking beneath you. She scoots closer to you, aligning her body along yours. Carrie's ankle brushes your calf, and you flinch. "Sorry." Try not to breathe in her face.

"Hey," she says, smirking.

"Hey."

She clasps your wrist with her fingers and lifts it straight up, then rests it against hers, frail in comparison. Every time she does this you think of that lunch game where you wrap your hand around your wrist and if you can get your thumb and your ring finger to touch, you're skinny. If you can't, you're fat. *You're just big-boned*, you can hear Angie saying. *Look, I can touch my pinky.*

"I like how you're so much bigger than me," says Carrie matter-of-factly.

It is a fact, isn't it. But you're supposed to be the same, you think. Stung. You've been trying so hard to be the same. You fight the desire to get up, get away. She drops an arm and runs her hand through your hair and you stay, pulse quickening. Moments like these you think the scene in the utility closet was serious, it had to be. Your heart going bonkers, you might faint. Or you might— No. Your bowels must not betray you. You place a palm on your lower abdomen, tense. Then her mouth is on yours, grasping, pushing into your shock until you come alive, your tongue meeting hers. You squeeze your eyes shut and taste banana. Ninety calories. Stop. When you open them she is straddling you, the sharp points of her tailbone grinding into your pelvis. She grabs your hand and places it on her black ribbed shirt, over her chest. When you freeze, she guides you until you catch on. Then she's lifting her shirt and looking down at you with a slippery grin.

Whoa.

You want this, you think. You could. A tiny internal flame is sputtering but there's this noise—fog—freeze—clamping down. Just. You wish you were different. You're not there yet. Your body's not there. The flame chokes out. You see yourself from above, distressing, and you want to stop Carrie, warn her. Slow down. Don't do that. Don't touch me. Don't touch my chest, or anything. Stop. But she should know, right? She should know you. Understand you. You're destined for a great and revolutionary love. Just not yet. Not now.

Now you are flinching, recoiling, then frozen, huddled against the wall hugging a pillow against your chest, and Carrie is on the floor.

"Ouch," she murmurs. "I thought . . ." Her eyes harden and her face goes flat. She runs the back of her hand over her mouth. "Never mind." She stands shakily. "I'm going."

You are eating breakfast with Carrie, Evie, and Suze, who has taken an important step forward by removing her feeding tube.

You focus on your tray. English muffin, scrambled eggs, two butter packets, two jelly packets (grape), banana, orange juice. Carrie has been giving you the silent treatment for two days. When she returned to your room the other night, you watched the ceiling hoping she would say something, ask what happened. Make it better. Easy again. She slid into bed in dead silence and hasn't spoken to you since. She continues to sit with you at meals, presumably to supervise your intake.

If she would just talk to you, let you apologize, explain.

You aren't there yet, but you will be. You need to lose five pounds first. Can you do it over then, do it right?

"Irene!" Carrie says sweetly. "You're back. Will you show us how to play spades today? Me and Suze, I mean."

Irene gives you a curious look but grins good-naturedly. "That'd be my pleasure."

"Marvelous," Carrie said. "And you can tell us all about Lily Fair."

Your eggs get stuck in your throat. You know she knows what it's called. "Lil-*ith*," Irene corrects. "And since when do you care about that?"

Carrie protests. "I love Sarah. Her new album is deep. That song about the angel makes me cry *tears*. Did she play that?"

You cough. You've heard her describe Sarah McLachlan as *cheesy lesbo shit*, though in fact Sarah McLachlan is married to a man.

A clatter from the right startles you. Suze is sitting very straight, hands in her lap. While Carrie has been sweet-talking Irene, you realize, Suze has been swiping food.

No way. Since when did Carrie rope Suze into your private plans? She hates Suze. You hate Suze together. Well, it's clear that Suze has now replaced you. And she's doing a shitty job.

Irene has caught on. "Suze," she starts in a warning voice, "where did your English muffin go?"

"Down my throat. Wanna see?" Suze opens her mouth haughtily, sticks out her tongue and says, "Ahhh."

"Thank you for that. So if I searched your pockets, I wouldn't find it?"

Suze shakes her head nervously.

"Up," Irene orders. "Pockets out."

Suze complies. Under the table, Carrie touches your knee and slips the disc of bread into your hand.

You

— inform Irene that the contraband is here, in Carrie's hand. If Carrie's going to be a jerk, you can be one too.

— cross your arms across your chest in refusal. You no longer wish to involve yourself in these self-sabotaging schemes. You want to get well.

— shove it up your sleeve without hesitating. You're just grateful to be included.

Obviously you take it. Fine.

"Huh," Irene says when Suze turns out to be clean. She frowns at you and Carrie but doesn't push it. Win.

"Maybe Nell took it," Evie says, shrugging. "You know. The ghost?"

Carrie rolls her eyes in your direction. You grin, relieved.

As you're lining up to get your trays checked, you hover hopefully near Carrie. You were loyal; you collaborated. Surely you've earned back your spot. She ignores you and whispers, giggling, in Suze's ear.

Dear Mom and Dad,

My therapist and I have been talking about gender roles in the family in preparation for your visit. Mom, this one's for you. You probably don't remember but I do, probably because it's the first time I figured it out, that it's not fair. I was seven or eight and you had overslept but I was up, showered, dressed, breakfast made and eaten, homework done and with time to spare before the bus so I'm working on my dolphin puzzle in the other room, three thousand pieces, by the way, very impressive for a seven-year-old. Here comes Brian, plopping into a kitchen chair with sleep in his eyes. I call good morning. He grunts. When you trudge down to join us you see Brian and roar at me: What am I doing? Why haven't I made my brother breakfast? So okay, whatever, I get up and put cereal in a bowl, pour milk on top, plop a spoon in, and set it in front of my brother. Who, again, grunts. It's not a big deal, I know, how can I complain when some kids are starving or have real problems like divorce or abuse or drugs, but come on. Brian is older than me. It's the 1990s and this kind of bullshit is supposed to be done. Girls rule, boys drool, and they can certainly pour their own cereal.

Dad, this one's for you. Remember that time you took me to your office for Take Your Daughter to Work Day and left me with your secretary, how I didn't get to sit in on your very important meetings but I did get to help with the refreshments? That reminds me of the twenty-four-hour math contest I participated in at Mrs. Lytell's house, because while the boys put their heads together I somehow found myself in the kitchen with the other smart math girl putting out all the snacks, a decadent spread. Nobody had told us to. We just did it, naturally. When Mrs. Lytell came in from wherever she was, she gripped our arms. *What are you doing?* she hissed. *Go join the boys.* By the way, your secretary Patricia was very smart, very pleasant. Her main career advice was not to let my body go in case one day I get divorced. But don't worry. We snuck some cookies for ourselves.

Love,
Margaret

Your first Visiting Day. You are, as you shared that morning, *looking forward to showing them that you're a different person when they're not around.* You always feel so cold and closed off in their company. *But in reality, you're funny, and interesting, and generous, and kind.*

Group nodded supportively. Except for Carrie, so withdrawn from the conversation she couldn't even manage an eye roll.

You wait with the others in the lounge, watching as various sets of family members arrive. Evie's mom is as she described. Tiny and precisely, exquisitely feminine, reeking of some floral bouquet. Evie is delaying going home. *They think I should be all better now*, she had said. *And I want to make them happy*—she added quickly—*but I don't want her to see me eat.* You watch as Suze rises slowly to greet her parents. That morning, she shared: *I think if my parents look at me and say, "Gee, you are putting on weight," I will jump out of the window and off myself. If they say, "Gee, Suze, you look good, your face looks better, your butt looks better," you might as well take out a gun and shoot me.*

Ian is flipping through a *National Geographic* with his gaze on the front doors. You notice he's taken off his nail polish.

Carrie ignores all of you, coolly playing solitaire on the other side of the lounge.

You feel heavy this morning. You've gained more than your usual half pound. For last night's evening snack you had yogurt with cereal and a juice. You also ate one of your two required weekly desserts: a dense, fudgy brownie. You envision it coating your stomach with sludge.

You treated yourself to a dessert because— Oh yes, you had just come from a productive therapy session with Dr. Holly, who had been so delighted with something you said. Something about Carrie. About realizing you and Carrie were on separate journeys. Dr. Holly responded with a nod so vigorous her head threatened to pop off. Of course you had only been saying that. It didn't mean anything.

Ian stiffens as his parents step inside. His father is white with military carriage, clean movements, rigid posture, crew cut. His mother's Filipina, short and solid like Ian. She charges ahead with a forced smile when she sees him. He shrinks.

You wish him luck. He glances over, surprised.

His mom wraps him in a big, long hug. Though he's bigger and taller than she is, somehow she manages to engulf him. "You made a friend," she says happily. "Introduce us." He gives you an imploring expression.

Wave. "Hi." His dad's handshake crushes your hand.

At the sight of your own parents you jerk toward them, then pause, waiting for them to spot you first. Your father guides your mother inside with a light touch on her lower back. Both hold sweaty Big Gulps. You greet them with loose hugs, unprepared for the wave of warmth that hits you.

"I'm really happy to see you," you start, with an earnestness that may register as sarcasm. Smile. Your gladness looks fake, but it isn't.

"Hey, point me to the restroom," your father says.

"I've got to go too," says your mom.

You show them to the common bathrooms and wait, watching Carrie. She professes not to care whether her mother will show but she does, you know she does. She glances up and you're caught. Her face darkens. You drop the gaze first. When you look up, Irene has joined her on the couch with a new deck of cards.

You lead your parents outside for a walk around the grounds, avoiding other families.

"I've told everyone you had complications from the wreck," your mother tells you. "Nobody needs to know, right?"

"Uh, okay." Shake your head. Step into a pensive pose on the bridge. "I come out here sometimes to think," you share. "That's part of my Level Two privileges."

Your father produces an *aren't you precious* chuckle. "I'd have thought you could think at home."

You direct your glare downward, trusting the pond to absorb it. Already you can feel yourself becoming cold and closed off. Don't let them suck you back in, you think. You are not that person anymore. You are someone you like.

"This place seems very nice," your mother says quickly.

"They treating you good?" says your father. He eyes your stomach and you're glad for the baggy sweatshirt you pulled on at the last minute.

Aim another glare at the pond. "I like my therapist a lot," you say. "She says I'm doing well. I'm already at Level Two," you say again, and wait a beat for praise. Your parents nod blankly. The others are heading in. Time for lunch.

"Sandwich isn't bad," your father says. "Good to know they're feeding you."

You stare at your turkey-and-swiss panini.

"How much longer is this going to take?" he asks.

This what, you want to say. This lunch? This day? This problem? This treatment? One should avoid the ambiguous "this." You shrug. You'd be happy if this never ended. This stage of your life. It's nice, almost. You don't have to think about anything else.

Your mother shoots him a look. "I'm enjoying my soup very much," she says.

You take a bite and focus on swallowing it. "How's Brian?" you offer.

"His expulsion is over," she says brightly, glad for the new focus. Brian, the comfortable disappointment, a topic well worn and at the ready.

"That's good." You take another bite.

"He's got a new job as a line cook. You know that place Gino's, in the square?"

"We're hoping he keeps this one," says your father through a mouthful of chips.

You mother slurps her spoon. "You know Brian," she says to you almost apologetically. "Always the problem child. We never have any problems with—" She stops abruptly.

Your father laughs roughly. "Excepting the obvious."

Which is a stupid problem, you imagine him thinking. Not a problem at all.

"You're looking very well," says your mother with a pained smile. "You've got color in your cheeks again."

That's blush, you want to say. You aren't fat. You are serious. You put down your sandwich.

Irene swoops down, concerned. "How we doing over here?"

"Fine." You cover your plate with your napkin and push it away.

Irene squats down to eye level. "That's two Boosts . . ." she whispers.

"I know."

She moves away.

"Is that one of your nurses? She looks very"—your mother lowers her voice and leans in conspiratorially—"butch."

You roll your eyes, feeling sharply protective of Irene. "So?"

She gives you an irritated look and rummages around in her purse. "If you're done eating," she starts, and pulls out a tube of the softest coral-pink lipstick. "*Mom*," you manage, but don't bother putting up a fight.

Then they're gone, and Carrie is MIA, probably with Suze. You Suze, you lose, you tell yourself stupidly. Suzing for a bruising. Fuck Suze. Fuck Carrie. Fuck Mom and Dad. Irene. Dr. Holly. The Grunch. You're hungry. You've got two Boosts sloshing around in there, sick, but you need something in your mouth, something to bite down on. Prop your desk chair under the doorknob. Lift your mattress to expose the packets of food you've been hiding in the bedsprings. Survey the spread. The half biscuits wrapped in greasy napkins. The cheese sticks, the half-eaten cookies. Half a veggie burger. Some of it spoiled and rank. You don't care. Make a line of food on the rug and shove it inside yourself methodically, two-fisted, an eating machine. Taste nothing. It's pleasure. It's punishment. It's content. It makes you feel full.

The handle jiggles.

Pause. Pause. Reset. Your teeth in a stale, crumbly cookie.

"Hey." She bangs twice. "Open up." It's the first thing she's said to you in days.

Ball up your napkins, the crumbs. Flush. Splash water on your face. You're perversely calm though your guts are inflamed.

You open the door. She gives you a long, suspicious look. You meet her eyes defiantly. You can't help it. You burp.

She screws up her face in disgust and drags her chair to the closet. "Correctol?" she asks, rummaging around on the top shelf.

Shake your head.

"It's just going to sit there. Here." She tosses a rack of tablets on your desk.

You

— take them.

— leave them.

— toss them onto Carrie's bed.

Leave them. Leave them.

Journal. You can't focus with the candy-pink tablets gleaming in your periphery.

You take them and toss them in the toilet. One by one. Pop them out of their foil cells and drop them in the toilet bowl. Flush. Wait, not yet. You fish out a few. No, no. Toss them back. No, wait. Fish out one, two. Swallow. Flush the rest.

In the mirror you lean closer. The slow blink. Stare. The image contorts, becomes a series of mirrors, a descending hallway, a well. Oh no. You're stuck in the mirror; will you ever get out?

Look. Above you, to the left of your reflected head. There's someone there, floating on the edge of your vision. A woman with a forlorn face and old, old eyes. Her body big like yours, faded gray dress taut over broad shoulders. She's there but not there. Like you.

When you turn around there's no one. You're alone with yourself. And cold.

You wake with a jolt. Carrie hovers over you, arms akimbo. As soon as you register the yelping alarm clock you reach out, fumbling to turn it off. She intervenes, slams it herself. "You're welcome," she snarls.

You pull the sheets over your head. You feel disgusting. Heavy, sick, sad.

"Hurry the fuck up," she says. "We're late."

Well, you're finally back on speaking terms. "I was having this dream," you start groggily as you slide into your flip-flops. "I was pulling this plastic ribbon out of my mouth . . ." You trail off, remembering. As you watched it unfurl, you found a clue in tiny letters stretching from end to end, and you knew it said something important, something you ought to have already known. But you couldn't decipher the message.

"Maybe you're still dreaming," she says with irritation. "Maybe I'm not real. Maybe I'm a figment. Maybe this is all some big fucking joke. Don't forget your stones." She hands them to you.

Take them without thinking. Position them snugly in your armpits. They'll give you two pounds. Not that you need it after your binge.

"Right," you say. You're too groggy for self-censorship, and you don't know what you're saying until it's out. "Maybe this whole time you've been giving me the silent treatment, I've only been imagining it."

"Are you serious?" She stares at you. "*You* were giving *me* the silent treatment."

"No, I wasn't."

Carrie waits a bit. "Hey, remember that time we were making out and you shoved me off the bed?"

You don't say anything, confused.

"*You* rejected *me*."

"But . . ." You don't know what to say. She's the thinner one, which means she wins at everything? You know that's not true but . . . also it's true. Right?

"But what?" She shakes her head, scoffs. "You know, sometimes . . ." She stops short and steps into the bathroom, as if to check her face, as if to get away from you.

Follow her. This is important. "What?"

She confronts you in the mirror. "I just think that you don't get that your actions affect people too. Like, you give me so much power, it's like you think I know what I'm doing all the time when I don't. I don't know what I'm doing. I'm sick and I'm not getting better."

"But you don't want to get better."

"That's not—" She squeezes her eyes shut. "I want to *want* to get better. I just don't know how. Like, what else even is there?"

"What do you mean?"

She groans, frustrated with you. "I mean this world is fucking fucked. It's fucking bullshit. It's like there's no use trying to live."

"You don't believe that."

Her laugh is a disdainful snort. "I do."

"You're up," says Irene, fiddling with the counterweights. "Way up." Her soft brown eyes level gently with yours. "Anything you want to tell me?"

158

You step off the scale and consider her question, still groggy, distracted by your conversation with Carrie.

Oh. Right.

Your parents. Their visit. Your defeat. Your intestines churn.

"I binged last night," you confess quietly.

"On what?"

Resentment. Shame. Defeat.

All of it returns in a noxious, dizzying roil.

"I was hoarding food."

Irene sighs and makes a note. "Thank you for being honest," she says. "Is there anything else?"

"Nope."

Something brushes your shoulder. You jump.

"You okay?"

Behind your other shoulder, what feels like the brush of fingers. You keep your arms fast to your sides, trembling, chilled. There's a tap on your back, a poke at your right under-arm. Another on your left. "Stop," you mumble, twisting away. Above Irene, a figure flickers. The woman from the mirror. She's there then not then there again. She's a disap-proving ripple in the air.

You swallow.

"And I took some Correctol." The figure vanishes.

Irene frowns. "I see. Is that it?"

Tap-tap-tap. She's behind you again, poking at your underarms with growing determination.

Okay, fine. Message received. Enough. And maybe it's time. You're tired. You have never been so tired.

Lift your left arm. The stone drops to the floor with a smack. And the other. Another smack. The tapping stops.

Irene bends to pick them up, silent. You wait to be yelled at, written up, something slapped on your file. Wait to get sent to the Grunch. To prove it's not just Carrie. You do bad things too.

Any second you'll be punished. Irene's storm of anger will break.

You aren't prepared for the pain coursing through Irene's face when she rises.

It hits you like a gut punch. You flinch, your surroundings coming into sharp, unyielding focus. You see the pale gray stones in her hands as if for the first time, their stolid smoothness. Irene is new to you too, her bloodshot eyes, her defeated posture, the worry around her mouth. Her painful realness. The shock leaves you quaking. The stones no longer reflecting back your body heat, you're cold and empty, light. Then the numbness gets replaced by a roiling heat that threatens to burn you up from inside. Every hard, uncomfortable feeling, all bubbling up at once. You see yourself, your actions, through Irene's eyes, through everyone's. The icy embraces you gave your mother and father before they left. The cruelly oblivious silence to which you've subjected Carrie. No. Stop. You're revolted. Then this: this betrayal of Irene, and the program, and the cold indifference with which you confessed it. Irene, who only wants to help you. Grab the counter for balance. Apologize. "I'm sorry," you blubber. "I'm sorry. I'm sorry. I'm sorry."

Irene stares heavily at her clipboard. "That'll be all," she says finally, and waits for you to leave.

She's never made you wait before. The chill brings goosebumps to your arms. You pull your sleeves down and fidget. When she comes in, she seats herself neatly in the worn cloth chair and opens your manila file.

Oh, Dr. Holly. Your kindness. Your crinkly crow's feet.

She blinks at you like a friendly cockatiel. "You've been doing so well," she says.

Your voice shrivels up in your throat. Despite all evidence to the contrary she still wants to see the best in you. She shouldn't. She's wrong.

"What would you like to tell me?" She waits. "Margaret," she says softly. "Do you understand how serious your situation is?" You venture a glance. Her gaze gone stern. Disappointed. Hurt.

"I'm sorry," you finally cough up.

"Do you want to continue treatment, Margaret?"

"Yes."

"I'd like you to tell me where you got the rocks."

"The pond," you say, too fast.

She looks at you closely. "We've heard Carrie has been distributing them."

You pause. That wasn't inaccurate, but it's not like she did it alone. You helped. You all helped. She could get kicked out for this, you realize, which can't happen because she's only just started speaking to you again. Also she's sick. Really, terribly sick. She might not—if she leaves—she might not—

"It was me," you say. "I got them from the pond."

Dr. Holly lets out a short breath. Her sternness falters and she suddenly seems very tired. "Lying to us serves no one," she says.

"I'm not."

"And the laxatives? Where did you get them?"

Your heart beats wildly. You shake your head.

"If you want to continue," she says, "you need to be honest."

Now it's clear: they will kick you out too.

"I—" You can't go back, you can't. The pretense, the

remove, the emptiness: everything, all of it, will begin again. No. You won't do it.

"Yes, Margaret?" Her head moves toward yours incrementally, as though she might extract the information with her eyes.

"I got them from Carrie," you mumble. "But it's not like—"

She leans back. Her response is curt. "All right. Thank you. The team has discussed your situation and we've decided to move you into a different room. Irene has already moved your belongings. You'll meet with the full team tomorrow morning."

"Wait. That's not— What about—?"

"Don't worry about Carrie." She looks at you searchingly. "Margaret," she says, "you're here to get well. You can only do that by focusing on yourself. Do you feel you are doing that?"

"Yes," you mutter. That's the problem. You can't focus on anything else.

"Hi, Margaret," Evie says shyly. She stands at the foot of her bed, holding an arm behind her back. Her side buns are secured by so many pins, her head looks armored. The arms of her pink glasses get stuck. "Guess you're my new roommate. What level are you now? Oh, sorry." Her expression is apologetic, a familiar look for Evie. "*Obviously* you're Level One," she adds in a rush, without malice. "Sorry. I could have figured that out myself. I guess I did, huh?" She lets out a nervous whinny, her version of a self-deprecating laugh.

Evie still sleeps with stuffed animals. Her walls are covered in word collages like *EmPoWeRMEnt* and *seLF-eStEeM*. She watches as you put away your things. "I'm Level Three," she says, hovering close beside you, "but I'm supposed to be moving up next week or . . . at least the team wants me to."

Her sentences roll out like unevenly weighted balls. "But Level Four seems so, I don't know, scary, aaaah!" (You jump. Her grip on your forearm is startling.) "I don't actually know anyone who's gotten there. Do you?"

No, and how would you? She's been here longer than you have. But she's right. In the weeks you've been at Briarwood, no one has moved beyond Level Three. Those who have left the center have either had to, like Jess and Natalie, because their insurance ran out, or decided, like Suze her first and second times here, they'd had enough of the pesky rules and constant supervision.

"It's like, can I just stay at Level Three for as long as I want? But it's also like, I know, I know, I can't stay here forever. But maybe I could? Sorry. Sometimes it's all just extremely confusing." That whinny again.

The last level before patients are deemed sufficiently well to go home, Level Four does seem like a terrifying, unappealing place to be. But you have other things on your mind.

"Sorry. Of course you don't want to hear my blathering. I get it. I totally get it." She pauses. "You and Carrie were so close. Do you maybe want to talk about it?"

"Not now, thanks." You absolutely do not.

"Well, maybe we'll get close too," she says hopefully. "I miss having a roommate."

You don't reply. You can't, certain it'll set off an interminable sobbing. Already you're bereft. It's a split, a wound, a gutting.

It was all your fault.

Carrie's harsh laugh echoes in your head. She'd been leaning against the wall by the art room in her stretchy black cardigan, joking with Suze about something. You love her laugh. Big and wild. Jagged all over. She gave you a tentative half wave, testing you out, checking to see if the fight was over. Then she got a glimpse of your face.

"Keep moving," Irene grumbled.

For a moment you felt romantic and criminal, tragic, one part of a star-crossed pair ripped violently apart. You let your mouth fall open helplessly. Saw her see your backpack and duffel bag in Irene's hands, shift her eyes back to yours. She thinks the worst. That you've asked for the switch. That you've given her up, betrayed her, told them everything. In a way, you have.

But it wasn't fair. None of it was fair. *I'm sorry*, you mouthed. *I—*

There's nothing to say. She'll never forgive you. You'll never see Carrie again.

"It has come to our attention," the Grunch says with a sniff, "that a number of you have been acting in defiance of Briarwood's policies." The other girls murmur, some with shock, others dismay. You don't react.

"The nurses," she goes on, "are searching your rooms as we speak."

Dr. Grunch adjusts tiny glasses on bulging cheeks. With pursed lips she pauses dramatically. "As some of you know, we have made the difficult decision to discontinue Carrie's treatment. We've weighed this decision carefully and ultimately feel her presence is disruptive to the culture of care we strive to create. We will be meeting with each of you individually to discuss your involvement."

The kickback to Level One means no more outside privileges and no Internet, which means you won't be able to email or chat-request Carrie. You won't be able to explain.

Dr. Holly speaks up. "We'll open the floor now. If you

have thoughts or feelings you'd like to share, please raise your hand and wait for the speaking baton." She lifts a silver-and-gold wand with a fraying pom-pom rolling around on one end.

Evie reaches for it first. "Maybe I'm awful but I'm kind of glad she's gone? Sorry." She winces, as if prepared to be kicked. When she sees some of the other girls nodding, she relaxes. "She made me feel bad for gaining. I felt like she was judging me. It was really polluting."

Newish-girl Samantha agrees, not waiting for the baton. "You're not awful. You're right. She always had to outdo everyone and be the worst." Samantha is jealous and full of shit. *She* wants to be the worst.

Ian is staring at the carpet but you get the sense he's listening intently. He didn't tell anyone about the stones, you realize. He could have but he didn't.

"Yeah," Evie adds. "It's like she didn't really want to get better and was always, like, laughing at whoever did."

Past tense? Really? They're talking about Carrie as if she's dead. "She does!" you protest. "She wants to *want* to get better, but . . ." It's like they're *blaming* her for being anorexic. When everything in the world is saying, *Be anorexic, be anorexic.* This sucks.

"Thank you all for sharing," says Dr. Holly. "Let's honor the speaking baton."

Suze raises her hand and waits for the wand. "I agree with Margaret. Anyway I bet there's not one of you here who hasn't hoarded food or manipulated your weight at some point while you've been here. The end."

That night you curl up in bed and face the wall. You can't fathom social time or journal exercises. You just . . . hate yourself. And miss her. Why be here without her? You might as well go home and hate yourself there. You squeeze your eyes shut. Here it comes: the sobbing. But no tears arrive. Just ragged, panicked breathing.

Fingers graze your shoulder blade.

"Leave me alone," you growl. Carrie's is the only touch you want and you'll never know how to respond to it. Why, *why*, did you react that way that day on her bed?

"I'm so sorry," Evie says stiffly, "but this is my room too."

You spin around. Evie is reading at her desk, fifteen feet away. There's no way she could have reached you.

There. That ripple in the air.

You sit up. "Evie," you whisper. "Did you see a woman in here?"

"A woman?" she repeats, confused.

"Just now?"

"I don't think so," she says, looking at you strangely. She goes back to her book, some fantasy she's read three times already. She told you about it yesterday, gushing until she realized you didn't care.

"Wait." Evie looks up again, excited. "Did you see Nell?"

"Nell?"

"You know, the ghost of Briarwood. You saw her, didn't you?"

Briarwood's ghost. Of course. "I'm not sure what I saw," you hedge, undecided. Were you hallucinating? Possible but highly unlikely. The more you think about it, the more certain you are: you've been visited by a spectral presence from another dimension. You're being haunted. By a ghost.

Given your early and formative encounters with Angie's house ghost, you're no stranger to paranormal activity (see GCSA #3: Angie's Bug Secret). But if this is, indeed, the ghost of Briarwood, it would be helpful to know whether she's a benign ghost like Agatha or . . . something else?

"I've seen her too," Evie adds. "She tries to get me to follow her sometimes, but I'm like, hell to the naw, Nell. I'm not getting in trouble for that!" She whinnies.

You can't take her eagerness, it's too much. It's all too much. If there's a ghost, Evie can have her. You have more important ghosts to deal with: those of your dead friendships. First Gretchen, then Eisha, now Carrie. All of your friendships are dead because you keep killing them. You don't know how to keep anything alive. Not while you're losing. And you want to lose. More than anything, still, you want to lose.

"Never mind," you tell Evie. "It was nothing, sorry I bothered you." You squinch shut and face the wall.

"Margaret, I've got a job for you."

It's Irene. The others have gone out for a walk with Nurse Hannah, but you and Suze, privileges revoked, are stuck in the lounge, not talking. You're paging through a *National Geographic* but can't focus. You know Suze blames you for Carrie's departure. You understand. You blame yourself too.

Irene hands you a stack of mail—manila envelopes, some stuffed mailers. "I need you to give these to Dr. Grunch. And be *slow* about it. No running."

You put aside the magazine. You've never been inside the Grunch's office. "What if she's with someone?"

"Then wait."

Irene returns to the nursing station. Since the scene with the stones, she's been more brusque. You don't blame her, you think as you round the corner into the other hallway. That's your fault too.

Ian sits next to Dr. Grunch's office, favoring the floor over the two available chairs. He's bent over his sketchbook, head and shoulders pulsing to some internal rhythm. The door is propped open and you can hear snatches of a phone conversation. "I'm very sorry, Mrs. Weiss. I can recommend other treatment options, but that's all I can do."

"Hey." You sit down in the chair nearest Ian. He doesn't register your greeting, and you're annoyed until you realize he has headphones on, buried in his thick hair. He's working on what appears to be a self-portrait of some kind, distorted and nightmarish, the lines of the body crude and mean looking. Maybe an exercise. Hard to know if it's an authentic self-representation or what he thinks the Grunch wants to see.

You lean sideways and wave a hand over the sketch. "Yoo-hoo. Friend."

"Oh." He shuts his sketchbook and pulls down his headphones. "Didn't see you."

"What are you listening to?"

"Um. Tori Amos." His voice is cautious, flat.

You brighten, then pause, inexplicably annoyed. Tori is yours and Davina's. You don't want to share her with Ian. You ignore the information. "How did it go with your parents?" you ask. With all the hubbub over Carrie's departure, Visiting Day has been nearly forgotten.

"Um." He looks at you dubiously.

"Mine sucked," you offer. "My parents are the worst."

"Mine are all right," he says. You smile uncomfortably, caught off guard. He's supposed to first sympathize, then relate. Has he learned nothing from group therapy? "They're trying," he says. "They're doing their best. It's not their fault I'm . . . me."

You want to backpedal. Your parents are all right too. They're trying too. Just . . . sometimes not enough.

Dr. Grunch appears in the doorway. "Ian," she says warmly, "and Margaret. This is a surprise."

"I have some mail for you. Irene sent me."

"Ah, wonderful. Come in. I'll have that"—she unburdens you—"and send you back with some outgoing items."

Ian takes a seat on the worn gray couch. You wait awkwardly as Dr. Grunch gathers some forms and envelopes from behind her imposing desk. Her office is twice as big as Dr. Holly's, walls glossy with framed degrees and photographs, many of a much younger Grunch with what look like colleagues or mentors. Other photographs are not of the Grunch at all, but of faded young women lined up in jumpers. Are these classes? Cohorts? Each fronted by the same woman—tall and healthy looking—"robust" is the word—in a variety of sensible dresses. Her long, wizened face draws a gasp.

It's her. The woman in the mirror.

"Ah." Dr. Grunch follows your gaze with a twinkling eye. "That's Briarwood nearly a century ago. We used to be a school, imagine that! A Montessori-style school for girls."

"Really? Cool." You examine the photos. In the first few, the mystery woman is handsome in a sharp blazer and full skirt with a floofy cravat. But over the years, things take a turn. It's as though she's resigning herself to something, you don't know what. Her dresses become frumpier and dull, her eyes haunted, cheeks sharp.

"When did it turn into a treatment center?" you ask.

"The building has had a few evolutions. First it was the Briarwood School for Girls. That's one of the founders, the first headmistress, Nell Edmonds." She taps an image of the

169

woman with the long face. "Miss Edmonds died rather young, of symptoms related to a disorder called hysteria. I believe she refused to eat." Dr. Grunch delivers that last part with a wide-eyed, pointed expression. You take in the final photo in the sequence. In it, Nell seems shrunken, her shoulders hunched forward over a sunken chest, the skin around her eyes appearing bruised. "The school shuttered. Then, let's see, was it 1923?" Dr. Grunch continues. "Yes, that's right. One of Nell's colleagues expanded the building and reopened it as Briarwood Academy. That institution closed during the Depression. Later the building was converted to a respite care facility and finally to what we are today.

"So you see. There's quite a lot of history here. You just have to reach out and touch it." She winks and passes off a small bundle of envelopes. "Thank you, Margaret. Please have Irene send these out."

Your arms light up with goosebumps. Nell Edmonds. Founder and headmistress. Refused to eat.

Died.

You take the pile and move to leave, pausing again before that last photograph, where she appears painfully, dangerously thin, held up by the side hugs of the two girls flanking her; yet beaming with a kind of maniacal energy. Her blurry face glows, almost translucent, as though she's hovering between this world and the next. Hmm. *You just have to reach out and touch it.* The Grunch's words echo in your mind. You lift a finger to graze the image. The surface is cold. You shiver.

"Shhh."

You awake to a chill. Carrie? No. You shiver. Up close, Nell's face is kind; her eyes, dim and unblinking.

She lifts a see-through finger to thin blue lips. You sit up, lurching away from her. Evie is sound asleep. Nell floats toward the door, beckoning you. Then she slips right through it.

You huddle in the far corner of your bed, gawking at the space where she was. It would be easier, you think, to ignore this. Pull the sheets over your head and retreat. Let this mystery slide by unpursued. Focus on yourself. That's plenty. Besides, you are no longer a detective, and mysteries are for kids.

(*Are* they, Margaret? You seem to be ignoring key counter-evidence such as the undying popularity of extremely adult sleuths like Jessica Fletcher and Sherlock Holmes.)

The door opens from the outside. Nell waits in the frame, scorn rankling her brow. *Now*, she commands with flaring eyes.

Okay. Whatever. Fine. You slip on your flip-flops and follow.

She floats fast. You have to run-walk to keep up. You pursue her down the hall, quiet as you can, past the cafeteria, the lounge, around the corner, flip-flops softly slapping. When you reach the nursing station, you slow. The door is open a gap, and you can hear Nurse Hannah humming along to the *Robin Hood: Prince of Thieves* soundtrack. A surreptitious peek sees her positioned inward with her feet propped up on the counter, face in a *Marie Claire*. You sneak past easily.

Nell leads you past the therapy rooms, the offices, and finally to Dr. Grunch's door, which she passes through. You try the handle. It's locked.

"Nell?" you whisper. "Miss Edmonds? Let me in?"

You wait for a response. Nothing. The door stays shut. Well, this is stupid. She's brought you all this way without telling you to bring some bobby pins.

Bobby pins. Right. You smile to yourself. You can get in. You can solve anything. Well. You can probably solve this.

You tiptoe back to your room—past Nurse Hannah, who is now singing along to Bryan Adams—and quietly close the door behind you. In the bathroom you poke through your hair things. Nothing but red and blue elastic bands. You open the drawers one by one. Nothing. Think, Margaret, think!

"What's going on?" says a sleepy voice behind you.

"Evie." You whirl around. "Can I borrow three hairpins?" She has a million. She uses them to pull back her flyaways.

"Sure." She gets up, rubbing her eyes. In the bathroom she rummages through her overnight bag. "Wait, what's the emergency? What's going on?" When you reach for the pins in her hand, she clamps her fingers over them. "Sorry," she says mournfully, "but I think I need to know what they're for."

"Don't worry about it."

"Sorry but I'm on Level Three. I definitely don't need to get in any kind of trouble right now."

"You won't. I promise."

She raises an eyebrow.

"I promise. I'm not bingeing or purging. Or hoarding. I'm . . ."

"It's Nell, isn't it? She summoned you." Evie's voice is soft. She's hurt.

"You guessed it." You grin despite yourself. "I'm investigating a mystery. I've been summoned by the ghost of Briarwood to unlock the Grunch's door and search the premises—for what, I don't know."

"Okay, but . . ." She plants her hands on her hips. "Are you making fun of me? Because that's super not cool if you are." Seen as something of a gratingly sycophantic overachiever,

Evie has been the object of some scorn at the center. You've been there. But that was the past, before Carrie. Carrie. You feel the pang of her absence. You take stock of Evie's heart-patterned pajama pants, the pilled teddy bear she sleeps with. She seems so young though she isn't, she's seventeen, like you, but *young*, like she wants to defer adulthood. You can relate to that too. Adulthood is like the last stop on the train and you have to get off. All you can see is dark and then the train leaves without you. Yeah. Steer clear of that.

It could be fun to get her out of her shell. Like Carrie did for you. With Evie, you can be the leader, the mature one, the instigator. Anyway it's always best to have more than one sleuth on a case. She'll see things you won't.

"Come with me," you dare her.

Evie glares. "Yeah right. You weren't even going to tell me."

"You said you didn't want to get in trouble."

"Well, I don't."

"Okay, suit yourself." You turn to leave.

"Wait." She draws herself up. "Look. I *know* you all think I'm some boring goody two-shoes, but I'm not, I swear. I've just had *enough* trouble and I don't need any more." She waves her hands over her head and torso. "Trouble-free zone. But the fact of the matter is, Nell summoned me first, which means—I mean, I know I'm not the *first* first. Kristen and Christina saw her last year, or so they said. They wouldn't tell me anything and I really did think they were lying. But she summoned me before she summoned you! She appeared to me twice . . . three times! And so she's *involved* me. And now you're *involving* me too. And I'm not sure what it is I'm being involved in, so of course I'm going to be wary. What's her *deal*? What does she *want* from us? Why should

I trust her? She won't answer any of my questions. She just *stares.*"

You nod, considering. "All good points. In my experience—and I have some experience—a ghost shows up because they need to show or tell us something."

"But what?" Evie starts. "And why? And—"

"There's only one way to find out," you interrupt. She's wasting valuable time. Her Adidas slides are by the door. You grab them and drop them in front of her feet. "Come on."

Evie relents. She hands over the hairpins and steps into her slides, which squeak.

"On second thought, we'll both need quieter feet," you say, removing your flip-flops. You frown at her pale pink PJs. "And more suitable sleuthing outfits. Something dark."

"I don't have anything dark," she says, stepping out of her slides and rifling through her dresser drawer. "Will these work?" She holds up blue jeans and a gray-and-pink flannel.

You shrug approval. "Better. I'll change too."

Evie doesn't like getting dressed in front of other people either. While she's in the bathroom, you pull on dark jeans and your bulky black cardigan. You knock on the door to signal you're ready.

Glasses secured (Evie), bobby pins pocketed (you), you tiptoe barefoot down the dark hall.

"I can't believe we're doing this," she whispers, squeezing your arm. She giggles. Her laughter is nervous and irrepressible; it tumbles out and keeps rolling. She covers her mouth. "Sorry." She giggles again.

Your hear a creak ahead. Nurse Hannah. "Shhh," you admonish Evie. You freeze. The lights in the next hallway snap on. Your room is at the other end of the hall; you'll never make it. Quickly, cautiously, you open the nearest door and push Evie inside. You click the door closed behind you just as the hall light comes on.

"Who's that?" someone asks, and switches a lamp on. Ian lies blinking in bed.

"Turn it off," you whisper. "It's just us."

Evie waves cheerfully. She seems almost high.

"What is it?" Ian asks, alarmed.

"Lights off," you urge him. "Quiet. We'll explain in a sec. Pretend you're asleep."

You slink into Ian's bathroom with Evie and listen, breath held, to the soft groan of the door across the way—Suze's room—the click of the light on and off. Then Ian's. The outer door nudges open, the light flashes on, then off. The door swings shut. Will she roam down the hall? Check your room too? Evie squeezes your hand. Nurse Hannah's squeaky sneakers retreat.

"Whew," Evie breathes out.

"She's gone," Ian whispers on the other side of the door. You usher him inside and flick on the bathroom light.

"I'm waiting," he says. "What's going on?" His hair's in a topknot and you can see his face for once, dramatic mouth, intent gaze.

"Just taking a midnight stroll," you hedge, unsure where to start or what to say. He might think the whole thing is stupid.

"The ghost of Briarwood showed up in our room tonight," Evie supplies. "So we're following her. Wanna come?"

"Really?" Ian says, suspicious. "Where is she?"

"Yes, really." You cross your arms defensively. "Her name is Nell and she disappeared behind the Grunch's door."

"Whoa. Cool. And . . . I can come?" He meets your eyes shyly.

You consider the prospect. As the only one of you to have spent real time in Dr. Grunch's office, he might have valuable intelligence. And you know he can be very quiet when he wants to be. "Sure," you say. "Why not?"

You fill him in as he fishes around in a dresser drawer, finally giving up; it's too dark to see. He grabs a hoodie from the closet. "I'm guessing there's something in the Grunch's office," you finish. "Did you notice anything unusual when you were in there?"

"Not that I can think of. But she has a lot of stuff. Books, filing cabinets, photos."

"Whoa," Evie says. "I bet we could read our files if we wanted to."

"Would you want to?" Ian asks. "I'm not sure I would."

You grimace. "I can probably guess what mine says." *Run-of-the-mill EDNOS*, you imagine, *hogging a bed that could go to someone worse. Liar. Selfish. Narc.*

Evie makes a noncommittal shrug. "My file's probably pretty thick by now. It's like they can't get rid of me! Nurse Hannah said that once, actually. It made me feel sad."

You roll your eyes, annoyed at the brag.

"How long have you been here?" Ian asks.

"Two months, but it's my fourth time. So probably like six or seven months in all, but spread out over three years. God. I know. All that time. I'm so over it. But yet . . ." She shrugs. You're staring, dumbfounded. She doesn't look that bad.

"Whatever," you say. "Let's focus on the investigation at hand."

You swing the door open and together step into the hallway.

"I don't like this," Evie whispers as you crouch before the lock. "What if someone comes?"

"Keep quiet and no one will," you say. Evie has proven to be quite the chatterbox. You've had to shush her five times. You bite the round nubs off one bobby pin and drop them into the left pocket of your cardigan. You don't want to leave a trace. It's too dark to see more than the outline of the doorknob, but this is about feel and sound. You bend a pin like Angie taught you and guide the flat part into the lock.

"Coast is still clear," Ian says.

It's silent for a beat.

"I'm really glad we're roommates, Margaret," Evie says. "Have I told you that?"

"You're not being quiet," you say, and press a second bobby pin into an *X* shape. You slide one end into the keyhole above the other one, jiggling it to catch the first pin.

"Sorry," she whispers. "I babble when I'm nervous." She's quiet for a moment. "Ian, isn't it so lonely without a roommate?"

He shrugs. "I'm a guy," Ian says in a low voice. "Sharing a room with a girl would be 'inappropriate.'"

"Oh. Right." Evie pauses a long beat. You maneuver the first pin, pushing it up until it clicks. Evie hums softly. "I've been wondering," she blurts. "How can a guy be bulimic? I thought it was a girl thing."

You guide the pick in farther. You've been wondering that too. It's *supposed* to be a girl thing. Which is proof you are, in fact, a girl—unless you aren't really sick. But with

Ian here, *not* a girl (though sort of a girl?) and a verifiable bulimic (though he could be exaggerating), all sorts of questions pop up.

"Yeah," Ian replies slowly. "Supposedly it's a white girl thing, too, but you and I are here to show, anyone can throw up their food." His tone is bitter. Evie is silent.

You fit the profile, you remind yourself. White, and a girl. You get the second pin up. You *are* sick, you are. (As if on cue, a wave of fatigue hits you.) And Evie and Ian are sick too, which means . . . what, exactly. You don't know.

"Anyway," he says after a moment, "I'm not . . . normal."

"What do you mean?" Evie asks. "Are you gay?"

Ian sighs. There's the third pin. You hear the click.

"I like gay people," Evie says quickly. "Sorry if that was rude. I sometimes wish I were gay. It'd be easier, don't you think?" The question seems directed at you. You don't respond.

Ian's quiet, and you can't tell if he's upset or just thinking. "Maybe I'm gay. I don't know. It's more like I don't like being a guy."

Shoot. You pressed too hard, fucked it up. Ian's fault. How can he *say* things like that, secret things? Carefully you extract the top pick and reshape it. "Shhh," you say crossly. "Stop talking."

"Sorry," whispers Evie. After a moment, she starts humming.

You shake your head, try to clear it. You retrain your focus on the lock. Concentrate. First pin. Second pin. Third. Fourth . . . You're in.

You turn the knob gently and the door creaks open. Darkness. Cold.

As you pass the threshold, there's a blinding burst. You find yourselves in a bright, narrow schoolroom. Through skinny windows, sunlight streams. You blink. But that's impossible. Where Dr. Grunch's sofa and armchair were are three lines of wooden desks. The Grunch's imposing desk has been replaced by a compact teacher's model with skinny legs. Before a murky-green chalkboard, glowing a cool blue, floats Nell.

The Mystery of the Secret Passage

CHAPTER 1

"Come in, come in," says Nell, tapping a ruler against her palm. "You're late."

Evie covers her mouth with a sleeved fist.

"I sort of thought you were joking," Ian whispers.

Nope. "Meet Nell."

"Hello, Margaret," says Nell pleasantly. "I've been expecting you. And Evie! Splendid. I had nearly given up on you. I see you've brought a . . . companion." She squints at Ian with a frown. "Very well. Take your seats."

You glance to the door for reassurance, in time to see it melt into the wall. Ian palms the wooden paneling with a stricken expression. Uh-oh. That's not good. No use panicking, but you'll admit to some rising concern—not for yourself so much as for your friends. (Friends? *Are* they your friends?) What were you thinking, enlisting Evie and Ian in the pursuit of a mysterious and potentially dangerous spirit? They're laypeople, inexperienced as sleuths. And they're *sick*. They should be in bed, conserving calories and focusing on themselves, not wandering into metaphysical layers after lights out. Whatever danger they're in, the fault is all yours.

You appraise Nell from this short distance. She certainly seems harmless enough, this ghost of a teacher in a sad, empty classroom. But teachers have agendas, demands. So do ghosts. You approach the rear row of desks with your defenses up. Evie trails you.

Nell raps on a desk at the front, her attitude toward unmoving Ian turning swiftly to displeasure. "Now, please." She gives you a look of annoyance. Feeling responsible, you motion to him. "Class is starting," you tell him with a jerk of your head. "Come on."

"Up here, please." Nell raps again. "Don't be shy."

When you're all satisfactorily seated, Nell instructs you to take out your ledgers and pens. Ledgers? Pens? All you see is— Oh. You've always wanted a desk like this. Hands shaking, you lift the top and extract a fountain pen and a stack of rumpled looseleaf. Other students have preceded you, it seems. Their notes travel in layers, left to right, up to down, sometimes three or four different writing styles on one side. Kind of creepy. Where have they all gone? Nell is the only ghost you can see.

Her chalk clicks merrily across the board.

WOMEN'S SUFFRAGE
NINETEENTH AMENDMENT
NEURASTHENIA

Next to you, Evie turns the looseleaf this way and that, poring over the notes. Beside her, Ian stares at Nell, apparently mesmerized. They can do what they want; you're a good student. You find a clean half page and copy down the terms—familiar except for that last one—in tight letters.

Nell points with her ruler. "Women's suffrage." She hovers close by your desks. "This refers to the movement to gain equal voting rights for women. Though the suffrage movement began stirring as early as the 1840s, the women's vote was not established nationally until 1920, when the

Nineteenth Amendment"—she points—"went into effect. It took a woefully long time, the better part of a century."

You take notes on autopilot mode. You know this stuff. The Seneca Convention. Susan B. Anthony and Elizabeth Cady Stanton. Blah blah. Key terms and figures bolded in one gray-tinted supplementary page in your American history textbook, a page you memorized then forgot. In his zeal to recreate the play-by-plays of the Battle of Cold Harbor, the teacher flew right past it.

"I was there for the end of the campaign. I was there—" Nell pauses dramatically, with her hands clasped behind her back. She's floating a bit higher off the ground now. "I was there for the triumph of women." She peers down her nose at you expectantly.

"Wow," you supply. "That's amazing." You elbow Evie, who nods along. "Cool," she says. Ian stares at his desk.

"My grandmother," Nell goes on, "was a suffragist." She floats back and forth, mimicking pacing. "She marched with Lucy Stone." She returns to the board and writes down the unfamiliar name. You copy it. "In the 1850s, Lucy was one of the most famous women in the United States, a fiery orator who spoke passionately in favor of abolition and suffrage. Lucy was a visionary. She cut her hair short, wore bloomers, and refused to pay taxes without voting rights. She even kept her maiden name upon marriage. And my own grandmother organized with her. Can you imagine?" As she speaks, rickety blue-and-gray images unfurl from her mouth. "Marching the streets of Boston with VOTES FOR WOMEN sashes clipped to your lapel. Pasting up pages of the *Woman's Journal* to be read by women across the nation. Sitting alongside Lucy and Julia Ward Howe in AWSA meetings." She pauses to write the acronym on the board. The images disappear. "The American

Woman Suffrage Association, or AWSA, was formed in opposition to the more well-known National Woman Suffrage Association, led by Susan B. Anthony and—never mind. I can see I'm competing for your attention."

She raps the front edge of Ian's desk. He jumps. "Sorry," he mumbles and takes up his pen.

Nell floats to the center of the chalkboard. "Grandmother Shaw was my hero." A new picture materializes, of a dignified older woman hovering over some important-looking document, bifocals slung low. "When I was your age—one century ago—I wanted with all my heart to follow in her footsteps. I wanted to go off to Boston, attend a women's college, and join the suffragist movement. But I couldn't." The image breaks up, replaced by a panorama of tobacco fields, a chicken coop, a piebald hen pecking at the hard dirt ground. "My parents needed me on our farm. They didn't have the money to send me to college."

Nell moves to another area of the chalkboard and lists her name and birth date in a box. "I was born in 1881." She draws a line up from the box, and another across it, forming a *T*. "Ma and Pa met in Amherst after the war. Ma's family was well-to-do: Grandmother Shaw had married a renowned professor and spiritualist who died before I was born." She expands the tree, waves a hand dismissively. "I forget his name. Pa's family were less secure. You see, Pa's father, my grandfather, was a unionist from around here. During the war he left to fight for the North, a decision that tore a family rift wide open. Pa grew up barely knowing his southern kin." Nell adds lines to her father's name. You replicate the expanding tree on your looseleaf with growing reluctance. Why does family have to be so all-important?

"Pa met Ma through the church," Nell continues, "and

they grew to love each other. Of course Pa was beneath Ma in matters of class, but Ma's parents were egalitarians and did not hesitate to consent to the match. Well, they were married. Shortly afterward, Pa's grandfather"—she points to one of the new boxes—"died, and the family farm was passed down to him."

You shake your writing wrist. This isn't the sort of information you'd need to know for a test, you think. Is it? Maybe there is no test. Maybe you've been lured here as a captive audience for a lecture that Nell is destined to unspool again and again.

Evie nudges your foot with hers and slides a sheet of paper to the edge of her desk. You lean closer to her to read the note she's written: *WHAT is* HAPPENING*!?*

Nell is turned to the board, adding more branches to the tree. *I have no idea*, you mouth.

"Do you think we should ask?" she whispers.

You shrug.

She raises her eyebrows at you expectantly.

You grimace. Fine.

"Question . . ." you start.

Nell twists around. "Hand, please."

"Sorry." You raise it.

She straightens and smiles warmly. "Yes, Margaret?"

"I don't mean to be rude but—why are we here? What are you telling us?"

"Why, Margaret," Nell pauses, looking miffed. "I am Nell, the ghost of Briarwood. Has my reputation not preceded me?"

"Oh, it has," you say quickly.

"We are truly honored to be here," Evie adds.

"Totally. Yes." You nod gratefully to Evie. "But I think

we're all wondering," you say, gesturing to Evie and Ian, "what it is that we're doing here."

"Yeah," Evie says. "What do you want from us?"

"And will there be a test?" you add.

Nell opens her mouth to respond.

"Are we going to die?" Ian adds suddenly.

"Ian!" Evie hisses.

Nell casts a gaze of practiced patience over the room. "These are excellent questions, students. First: My aim is certainly not to harm you. You shall not be dying on my watch. And there's no test; only my story, which for whatever reason, I am compelled to keep telling." She sighs dejectedly. "I have only ever wanted to be part of it. History, that is. The great big record of time. But it seems my time keeps running out."

She approaches your desks, hands clasped at her back. "I have kept watch over Briarwood for decades and I have come to choose carefully to whom I appear. I cannot tell you how many times my mere presence has caused fainting spells and shrieks. You girls . . ." Her gaze moves from you and Evie to rest on Ian. She relents. "All of you, I suppose. You're not fearful. You're strong. You're driven by curiosity and yearning. I believe you're capable of absorbing what I have to share."

Ian relaxes somewhat. Evie is puffing up proudly. You tilt your head, unsure. Is *strong* euphemistic for *heavy*?

Nell scoops a timepiece out of a skirt pocket and checks it. "We don't have much time. Hmm." She frowns at the intricate diagram she has drawn on the board. "I'll have to skip over some things.

"Now, where was I?" She floats to the middle of the chalkboard and starts again. "After the war, the farm was nothing much to look at—but it was land. Ma and Pa resettled here in the hopes of rebuilding and making a family. Soon enough they had succeeded at both: they had a working farm, albeit much smaller and more economical than in its previous life, when it had run on the labor of slaves; and they had me, followed by my sister Agnes.

"Farm life is hard but rewarding work and I liked it well enough. But I yearned for a life like my grandmother's. When I was a girl we took the train north to see her in Boston before she died. I was young and impressionable, and the city fixed in my mind like a splinter. I would get there like she did, I decided, by attending Smith or one of the other Seven Sisters. A college education would mean knowledge and independence. It would mean joining a legacy of accomplished and promising young women. It would mean a life in the city, surrounded by other young women like me.

"Unfortunately only women from wealth and prestige went to college—like my grandmother. But that money was gone, and money on our farm was short. After a particularly difficult year, we became indebted to our neighbor . . ."

$, you write. *College. Debt.* You're not sure you trust where this story is going or how you'll get back before weigh-in, but your interest is piqued; you keep taking notes.

"When that neighbor, a widower with a young child, asked my father for my hand in marriage, my parents were pleased." As Nell speaks of him, the figure of a slight man glimmers in the air, clutching the paw of a small girl with a petulant mouth. "They would no longer need to worry about me, they said. I would be cared for while remaining nearby. But beneath their rationale lay the ugly truth that I was the collateral for Pa's loan. I was horrified. *Was this truly 1899, only ten months shy of the beginning of the twentieth century?*

Or had I been catapulted back into the Middle Ages? I had never meant to live my life as a wife and mother. Yet if I said no, I would become a drain on my family's resources. Although the idea upset me greatly, I agreed to the proposal."

Young widower proposes, you scribble. *Nell agrees.*

"When I was a young woman in the 1890s, the birth of the new century loomed large and promising. I was smart, ambitious, disciplined. I had grown up with the certainty of women's progress. I was sure of change, and of my own personal freedom. Yet it soon became clear that my options were far fewer than I had anticipated. My dreams and ambitions were naive. The bitterness that accompanied this understanding was staggering."

Yes. You know that bitterness. It comes with the realization that girls don't "rule" and they can't solve everything. "Girl power" is an empty promise and growing up isn't liberating. It's disillusioning.

"Soon I became very sick. Very deliberately sick. I stopped eating and cut off my hair. I had manic bouts of energy followed by periods of weakness such that I could barely walk. My menstruation halted. My body grew a strange layer of silky hair. I began to resemble a boy. Profoundly unwifely. No more Nell. That was my goal. It would certainly take care of the problem."

You shiver. Her story is close. You exchange disturbed glances with Evie. Ian is scribbling intently.

"For months my father would not acknowledge the seriousness of my condition. He thought I was being foolish and refused to spend money on a physician. Finally my mother convinced him to take a day off from farmwork and deliver me to our family doctor, who diagnosed me with neurasthenia."

She points to *NEURASTHENIA* on the chalkboard.

"A catchall for nervous conditions at the time. The doctor prescribed a noxious elixir that did absolutely nothing. My condition worsened until it became apparent that I was unfit to be a wife or mother. Our family agreed that my sister, who did not resent the idea, would marry our neighbor in my stead. With this weight upon me lifted, I could regain the weight I had lost. I began eating again. I returned to life, to myself."

Great. Good for Nell. She's making it sound so simple. As though if you could just figure out whatever the external "weight" upon you might be, you could get rid of it. Like dieting.

She taps out another term—*HYSTERIA*—on the board. "I began to, with my parents' blessing, work at a local bakery while still fulfilling my duties to the farm, eventually saving enough to enroll in Miss Ellett's School for Girls. A small, independently run organization, it was no Smith College, but I was pleased at the community and support I found there." She sniffs. "After earning my certificate, I joined a group of other women from my cohort to found the Briarwood School for Girls, with the goal of eventually converting it into a four-year college and working toward establishing a Seven Sisters hub right here in Virginia." She adds a new line extending from the box in the tree containing her name. At the end of it she writes: *BRIARWOOD*.

Another image unspools, this one similar to the photographs that line Dr. Grunch's office—except that it's moving, the girls laughing, grinning, pinching one another. Captivated by their vibrance and the clear affections they're sharing, you stop writing to take it in.

"How exhilarating it was to create something with friends

and watch it flourish almost before our eyes. We started small, in Bess's aunt's sitting room with our first cohort of just four students. In no time we had a full roster. Then a waiting list! So we raised funds and built a school. This school. This is one of four classrooms, by the by." She smiles tightly, with evident pride. "It was as though one day I looked up, as if from a haze, and realized my life had surpassed my dreams. For a little while.

"Not long after Briarwood opened some of us caught wind that a women's suffrage group had formed in Richmond. The founding group was insular, the usual elite women with enviable amounts of time and money on their hands, but within a year they'd grown in ranks. I joined with my colleagues Bess and Catherine and together we campaigned for ratification in Virginia." Nell adds BESS and CATHERINE to the board and connects her name with theirs. At their presence on the tree, something leaps in your chest.

Evie raises her hand.

"Yes, Evie?"

"Were you in love with them—Bess and Catherine, I mean—your friends? Is that why they're on the tree?"

"Why, no. Of course not." Nell lets out a shrill, strangled laugh. "Now you've distracted me. Oh yes. In many ways the Virginia campaign was embarrassingly behind the national campaign. It was an uphill battle just to educate our fellow women. The anti-suffrage movement was loud and vicious, and its most odious argument exploited white fears of Negro domination: by giving colored women the vote, the anti-suffragists claimed, equal suffrage would usher in Negro rule. This logic, though preposterous, put many white women and men against our cause. I remember the day when Lila—our president—authorized the circulation of a handbill that made the case against this fearmongering." A new image unfurls, a crisp flyer with the words *Equal Suffrage and the Negro Vote* printed at the top. "Only, to do it, we had to take the fearmongering seriously. The league argued that, because of restrictions such as the literacy test, white women would unequivocally outnumber Negro women at the polls; by this logic, the league argued, equal suffrage would actually contribute to *upholding* white supremacy.

"Bess, Catherine, and I often butted heads with the more conservative contingent in the league, but we believed in Lila, who, after all, had worked for decades to improve educational opportunities for Negro youth in Richmond. 'This is not a matter of principle but of expediency,' she said by way of justification. We all lost some faith in Lila that day, but Catherine, whose grandmother was Negro, felt the betrayal keenly and diverted her energies elsewhere, toward Maggie Walker's community-building projects." She adds the name to the tree and connects it to Catherine's box. "Have you heard of Maggie? She was a tremendous force."

Nell checks her timepiece again. "I'm always behind where I should be." She shakes her head sadly, then composes herself. "Well, long story short. When Virginia denied us the state amendment, we refocused on the national amendment. I caravanned to the nation's capital and joined the march for suffrage there. At last: I was following in my grandmother's footsteps." Her pacing has accelerated to a brisk clip.

"Still I yearned for more. I would have been thrilled to join Alice Paul and the Silent Sentinels daily in front of the White House. But I had an academy to run, the personal and intellectual growth of young women to support. When I learned of Alice's imprisonment and the hunger strike she implemented in protest, again I felt that bitterness rise up.

Again I understood I was stuck on the periphery, unable to participate in history unfolding in the way that I wanted. What could I do from lowly old Central Virginia? In solidarity I initiated my own hunger strike. A private strike, staged for myself. An excuse, I suppose, to sink back into the miserable pleasures of my old behaviors.

"Alice's hunger strike ended, forcibly, with force-feeding. Mine continued, persisting long after the Sentinels were released from prison. Not until Bess intervened and talked some sense into me was I able to return, the full Nell. She sat with me and scolded me and made me drink bone soup. She kept me alive." Nell brushes away phantom tears.

"What about Catherine?" Evie whispers to you. "What happened to her?"

You shush her. "I'm trying to pay attention." In truth, you'd already forgotten about Catherine.

Evie squints at you with irritation. She lifts her hand again. "What happened to Catherine?"

"Catherine?" Nell seems caught off guard. "Oh yes. I suppose I have conveniently left out that part of the story." She pulls out her timepiece again with a stricken look. "Catherine married well and bore three beautiful children." Her voice is edgy, defensive. "That's what happened to Catherine. Oh, blast." Nell starts sobbing. "That's not the full story. Of course it's not. Catherine could not forgive me, nor Bess, for continuing to support Lila and the league after the publication of that regrettable handbill. Our political differences led to such a rift that she felt she needed to extract herself from our friendship and lives." She blows her nose loudly on her cravat. "I suppose I'm still a wretch about it but, well, we made our decisions. I respect hers."

Nell resumes her steady back-and-forth before the

chalkboard. "On August 26, 1920, the Nineteenth Amendment was ratified. The triumph! After decades of organizing and sustaining hope in the face of continual disappointment, finally, at last, we succeeded. Bess and I danced in the streets, flinging ourselves and each other around with abandon, hooting wildly, unencumbered by obligations to frilly propriety." Nell's words make the images dance with warmth. "I returned home that evening assured of progress, confident that our conditions would at last improve."

Nell laughs bitterly, and the scene evaporates. "After ratification, the anti-woman sentiment rose up more viciously than ever. Virginia refused to ratify the amendment, one of nine southern states to do so. Though we won on the national level, our home state sneered in our faces. I did not live long enough to see our state's ratification. Nor did I live long enough to see women elected to office. While I did, in my lifetime, exercise my right to vote, I did not live long enough to see colored women freely exercise their rights."

Nell pauses, lost in reverie. "Perhaps I could have—if I hadn't—" She gives a low moan, then checks the timepiece and continues with fresh urgency. "The 1910s were difficult, what with the war and the rancor around suffrage. They took their toll on Briarwood. We felt Catherine's loss heavily: she had done such a brilliant job gathering funding. Eventually Bess proposed we shutter the school, which I simply could not fathom." Her voice has clotted with feeling. "How could she give up so easily? These setbacks were predictable; we would recover. But she wouldn't see reason. She wanted more, she said, a richer and easier life. Open and honest and—she was telling me these things and . . . I was afraid! Oh, Bess. I was afraid."

Nell is now sobbing vigorously. "She left me to run Briar-wood myself. And I did. I did . . ." She trails off, honking her nose on her cravat.

Poor Nell, you think. Abandoned by her friends to run the school solo. How awful. The whole point of clubs is the club. New reasons to spend time with your friends. Without the friends, there's no club, no group, no belonging.

"I miss her," Nell manages to get out through her tears. "I miss them both."

You miss them too—your friends. Carrie. You wish she were here, swiveling toward you to mimic Nell. *Bess! Bess! Come back to me, Bess . . .* Imagining it draws a tiny snork of amusement to your nose.

Nell frowns. Remembering her audience, she composes herself. "It was a pale imitation of what it had been, but I kept Briarwood going." She shakes her head in agitation. "Again, my long-cultivated dreams collapsed and I fell into a new bout of my sickness, one I couldn't find my way out of. I simply could not bring myself to eat. This time, lethargic and morose, and suffering an awful hacking cough, I was diagnosed with hysteria and prescribed another nasty elixir, but nothing helped. I grew worse and worse until, one dreadful day, I extinguished."

You look up sharply. What?

"By which I mean, I died. At the young age of forty—I assure you, that *is* young—I died. Right here at this desk, I died. I also assure you, in the event you are conjuring false notions, my death was not in the least romantic or beautiful. I didn't fade away, a pale, dying rose. I didn't collapse lightly, crumpling like a doll. I frothed at the mouth and evacuated my bowels, directly before my dear students."

You take this in, heart thumping. In the desks around

you, the images of Nell's former students have material-ized. Some are taking notes. Others scribble on desks, their heads propped on elbows. Staring out the windows. Pigtails and ponytails. Suppressed giggles. When you pick up your pen, your forearm is superimposed onto a blue limb. You look down to find your torso covered in a blue-and-gray jumper with navy buttons. Gross. You shake it off. The image dissolves.

"It was perfectly gruesome. I am telling you this because, unlike many ghosts of my generation, my wish is not to take you with me unto death, but precisely the opposite. I wish for you to live.

"You girls now don't know how fortunate you are," she says to you. Evie is bent over her notes, writing furiously, no longer paying attention. "Thanks to your feminist fore-mothers you can vote, wear pants, enjoy more equal access to education. You can abort pregnancies. You can divorce and be spinsters. Yet girls like you continue to starve yourselves and compulsively purge your innards: Why?"

Is her question literal or rhetorical? You're not sure. Ian is doodling distractedly. You can tell by his slight frown, he's upset. Well, Nell is not much acknowledging him. You shoot your hand up.

"Over the years," she goes on, pretending not to see you, "I have come to understand neurasthenia and hysteria, anorexia and bulimia, as varieties of the same illness. And I have come to see them all as forms of feminist protest."

"What about boys?" you blurt.

"Excuse me?" Nell is displeased.

"It's not just a girl thing. Guys do this too."

"Self-starvation is historically a women's problem."

"But guys are affected too. Right?" You look to Ian for

backup or perhaps an appreciative nod. He scowls at his desk, avoiding your eyes.

Nell holds up a pointer finger, a signal for you to wait. On the chalkboard she adds new terms and statistics. You sigh and hunker down, copying without thinking. Evie is still scribbling. Ian glares at his feet, hating the world. Well, whatever. You tried.

You've run out of room, so you rifle through the other sheets. They're all full—no, more than full, they're written over in every direction. There's a layer in illegible shorthand, but the others begin with notes from the same lecture you just heard, are still hearing. Then they each veer into something else. Hidden passages that become stories, personal narratives. Testimonies. *Neurasthenia. Then hysteria. Now anorexia. A form of feminist protest (?) hmmm. My name is Theresa, and I am sixteen years old. The year is 1980. I've been at Briarwood twenty days.*

You read. You keep reading. Suddenly you can hear Theresa's voice alongside Nell's, growing stronger with each word. Soon you can hear many voices, a chorus, as though you've tuned in to some frequency.

CHAPTER 2

My name is Theresa, and I am sixteen years old. The year is 1980. I've been at Briarwood twenty days. It started—the food stuff— when I was around twelve. I was helping with breakfast and when I cracked open an egg, I found a tiny baby chick inside. I guess I had realizations. I vowed never to eat animal products again. Unfortunately my vow has proved difficult to honor as my parents do not understand veganism and do not approve of my diet. They say it's bad for my health, and weird, and sometimes they make me eat things I don't want to. So I started throwing up. It quickly became

The next word is illegible. The lines become blurred, the voices layered. *It's like you've been hungry your entire life and you'll never be satisfied . . . Your body takes over and you are living like in a trance. For yourself you have tunnel vision . . . You become amazed how much your body can take and you kind of test it out . . . The whole life is like you are carrying a cross . . . something heroic, something that is very difficult and demands admiration . . .*

You rotate the page.

My name is Patricia. I'm twenty-nine, it's 1989, and I've been here six days . . . Leaving tomorrow. First time I've had insurance that covers this kind of thing—figures it would run out on me before I make it to solid ground. I don't fit in anyway. The other girls are young and privileged. Whining about how there's so much food at home, they can't stand it. My experience was the opposite—there barely was any food in my house, and what we did have was disgusting. Canned spinach, stale cereal. Powdered milk. I learned to be strategic about getting myself invited to friends' houses for dinner.

Your attention snags, caught on something Nell is saying: "As women," she intones, "we must claim these illnesses as political damage done to us . . ." Yes. Political damage. As women. But Ian, you remind yourself. He doesn't give a shit. He's doodling directly on the desk now; you're surprised Nell isn't reprimanding him, but she's on a tear. You hook back in to Patricia's story.

I learned to be likable and charming, the only way I'd get a good meal. I'd go over to Kay's to play Barbies . . . You're sitting cross-legged across from your friend now, your stomach punching you from the inside, all you've eaten today is Pop Rocks and Cheerios. Focus. You need things from her. "Look at you," you tell Kay's Barbie, "you're perfectly stunning." You've adopted a vaguely British accent, it seems richer somehow, whiter. "And what divine plans do you and Ken have this evening?" When playtime is over, you stall with your coat in your hands, stage a cartoon seizure as though overwhelmed by the smells of the kitchen. "Great Scott, Mrs. H"—(still in British mode)—"I'm quite sure you've outdone yourself, what *is* that wondersome smell?" Endeared, she invites you to stay for dinner. You chat obnoxiously through the meal, annoying Kay, who wants her parents all for herself. She won't invite you back, you understand, but it's okay. You've got dinner at your uncle's on . . .

The scrawl becomes too tiny to read. You rotate the page, jump into another story.

I grew up fat, I've always been fat. It was never a big deal. My whole family's fat. Both sides. Then we moved up in life, I guess that's one way of putting it—Dad got a better job and we got a house in a better neighborhood. My sisters and me had to play the role of the attractive, intelligent, well-behaved daughters so he could show us off to his new coworkers. Suddenly there was all this pressure to be thinner, more presentable, upper crust. But it's not like our habits at home changed. We still ate the same big meals, our parents telling us, Eat up, eat up, do you think we're rich, no wasting . . .

The words become unintelligible, obscured by someone else's narrative. You rotate the page again, can't separate the handwriting. The voices swirl. *I remember all the things that are symptoms of eating disorders being taught by my family . . . You start thinking "fat" means the same as "not being good enough.". . . You call "fat" everything you are dissatisfied with*

. . . It's kind of a reverse swallow. It's as easy as swallowing, almost.

My name is Laura, I'm seventeen. Day twelve. From Midlothian. It's 1997. What else. I'll just say it. I was raped.

This sinking feeling in your gut. You know this handwriting. The *a*'s with their hats, the *e*'s like three-pronged forks on their sides. The *j* with its seahorse tail and open-circle dot. Tenth-grade Latin class. Laura Graber.

You're getting into Rick's car after a show at the Carpenter Theatre—you've both been ushering and he wants to go to some house party. You have a boyfriend, he knows, it's fine, fine, relax. The place is packed. VCU kids, so old acting, pretending at being adults. You shrink. There's drinking, a lot of it, you're nervous about getting home. Rick brings you a High Life and you sip cautiously. He's watching you. The next time you lift it to your lips, he tilts your head back, holds the can up. You glug, sputter. He laughs. You hate him. "Rick!" you protest, laughing it off, and you hate yourself too, playing the cool girl, unbothered, ha, but what other option is there? Now he's acting weird, too attentive, hand at your elbow, then at your waist. "It's loud in here," he says, breath sickly sweet, sticky on your cheek. "Let's find someplace quiet." You shrug. Fine. He leads you away before you realize how difficult it is to move. Your legs are woozy and leaden. You grin, sleepy.

No. It's too much. Like group therapy but worse. More real. You jerk out of the story and flip to the other side. The ink of the top layer still wet.

I'm Evie. I'm seventeen. This is my fourth stint at Briarwood. Day fifty-two. What am I even doing here? I'm not sure I count. When I was fourteen I read an article on eating disorders in a magazine and it gave me "ideas." I guess that means I'm a faker, right? I didn't develop an eating disorder on my own like some of these other girls. I deliberately and strategically gave myself one. I wanted to lose weight. Since I gave it to myself, I can stop anytime. Right?

I have stopped it, lots of times. Then I start it again.

I've always been big for a Vietnamese girl. My mom's tiny and delicate like a baby bird. Everyone comments: How'd someone like her make a big daughter like me? I honestly can't blame them. I don't understand it either. What sucks is that even now that I've lost weight, it's never enough! Even when I'm shrunk down like a shrinky-dink I still feel like "the big girl" wherever I go. It's just who I am, how people think of me. That's why I make a point to be nice and easy all the time. Ava (she's my best friend) says I'm just full of love. But I'm not really. On the inside, I'm rancid, and on the outside, I'm compensating. Like, "I'm sorry for being big. Please love me anyway."

Even at home.

You're Evie now, sitting at a round kitchen table with your parents and aunt. Your mother and aunt speak harshly, always jabbing in Vietnamese, too swiftly for you to follow. Your father is silent. The air's gone sour and you need to fill it with something else, something lighter than this rankled mood. You start in on your usual stream of chatter; it helps to keep the peace. "So we're reading the Gospels in youth group, and they're kind of amazing." You rattle off a few choice passages, definitely inaccurately. "Jacky says we must learn to identify our temptations before we can fight them. Like Mark said. Or maybe Luke." Jacky is the church's youth leader, blandly attractive and spellbinding when he speaks. Your mother nods along emphatically, shushing your aunt when she interjects. Your father packs away his rice with fluid movements. You chatter and chatter until the air is clear and the meal is over. You've barely touched your food. "Not very hungry tonight," your father observes. You smile and shake your head. Your mother pats you on the hand with approval. You don't deserve it, you never do, especially not today. Today you got another demerit; one more will mean detention. You couldn't help being tardy to orchestra: you needed the girls' bathroom to yourself. So you skipped last period to binge at Dairy Queen, but your usual booth, the most private booth, was already occupied. You ate your burger in the open, threw the fries and Blizzard in the trash, and walked home off-kilter and upset. "Hi, Mom. Hi, Auntie." In the bathroom, you got your kit, which you never bother to *really* hide, and sitting on the side of the bathtub, you pushed up your left sleeve, exposing a column of raised scars. No. Not there. You unbuttoned your jeans, dragged your underwear down, and brought the straight razor to the soft flesh of your lower belly. Pressed down.

The pain brings tears to your eyes. You blink the scene away, guilt crashing through. "Evie is so desperate to be loved," you remember saying to Carrie callously. "It's embarrassing to watch." So what. You're desperate too.

I really hate myself for all this . . . Just look at what I have done to myself . . . I wish I could die and go to heaven and eat ice cream forever . . . Years and years. So many voices. And more that aren't preserved in these pages. Voices from Briarwood, and beyond.

A stick figure materializes on one corner. A woman in a dress with an angry *V* over her eyes and steam coming out of her ears. *IM GAY*, reads a cartoon dialogue bubble. The woman is obviously meant to be Nell. Ian's doodles? Must be, though you're surprised he would be so childish. His scrawl spreads up the page. *SEXISM SUX. GENDER SUX. HISTORY SUX.*

PATRIARCHY SUX. EVERYTHING SUX. Irritated, you flip the page over and stack the rest of the pile on top of it.

Your turn. You smooth the rumpled top page and pick up the pen. Where to begin? Your name is Margaret Worms, and you are seventeen years old. It's 1998. You've been here twenty-two days and . . . what. Your pen hovers, uncertain. You have problems. You were a fat kid, and a girl, which are problems. The problem is you don't know how to grow up if it means . . . what. Cross that out. The problem is Sexist Society. The problem is Ian is right: GENDER SUX. No. The problem is you. You're weird. The problem is you have a body. It's a problem body. Your body is full of problems and you can't get them out. The problem is you still don't know what the problem is, or if there is even a problem at all. How can you tell that story? That's the problem.

"Psst." It's Ian, trying to get your and Evie's attention.

Flinching, you cover your notes with your arm, though there's no way Evie or Ian can read them from their desks—unless your writing has already magically appeared on their pages. You gulp. "What?" you say flatly.

"Something's up," he says. "Look." He points at Nell.

She's jerking back and forth now, stabbing the chalkboard and repeatedly breaking her chalk. Her spectral hair and spectral dress are coated in spectral dust. She turns, sputtering, spearing the air with each word, chalk dust puffing around her head. "How many times must I repeat this lesson?" Her pace accelerates. "Over! And over! And over! And over!" Her face flickers, streaks, morphs between ghost-flesh and skull.

The light in the classroom blinks. Your desk is there then not there. The chair flickers in and out of solidity. You rush toward the wall, where the door used to be, and feel for an invisible doorknob. Nothing.

Nell swings herself back to the board and smacks the chalk against it. "Things change!" she chants. The chalk shatters. "Things stay the same!" She begins scratching words into the slate with her nails, a wretched sound. You wince. The room is beginning to shudder.

Dr. Grunch's sofa flickers into visibility. "Take cover!" you yell, and crouch behind it. Ian and Evie follow.

"Looks like she's going to blow," Ian says, peering out from one side.

You're almost afraid to watch. Nell is jerking around like a windup doll, speeding up instead of slowing down. She hasn't noticed you're no longer paying attention. The schoolhouse shakes violently.

Nell froths at the mouth, shudders, goes still. The top of her head falls back as her mouth cracks open and splits, then collapses down around her body, like a snake swallowing itself from the inside out. With a dazzling burst of blue light, her body spills up and out and melts into the floorboards. You squint your eyes shut and grip the back of the sofa until the room stops shaking.

"It's over, I think," you say, taking a peek.

Ian gets up. "Whoa. That was intense and kind of upsetting."

"Also amazing," says Evie, breathless and giddy—with shock? With delirium? The thrill of adventure? All of the above? "Especially when she ate herself." Her grin wavering, she adds guiltily, "Do you think it hurt?"

The room has reverted to its former appearance as Dr. Grunch's office. The familiar bookcases. The wall of photographs. The circular rug. The armchair, the desk with its neat stacks and business telephone. Everything the way it was. Except the door is still gone and something—some design—appears to be gouged into the hardwood floor where Nell had been standing.

"It must be her cycle," you say. "She dies again and again. Which means she keeps coming back." You approach the etching cautiously, circling in to find a large wooden mouth, smiling mysteriously. Its lips are parted slightly to reveal large square teeth. You crouch down and run your hands over the etching. The lines are still warm.

"Think it's a way out?" Ian asks, joining you.

"I don't know." You trace the edges of the lips with your fingers. Nothing catches. You press your ear to the floor and rap your knuckles against the etching, then the floor beside it. Under the etching, the sound carries. "It's definitely hollow," you report. "Could be a door to a secret passage. I can't seem to open it." You press into the wood. Nothing happens. Ian tries each tooth, one by one. Again, nothing. You sit back on your feet. Hmm.

"Here lies Nell," says Evie, contrite. She stands over the etching with her head down, hands folded: she's paying respects. "She was a passionate and creative teacher who will be missed." She makes the sign of the cross. "Thank you for entrusting us with your story, Nell. Your lessons will forever stay with us."

"Speak for yourself," mutters Ian.

"Excuse me?" Evie says.

"Nothing."

"It was definitely something," you say.

"Fine, it was something."

"Well . . ." Evie waits. "What was it?"

Ian shrugs.

"It was 'speak for yourself,'" you tell Evie.

"Oh, okay." Evie considers. "What did I say?"

Ian groans. "Never mind. It just seemed worth acknowledging that she was speaking to you and not me. That's okay. That's fine. I get it. I'm not even supposed to be here."

You tried to include him, you would like to point out, and he did not seem to appreciate it. "Maybe not everything needs to speak to you," you say gently.

Ian drills a cold stare into the space between your eyes.

"Or maybe," you try again, "you would have gotten more out of it if you'd paid better attention."

He drags his hair across his face, taking a moment to respond. "I was drawing."

"Yeah. I saw. 'Everything sux.' So profound."

He squints at you. "Do you have secret superpowers of vision or something?"

"You didn't find any of the hidden stories, did you?"

He looks to Evie for an explanation. Not getting one, he throws his hands up in defeat. "I guess not?"

"Did you read mine?" Evie asks you, her expression tense.

"What hidden stories?" says Ian.

"The notes turn into stories," you tell him. "The stories of past residents. And somehow they all appear on all the notes, like they're connected. So when you were drawing, your drawings showed up on my pages. Evie's story did too." You turn toward her apologetically. "And I did read it, yeah. I hope that's okay."

She relaxes. "Good. I wasn't sure if it got added or not. I thought maybe I didn't count."

Spoken so casually, the comment makes you wince. "Well, you do." Kill eye contact. Sincerity is embarrassing. "Did you read mine? It was kind of a mess."

"Sorry," Evie says quietly. "I guess I was too busy writing."

Ian seems disappointed. "That sounds cool. I may be regretting my choices."

You can't help yourself. "Would you be referring to your very mature slogans or your mean sketch of Nell?"

Evie raises her eyebrows.

"What's mean about calling a gay person gay?" Ian says with exaggerated exasperation.

"How do you know she's gay?" you ask.

"Oh, come on. You heard how she went on about Bess."

So he had been paying attention. "And? Maybe they were just friends." Not *just* friends. The best of friends. You've had those. The connection is deep.

"Do 'friends' make lives together? Do 'friends' die of broken hearts?"

The answer is so obviously yes, you're confused by the question.

"Jesus did," says Evie. "What? It's true."

"I can't believe you two. Nell is the gayest gay. Anyway, sorry. I didn't realize I was desecrating an entire archive with my dumb fucking art." He takes a deep breath, his expression regretful. "I honestly didn't."

Evie smiles agreeably. "Apology accepted. Onward and upward. Outward, in this case. How *do* we get out?"

The door has yet to reappear. "Let's regroup," you say, taking a seat in one corner of the cushy sofa. Evie sits officiously in Dr. Grunch's worn armchair.

Ian sprawls on the rug. "It's just— You heard Nell. I'm a guy. I'm not supposed to be here. Eating disorders are 'for girls.'"

"You're missing the whole point," you tell him. "We're all part of a much bigger history. You are too."

"Maybe," he says, unconvinced. "I'm not sure that history is mine." He glances coolly at Evie. "Does it seem like yours?" he asks her.

Evie shrinks. "Sort of?" Her voice is shrill, uncomfortable. "I mean, Nell is a white lady from a much different context than I am. I don't *expect* to see myself in her history so it's fine when I'm not there? My ancestors were on a whole other continent, so. Whatever. Catherine sounded cool, though. I wanted to hear more about her."

"Wasn't that part of Nell's point?" you offer. "Like, what she was saying about how only certain people get to participate in the big things and go down in the record? And so many others get left out." You pause, thinking furiously. "Nell can't speak for everyone. She can't speak for us. That's why there are the notes. For us to add our experiences. So we become part of it. We add to it. It's ours."

"Right," says Ian. "But it's still Nell's story. Everyone else is just appendages."

"How about this," you counter. "When *you're* a ghost, *you* can tell the story." You're embarrassed to find yourself shaking. It's been so long since you've felt much about anything. Besides Carrie. And food. You breathe out. "But, like, don't die yet," you add. "That's not what I'm saying."

"Yep. Got it."

There's an awkward silence. Evie jumps to fill it. "Question for the group," she says brightly. Peacekeeping. "Do you or do you not think eating disorders are a protest?"

Ian shrugs. "Yeah. Maybe."

"Maybe sometimes," you say grudgingly, not ready to leave the other thread behind.

"That seems right," she agrees. "Sometimes they're a lot of things. They're like—a coping mechanism. And an addiction, something you have to do. And sometimes just something to do."

"And sometimes they connect you to a larger history," you add pointedly. You're determined to convince them. "A history of oppression."

Ian shrugs. "Sure, maybe. Sometimes they're a reasonable response to stupid cultural expectations. Whether they're like a capitulation or a rejection of those expectations. Sometimes both at the same time." He considers. "Do you ever wonder what it would be like to have a body that's not so defined by society?"

"What do you mean?" Evie asks. She shifts to a sideways position, her calves dangling over one arm of the chair.

"Like what would it be like to experience one's physical being outside of— I don't know. Culture? Take fat, for example. What if fat were just fat and not seen as a sign of self-indulgence or laziness? Or what if— what if a person were just a person and not defined by their, I don't know . . ." He coughs over the word "genitals." "You know?"

You roll your eyes. "But we can't get outside of culture. Or gender. That's the problem. We're stuck in it."

"But what if we're not, or don't have to be. What if I don't *have* to be 'a guy'? What if I'm just *not* one?"

"You guys," Evie says.

"You've still been *treated* like one," you retort. "All your life."

"Exactly. Which means I've been punished every time I've failed to live up to the ridiculously stupid expectations of"— he drops his voice—"'manhood.' No crying. No feeling. Quit being a wuss. At all times, scheme to get sex from girls. It fucking sucks."

"Being a girl sucks too."

"I never said it didn't. I'm just saying—"

"You guys!" Evie points. You see what she sees: a spurt of cloudy air coming from the mouth etching. And you hear it: a hiss, like a release of gas, first faint then intensifying like a rush of compressed steam. The hiss dissipates as the room fills with the noxious odor of centuries of concentrated morning breath.

"Oh my god." You bring your collar over your nose to avoid breathing it in. "What *is* that?"

Like a groundhog in a game of whack-a-mole, a quivering purple-pink lump is bobbing out of the wooden floor. Ian yelps and scrambles over to the sofa, bringing his legs and feet off the rug.

"What on god's earth . . ." Evie says. "Should we see what it is?" When neither you nor Ian moves, she gets up and creeps deliberately toward it, lunging to keep her weight close to the ground.

"Evie, don't," you whisper. She keeps creeping. "Don't get too close. It could be volatile." You make yourself leave the sofa and follow close behind her, fear rising.

Evie stops a short distance from the mouth. "Looks like a . . . tongue?" she says, peering down at it. "I think it's stuck. It can't get us."

You see what she means. The wooden panel between the upper and lower teeth has disappeared, and the pink slab is sliding around in the space it has left, repeatedly bumping up against the teeth and retracting.

From behind the teeth and tongue, a groan of displeasure.

"I think it wants out," says Evie. "Let's see if we can help it."

"No fucking way," says Ian, still huddled on the couch. "It wants to eat us."

"I'm with Ian on this one," you say. "We have no idea what this is."

Evie ignores you. She drops to her stomach and nudges herself closer to the mouth. "I want to see what happens."

"Evie, stop." Oh god. You can't look but you can't look away. You watch as Evie reaches for the lower set of teeth and tugs. The jaw creaks open, then sticks. The tongue stretches out with the additional room but it's not enough. The next moan reminds you of the impatient yelps of a frustrated dog.

"Okay," Ian says. "It's working. But do we want it to work?"

Curiosity overtakes your fear. This mouth is trying to tell you something—something important. "I'll get on the other side." Crouching down, you step carefully around to the upper lip.

"Now wait a second," Ian intercedes.

"It's the way out," sings Evie confidently. "It has to be."

"It's a secret passage," you say.

"Or it's a throat," says Ian. "That leads to a stomach. That leads to our death by acidic decomposition."

"Look," you tell him. "Trust me. This is how mysteries work. I used to be a sleuth."

Ian hesitates. "And— Wait, what?"

"This is our only lead. We have to follow it. It's not like we have other options."

"Other option: We stick around and hope the door shows up again. Maybe it comes back at sunup?" His voice is pleading.

The tongue slips through the teeth again, desperate for release. The impatient moan sounds. The tongue retreats.

Maybe you should give Ian a job, something to focus on instead of his fear. "What you can do is . . ." You search the room. "Grab the scissors. As a weapon. Just in case."

"I can't believe this," Ian says. "You people suck." But he grabs Dr. Grunch's heavy-duty scissors from her desk and kneels, quivering, next to Evie.

Evie keeps hold of the lower teeth as you crook your fingers around the front upper teeth—slick and smooth, they're sturdy and solid. On the count of three, you pull. The jaws separate and the three of you clamber away, watching as the tongue elongates into the air thickly, moist and quivering, stretching, stretching, teetering first forward then backward before falling and crashing down near Evie with a thwack and a soft, sour-smelling exhale. After a moment of stillness Evie pokes the tongue with one foot. It's silent and seems to be at rest. You hear strange squelching sounds from below and peer into the wide, dark tunnel of the throat. A rippled chute leads downward at an angle.

Stepping up behind you, Ian stares down at the chute. "I guess this is our future."

"Look at this dip here." Evie points to a depression near the back of the tongue. "I bet we just sit on the tongue and push off. Like the slalom ride at Kings Dominion. That's one of my favorites."

"We're really doing this?"

You are.

You, Margaret, the tallest, take the rear position, straddling Ian, who straddles Evie in the front. As a unit you balance on the edge of the tunnel, and one-two-three, you push off. You slide down, down, at a brisk but not death-defying pace. The mouth closes above you with a clang. Your shrieks relax into laughter. It's too dim to see much but you hear all kinds of interesting noises: drips and trickles, sizzles and booms.

Then the tunnel ends. Releasing your grip on Ian, you sail through space screaming, to land in a pile of loose chunks.

"Gross." You chuckle nervously and push yourself up. Evie reaches over to peel off the splotches of muck plastered to your forehead. You wipe your face on your sleeve and behold your surroundings.

You've dropped down into a glistening, pinkly lit chamber. Around you, the floor slopes up. When you step onto it, it pushes back like a trampoline, rubbery, springy, with give. The walls stretch high above you to form the opening through which you arrived. Along the ceiling, globules dangle, producing a viscous, drippy ooze. The walls are wet and irregularly ridged, a darker pink than the mouth, rippled through with crimson, brown, electric blue, and waxy yellow streaks.

Peripheral movement drags your attention. Along the walls, an array of holes open and close. Not holes: Mouths. A cacophony of them, all different shapes and sizes, slurping, salivating, chomping, murmuring, licking their lips, sighing.

You turn slowly, taking it in.

It's breathtaking. It's beautiful. It's wretched. It's like stepping inside oneself, if one's insides were disassembled and reconfigured by a mad scientist.

Or an artist.

It's art.

It's a body. A giant mutant body.

And you're stuck inside it.

LEVEL ONE

"We seem to have entered a body," you observe. "Or some kind of circus mirror of a body."

"You think this is Nell's stomach?" Evie wonders.

"Nah," Ian says. "She seemed pretty dead. And this place seems . . . alive."

The longer and stiller you stand, the clearer it is: a beat, slow and steady, hanging in the air. You touch the wall. It's slick and warm. It twitches.

"If it's not Nell's," says Evie, "whose is it? Are we inside ourselves? We could be, or even inside all of our bodies together. Like we've merged. That would be trippy."

"I don't think it's anyone's actual body," you say slowly. "Or bodies. I mean, whose stomach is lined with mini-mouths? Not mine."

"That you know of."

"True."

"Y'all," Ian says, with a barking laugh. "It's disordered. We have landed inside a disordered body. Get it?"

Evie gasps. "Oh my gosh, you're right. Wow, that's super literal."

You give them a tight smile, sharply annoyed. You're the sleuth here. You should have been the first to figure it out.

Ian's still laughing. "So what's our plan?"

You look up to see that the opening at the apex has closed: the chamber appears sealed. "Uh . . . find the nearest exit?" you say with a *duh* tone. But you have a feeling it won't be so easy. The chamber is set up like a puzzle or obstacle course, like a game-show physical challenge. The only thing missing is a host delivering the instructions. Without them, you're not sure where to begin.

A growl rumbles through the chamber, starting at one mouth and spreading like The Wave.

"They seem hungry," says Evie. "I bet these chunks are food."

You inspect the pellets. They're rubbery and gelatinous, with the good-for-you smell of vitamins, minerals, spinach. You follow her logic, letting your irritation pass. "So we should feed them."

Ian shrugs. "Seems reasonable."

"Or maybe not," says Evie. "If it's a disordered body, then maybe the hunger is a lie and feeding it is enabling a binge or something. You know, like it might just be pretending to be hungry when in fact it's already eaten. A lot. Which is . . . Oh wow, I just heard myself. I'm totally projecting. Sorry, Body." Evie nods. "Yes, let's feed it."

You scoop up an armful of pellets and make your way to the wall, where you form a small pile. Up close the mouths appear obscene. Slavering, murmuring. Maybe this is a bad idea. Evie and Ian are watching and waiting. Without pausing to think too hard, you toss a pellet at a pouty mouth. The mouth catches it, pulls it inside, and chews. *Mmm.*

"I guess that's right," you say. "All right, team. Let's split up and feed them in sections. I'll take this one. Evie, that one, and Ian, the rest over there. Got it? Good. And be careful. Some of these mouths could be dangerous." Evie and Ian get to work but you stay still a moment, unsettled by something you can't quite pin down, some sensory memory maybe. Oh. It's that voice, you realize—a familiar voice. You sound like that other Margaret, the one who takes charge, takes action, takes risks. After a long absence, she's back.

You don't like that Margaret. That Margaret is fat.

You shrink her down to pellet size, hold her in your throat, and swallow, sending her deep within you to be broken down, disintegrated, and eventually evacuated. Bye.

You move to the next mouth, which has puffy lips and small square teeth. It greets you with a low murmur. Leaning toward it you make out syllables. Words. A pulse.

gree / un / gree / un

You inspect your pellets. They all share the same composition, a blurring together of blue and green and purple particles.

"See any green ones?" you call to the others.

"Green?" Evie says. "No, they're all the same blend."

"It keeps saying, 'Green, green.'"

She trots back over and listens. "Not 'green.' 'Hungry.' Hear it?"

hun / gry / hun / gry

"Oh." You lift the pellet to the puffy lips. The mouth opens wide, thrusting its lower jaw out to grab the food and stretching the wall out with it. It chomps noisily. *Mmm*, it says, licking its lips. *More?*

You give it another.

Yummies. It licks its lips happily. *More?*

You give it one more. It chomps it down, then burps. *All done.*

Around you, the chanting becomes louder.

hun / gry / hun / gry / hun / gry

You toss a pellet into another mouth, open and waiting, and slide another into the one above that. The number of mouths and voices is dizzying; they're all the same but a little bit different. Tongues moving over lips. Thin whispers of please. Impatient snarls.

hungry hungry hungry

You find a rhythm that matches the beat. There are so many mouths *hungry* loose, sloppy mouths *hungry* tense, nervous mouths *hungry* strong mouths *hungry* mouths with firm, geologic musculature *hungry* lips that hang heavy *hungry* dry, chapped lips *hungry* lips that shine slick *hungry* lips that in their curvature seem positively lascivious *hungry* lips that quaver and hum *hungry*

hungry hungry hungry

Soon enough the three of you have gone through all of the pellets and you're hoping that means you're done. Nope. A loud squelch sounds, and a new batch pours in.

"Should we keep going?" Ian asks.

more more more

"I guess."

This hunger has no end. It's excessive. It's greedy. It's wrong. When one of the mouths asks for a fifth helping, you don't want to give in. *MORE*, it insists. If Carrie were here, you think, pausing, she would stay strong, she wouldn't give it anything. Wait. You shake your head. As far as you can tell, restriction isn't the goal here. And it's not fair, you remind yourself, to make Carrie into the best, the worst, to give her all that power. She doesn't have the answers. You feed the mouth grudgingly.

hungry hungry

more more more

How much more can they eat?

You resume your rhythm, fulfilling the mouths' demands, until you get to a mouth with twitchy, thin lips, wide and dramatic and utterly amused. *What are you doing here?* it says. *You don't belong.*

Startled, you pause, holding a pellet near its lips, which are curled up in a mocking smile.

You're not a Briarwood girl, the mouth goes on matter-of-factly. *You're not even a girl.*

"Yes I am," you reply, insulted.

I don't think so, it sings. It grabs the food and chomps noisily. You wait and watch. The mouth swallows and repeats its amused smile. *I'd like another.* It waits expectantly.

Unmoving, you glare. You'll teach it a lesson. "No more pellets for you."

The mouth snarls, opens wide, and snaps. Its lips clamp onto your hair ends and it slurps them in like spaghetti. You jerk away but it has you by the roots, then the head, then you're gone. You've been eaten.

Back in Dr. Grunch's office, you stand before the open, grinning mouth, alone this time. If this is some sort of game where you need to pass the levels, there ought to be a save point, or it's a stupid game. There should be an escape key, too, an obvious exit. You probe the walls, in search of some button that you can push to get out, to get back to your room, your lumpy mattress, your pillow with its faint moldy smell. You want out of this weirdness and back to that other world, that other game. The one you're good at.

But the walls hold no secrets and there's no way out but down.

Ian and Evie are waiting for you. "What happened?" Ian asks as Evie helps you up out of the pellet pile.

Wiping the muck from your face and arms, you tell them.

"What a jerky mouth," Evie mutters. "I wouldn't want to feed it either."

"But that's the test, right?" says Ian. "We have to keep feeding them until they aren't hungry anymore."

You roll your eyes but say nothing. Know-it-all Ian knows all.

hun / gry / hun / gry

The murmur rises. You heave an exasperated sigh and trudge away to restart your work. "What'd I say?" you hear him whispering to Evie behind you.

hun / gry / hun / gry / more more more

You get back into the rhythm of listening and feeding. This time, when you get to the bad mouth, it puckers up for a kiss. It strikes you now as familiar, its shape so like Carrie's. Is this a hidden sublevel? An opportunity to make things right, a do-over? Or do you just miss her that pathetically much? *I'm sorry*, you imagine telling Carrie. *I didn't mean to get you in trouble. I'm sorry, I'm sorry. I didn't mean to push you away. I love you. Please, can we try again?* You lean cautiously toward the mouth, shutting your eyes and parting your lips. Something wet—a tongue—licks your cheek. Your eyes spring open to find the mouth wrenching its jaw out. Soon it's wrapping its lips around your head and sucking in—a warm, not unwelcome feeling. When blunt teeth graze the crown of your head, you panic and extract yourself forcefully. You're panting, trembling, hair dripping with spit. The mouth whines and slavers, runs its tongue along its lips. It's not Carrie anymore. It never was Carrie. It's slabs of muscle with teeth, an eating machine. Taking advantage of your confusion, it springs from the wall, opens wide, and snaps you up in its jaws.

Evie frowns down at you, concerned. "What happened that time?" You shrug. You can't explain. But you're determined. You're going to beat this level.

This time when you get to the bad mouth you shove in pellet after pellet before it can say or do a thing. Finally it locks shut and you move to the next. Feeding and feeding and feeding. You go through the mouths in your section again and again, soldiering on after you've hit your exhaustion point.

You're pushing a third pellet into a small mouth with crowded teeth when it spits it out and sighs. The mouths are all sighing. A contented sigh, full of fullness. In sync they snap shut and stretch into smiles.

You laugh. Evie cheers. You've done it! You've finished the level.

One of the mouths flies open to let out a belch. You keep laughing. Ian breaks out into an awkward happy dance and you laugh harder. "What?" He freezes, arms crossed, but he's smiling. Around you, the mouths purr.

"Go, team!" Evie pumps an arm up and joins you and Ian by the chamber's wall. The three of you lock arms and jump up and down. "We did it," you say. "We won."

You catch your breath and collapse to the springy ground. "I'm still not seeing an exit," you observe. "Do you?"

"Last time it took a minute to show up," says Evie. "Maybe we just need to chill out."

"I hope so," says Ian. "I could use a breather." He and Evie join you on the floor.

"So, thoughts? What was this? What did we achieve?"

Ian shrugs. "I guess we were being challenged to listen to the body, right? Learning to give it what it needs. The standard 'the body is always right' lesson."

Evie snorts. "Like we haven't heard that before. I'm not sure it's that easy, Body."

"Yeah," you agree. "The body is *not* always right. Sometimes the body wants to binge. Sometimes it wants, like, heroin. And that's not right. Right?"

"But wouldn't you agree," Ian suggests, "that people like us have a hard time listening when our bodies communicate anything at all? Whatever this is, it seems to be asking us to live inside it and listen. And maybe even to help."

"Maybe," you say, irritation at Ian rising again. He's not saying anything wrong, but it's the way he's saying it. With such confidence and self-regard. Why does he get to be that way? And why does it *bother* you so much? "It's not asking, though. It's forcing us to be and act a certain way—just like everything and everyone else is doing."

"Yeah," says Evie. "It's not like we can leave."

As if on cue, a mouth on the wall behind her yawns open, jaw distending and tongue rolling out. Together you get up to investigate. Peering into its maw, you can see another chamber. Evie points. "Looks like we go through here." You step through. There's an ominous rumble as the ground tilts beneath you. You jostle for balance but the floor is moving: rippling and rolling. You fall to your butt. And slide.

LEVEL TWO

Down, down you drop, coiling around a smooth corridor until you collide into a warm, sticky wall. "Ouch," you say. It doesn't hurt; it's a word to indicate contact, which you've been experiencing a lot of in this weird place. Hugging Ian to your chest for the descent. Letting Evie peel the muck off your forehead. Getting licked and swallowed. Somehow it's easier to manage here than out there, in real life.

The ground settles around you, and a sphincter closes off the passage.

"*Now* where are we?" Evie says. She wipes at yellow residue on her arm. "Ew."

You're in a much smaller chamber, facing a wall made up of a glistening, waxy substance like melted yellow-orange crayons. The air is rank, thick with a raw-meat smell. And warm.

Ian pokes the wax. "What *is* this stuff?"

You slide a hand in, grimacing at the gristly texture and the way it molds itself around your fingers. "I think," you say slowly, with dread, "it might be . . . fat."

Evie recoils visibly.

"Of course it is," Ian says wryly. "Either of you get the feeling we might be on *GUTS*?" He waits a beat. "You know? The Nickelodeon show? Never mind."

Evie shoves at the sphincter. It's sealed tight. "There's no turning back, is there?" She goes back to wiping at the residue, which won't come off.

"And forward is . . ." Ian nods at the wall.

"Yeah. We may have to go in."

"In where?" Evie says nervously. "Looks pretty solid to me."

Ian plunges a hand in. "It's warm," he observes. "Sticky." Then his forearm. "I can't tell where it ends."

"Gross." Evie shakes her head. "No way."

"It's got to be some sort of passageway," you conclude. "There must be something on the other side."

"That's not a passage, it's a massive fat deposit," Evie says. "We could get trapped."

Ian retracts his arm, which is now streaked with glowing yellow. "Everything we've learned about this place tells us it adheres to some kind of logic," he says. "This has to lead us somewhere. Why else would we be here?"

"Why are we here at all?" Evie retorts.

She has a point. "Blame me," you say. "I'm sorry. If I'd had any idea this is where we'd end up tonight, I would never have invited you to come along."

Evie softens. "I know. It's okay. I'm sorry I'm so bent out of shape, but this is, like, worst nightmare–level stuff."

"I'll go first," Ian offers. "Margaret, grab on to me in case it sucks me in. Evie, hold on to Margaret."

You look at him sharply—since when is he in charge?— but don't object. You're certainly not jumping at the chance to go first. You clasp each other's wrists and squeeze tight. Ian steps into the substance. You hold your ground as he yanks your arm this way and that, searching. He steps out again, glistening.

"It seems safe to wander around in. A bit hard to see." He rubs his eyes. "I can't tell how far it extends, but I'm 99 percent sure it's the right way to go. Mostly because there's no other way."

"I'm gonna barf," says Evie. When no one reacts, she adds, "It's *fat*."

Ian rolls his eyes. "Hello. Fat person in the room."

"Sorry. But, like, what if we *suffocate*? What if we swallow it down and *drown*?" It's a reasonable fear. You settle on covering your heads with your shirts; there's nothing to see anyway. Evie's still reticent but recognizes she doesn't have much of a choice, a situation you're all familiar with, thanks to Briarwood. You take a big gulp of air, shut your eyes tight, and grab hands. Ian steers you behind him. The substance is sticky and buoyant. It stinks. Do *not* seep through my skin, you think, cringing. You lead Evie behind you. After a moment she yanks your arm and reverses course.

"Sorry," she says when you've regrouped at the edge of the wall. "I needed air. It smells so awful in there."

"Maybe you should go between us," you suggest.

"Not yet." She grimaces, shaking her head as if trying to erase this reality. You give her a moment. When she's ready, the three of you plunge back in.

The fat settles like a jelly mold but doesn't congeal; you're in no danger of getting stuck. In fact it moves smoothly in response to your movements, guiding you, almost as though it's gliding you along. Soon you're moving at walking speed.

Until Evie starts gasping and kicking. "What's wrong?" you yell back at her. Then Evie's hand is plucked from yours. She's gone.

"Wait!" You fling your arms around wildly, violently, in search of her. Now you're being pushed out too. The substance collapses around you, shoving you out. You can't breathe—the viscous liquid slips into your throat and nose—

You're back in the chamber on your knees, coughing. Next to you, Evie is sniffling. After a moment, Ian gets pushed out too. "I tried to get to you," he explains.

"I hate this," says Evie. "I want to go home. Not home-home. Just anywhere but here."

"We just need to figure out the trick," you reassure her. "Like we did with the mouths. So let's recap. What happened? Why did we get pushed out?"

"Evie, what was going on when you vanished?" Ian asks.

"It was just clinging to me all over. I freaked out and started flailing around like, well, kind of like when my dad tries to dance. Which is hilarious. And then I felt . . . *it* . . . moving me out."

"I was fine until I started smacking it," you say. "Then I got pushed out too."

"I bet that's the problem," says Ian. "Like if we move too—"

"Violently—" You cut in, not willing to let him get there first.

"—it pushes us out. Like, we have to be *kind* to the fat." He lets out a strangled laugh. "This is like one of those tediously oversymbolic dreams."

"We're not dreaming," you say with an edge. "Obviously."

"I know, I'm just saying."

Evie shakes her head. "I don't know if I can do that again. We don't know how far we have to go or how long it will take."

"We could split up," Ian suggests. "I'll find the exit and come back for you."

"We're not splitting up," you say flatly.

"It'll be fine. If something goes wrong, I'll just start punching around and it'll push me back out here."

"No," you repeat. "Trust me. I used to do this sort of thing a lot."

"You used to wander around a giant mutant body?"

"Obviously not. What I'm saying is— Never mind. I don't have to explain myself to you." You don't want to get into it. He wouldn't get it and it's stupid anyway. You shouldn't have said anything.

"Uh, okay." Ian waits. He's not going to ask a follow-up question. Neither is Evie, who's still sniffling. "Well, in the absence of a better idea, I propose that you stay here with Evie while I go for a swim."

"I said no. We're not doing that." Suddenly you're livid. "Who put you in charge, anyway? I'm the one with two years of solid detective experience. And trust me"—now you're yelling—"while sometimes it is wise to split up for the purposes of dividing tasks or providing backup, skilled sleuths *never* explore a secret passage alone. Duh. Fast rule. Too many things could go wrong. Like, catastrophically wrong. There could be booby traps or the floor could drop out or you could trip on a stick and shatter your arm or your head and we wouldn't know how to find you." You're trembling. "So no, we are not splitting up. You got that?"

"Whoa," Evie mumbles. "Scary."

Ian's shoulders slump. "Yep. Message received. We won't split up. I'll just get the fuck out of here." He pulls his shirt collar over his nose and steps into the hall of fat.

You're too embarrassed to look at Evie. "Sorry. I don't know where that came from."

"Well, clearly you have to follow Ian and apologize to him.

Which means I have to get over myself and come with you because I am *not* staying here by myself. *Ugh.* Okay, okay. Okay. Okay. Okay." She breathes out. "Okay. Let's go."

This time you sink your fingers in gently and wave them, like saying hello. Around them, the semiliquid stirs. You extract your hand and slide it over the surface. The fat stirs again, loosening and becoming more fluid. You lean in and slide an arm through it softly, curiously. Interested. Then you're in.

That's it. No slapping, no smacking, no kicking. And just like that, it's easy. The substance buoys you, cooperating with your motions, pushing you ahead as you move, warm and rich against your skin.

"It's working!" Evie says through her shirt. She has followed your lead. A few moments later you hear her groan in disgust and squeeze her wrist reassuringly.

"Calm down," you tell her. "Deep breaths."

Evie has slowed and is starting to panic. "I can't," she gasps. "When I breathe it—ew—gets in my nose and mouth."

"It won't if you stop trying to shake it off."

"Okay, okay. Got it. Okay." Evie softens her movements, and the fat loosens its grip. Better. You regain momentum.

The soft, creamy semiliquid feels almost good, almost luxurious. Almost soothing, after the heat of your ugly outburst. It did feel momentarily good, saying those things. It felt like being real, being okay with being ugly, *not nice*. But when you think about Ian's dejected slump, you want to cry. He didn't do anything, not really, to deserve your anger. How could he have known things you never told him? Besides, you aren't that person anymore. You don't even want to be that person. Right?

"I can't—" Evie is slowing down again. "How long is this going to take? Sorry, Margaret. I can't hold it in." She's on the verge of tears, you can tell.

"Evie . . ." you start. "Calm down."

But she's already kicking and punching and screaming. She vanishes.

"Fuck," you mumble. It's starting to get to you too. Now you can't remember which direction you were going in. You move this way, then that. The fat contorts around you and you think it's sending you back before you realize it's signaling which way to go. You slow down and follow its guiding pulses.

Then you hit a barrier, a springy, solid wall. Finally. Yes.

"Ian? Are you here? Ian?"

"In here." His voice, close, seems to be coming from behind the wall. You feel along the barrier until you find an irregularity, a thin, permeable slit the width of your frame. You insert first one arm, then two, then squeeze your head through and you're in another chamber, this one grayish blue. The floor is uneven with raised lumps, on the tallest, flattest of which is perched Ian, arms crossed and squint-faced, glowering. You wriggle all the way in and crumple to the floor.

"Evie got sent back," you say.

"Okay."

You stare at your feet uncomfortably, then busy yourself by peeling off your oil-saturated cardigan. "Think I can just leave this here?" Ian doesn't respond. "Right. So. Sorry. I don't know why I blew up like that."

He stares. "I don't know why you did either."

"Well, it's— I'm just—" You're stumbling. "It's my own bullshit. I think it was even maybe good for me to yell because it's like personal progress, you know. Like I'm actually expressing myself whereas I usually let things go unsaid."

Ian is unmoved. "I'm glad it was helpful."

You heave a sigh and try balancing on one of the lumps, which collapses under you with a spurt of chartreuse pus. "Gross." You stand. "You're right. That was a bullshit apology." You rack your mind for a suitable entry point. "I'm sorry I yelled at you. I think"—it's hard to say out loud—"you were reminding me of me, before I . . . this." You gesture vaguely to your body. "I used to be confident and assured and—well, kind of bossy. I used to be fat too. And loud. And a know-it-all. I feel like I've killed that person in order to . . . lose weight. And you were— This whole situation is reminding me of her. Bringing her back. Which is a lot. So yeah. I'm sorry."

Ian meets your gaze warily. "I don't feel confident or assured. It's actually bizarre to me that you'd perceive me that way."

"Really?"

"Uh, yeah. I feel like such an alienated fuckup all the time."

"Oh. Sorry." You pause. "Me too."

"Yeah. That figures."

You laugh nervously.

He smiles sadly. "I was actually hoping we would be friends."

Friends. The petty resentments you've been harboring toward him vanish, replaced by a familiar thrill. "We are friends," you tell him eagerly. "I mean, I want to be. Do you?"

His smile deepens, wobbles. "Yeah, sure. Why not?"

"Awesome. It's settled." A too-big, kiddish grin takes over your face. "Is it just me, or do you feel a hug coming on?"

Ian's groan is a put-on. What a great hug. Long and good

and sticky. You pull back, smiling with relief. A new friend. A good, important friend.

"So you were a detective?" he asks.

"I was, yeah. Just in the neighborhood. It was stupid, I guess, but I miss it. We called ourselves Girls Can Solve Anything and solved forty-eight cases. Just me and three friends of mine. And you know what." You elbow him lightly. "You would have been a perfect fit."

He smiles shyly. "It would have certainly beat playing *Doom*." He returns to his perch. "You think Evie's doing okay?"

"I hope so. Let's give her a bit longer, and if she doesn't show up we'll go back."

"I was going to suggest the same thing. And also propose that we yell? Let her know where we are?"

"Good plan." You crawl over to the opening and cup your hands to throw your voice. "Evie!" you shout. "Can you hear us?"

"I'm here," she says, her voice faraway. "I'm getting it!"

"This way," Ian calls back. "Keep going!" You and Ian keep cheering until you see her slide inside. She pulls down her shirt collar and flops to the ground, beaming, proud.

"I thought it would never end," she says between gulps of air. "Sorry to be the weakest link."

"Not even," you say. "I was the one holding us up with the mouths. And instigating conflict," you add sheepishly. "I apologized."

"We hugged," Ian reports.

"Good." Evie grins, her eyes bright. She lifts a knuckle to itch her nose and smears fat residue on it. "Ugh," she groans. When you reach over to help, you make it worse. Evie starts giggling. It's contagious. Soon the three of you are laughing in big swells, and it occurs to you that you may have found a new club, an unnamed club. The only member missing is Carrie.

"It doesn't taste that bad, actually," Ian says, laughed-out and licking his lips.

"Oh no," Evie says. "That's my limit."

"Do we want to know what's next?" you ask.

"Whatever it is, it can't be as bad as that," says Evie.

"I don't know . . ." Ian says. A loud squelch interrupts him. "I can think of worse." Behind him, a hitherto unnoticed sphincter is gaping open.

"Right on time," you say. "I guess we're about to find out."

LEVEL THREE

You've entered a tight tubular corridor that curves down into darkness. The floor is slippery with semisolid goop, and the air is charged with forward-tugging friction.

"Ah-ha," Ian says. "We've reached the guts."

"Oh good," says Evie. "We know where those go . . . Out."

You're quiet, mulling this over. While you mustn't ignore the possibility that "out" could mean something else— another passage to another world, for example—you have a feeling that this is it. The last level. An "out" that means return: to Briarwood and everything that comes with it. Terse weigh-ins with Irene and painful, exposing sessions with Dr. Holly. Traces of Carrie everywhere. The inevitability of home. These thoughts leave you stricken: all the joy of a few moments ago now jeopardized, set to adjourn. You walk for a while, deliberately slowly to resist the downward flow.

"Hey," Evie says suddenly. "Do you think this might be Level Four? I mean, this whole experience, and the thing with Nell too."

"I'm at Level One," you remind her.

"Yeah, but . . . does that matter here? If you didn't notice," Evie tells Ian, "no one in Briarwood reaches Level Four. At least, no one has while I've been there, and I've been there the longest."

"So you're saying Level Four could be, like, metaphysical?"

"I guess so. But that would mean we're recovered enough to go home, and I'm *definitely* not ready for that yet."

"Me neither," you jump in, relieved. "Maybe we should turn back. Keep exploring."

When they say nothing, you go on, making your case. "There has to be more to this place. We haven't visited the heart. Or the lungs. Or the brain. Imagine what they look like. Wild, I bet! And full of hidden passages."

"I don't know, Margaret," says Evie. "We don't seem to have much control over where we can go in here."

"Yeah. And what if we got sent all the way back just for trying?" adds Ian.

"Right. It would be like having to start over at Level One. Better to just keep going."

"But . . ." you start, the questions forming anxiously in your mind: What if leaving means club time is over? What if there are no more adventures and you're no longer friends?

"But what?" Ian asks.

You shrug weakly, say nothing. They don't feel the same. They want out.

After a beat, Evie goes on. "Do you think this has been healing in some weird way? For me it's like something has shifted, but I'm not sure I can say what it is."

Has something shifted? Maybe. You've been wondering, in the back of your head, how many calories you've burned while here. It feels more like a habit, though, than it does a real concern.

"So I'm still thinking this out"—Ian is gesturing animatedly—"but if we're talking about healing. The main thing I've noticed in here is a kind of relief from having a body, like, in the world. That's healing for me, at least. Because it's like being inside a body is giving us a way to be outside of society, and, like, social hierarchies?"

"Like . . . ?"

"I mean, weight, for one thing. And gender. And race too. But I get tripped up because it's not like those things are *only* social. Physiological differences exist. So I don't know. What do you think?"

"Right. And we're here and *we're* social," Evie says. "We can't get outside of that." The ground has tilted down, making it difficult to walk. "Want to slide for a bit?"

You sit down and push off, sliding around the corner. Then you're in another corridor, going the opposite direction.

"I guess I see what you're saying," Evie continues. "If we're in a body that is outside society, it's easier to respect the body and its needs on its own. Outside of all the meanings attached to it. And judgments, like girls should look this way, boys should look that way."

"Or like you were saying," Ian adds. "These expectations that Vietnamese girls are supposed be small-boned and skinny. All that stuff."

The corridor trembles. It's already happening, you think as their discussion goes on without you. You're being shut out of the club.

"Do you think this body is male or female?" Evie asks. "We haven't been inside the reproductive system."

"That's my point," Ian says. "We don't know what sex it is, or if it even has one. And if it does, it would be outside of the cultural meanings attached to it—like what we think of as gender. Right?"

You haven't ascribed gender to this body at all, you realize. Or anything. It's just like, organs and mouths and shit. Literally. (Fecal matter floats past.)

You crouch to a seat to slide around the next turn. The corridor trembles again, and this time the momentum drags you with it. You coil around and around.

"Woo," calls Evie in front of you. "Getting dizzy."

You come to a stop behind Ian. "Are we sure we're not in the brain?" he says. "It seems to be reacting to what we're saying."

You haven't been saying anything, you would like to point out. It's been the Evie and Ian Show for a while. Has either of them noticed? Nope.

"The fat was doing that too," Evie points out. "Maybe the whole thing's a big brain."

"But this has to be the guts," Ian says. He pauses to side-step a stream of rank-smelling excrement as it slides by. "This is where the small intestine meets up with the large intestine."

You've been deposited at the bottom of the tube apparatus, which connects through a sphincter to a wider, upward-swooping canal. If this is, as you suspect, modeled after the colon, the next step will be to climb up the vertical tube, pass through the last segments of the colon, then exit through the rectum. The end.

A sour-smelling wind catches you in the face. The whole tube system is atremble. "Something's up," Ian says. "Do you feel that?"

Yes, you feel it, the queasiness. The gut feeling.

Evie glances behind her worriedly. "I think we need to leave."

"No," you bark, surprising all of you. You pause to get your volume under control. "Maybe we're not supposed to leave yet. I think we should stay."

Ian and Evie look at you oddly. "And do what?" asks Ian.

It's like they don't *want* to stay together. You don't trust yourself to speak without a wail in your throat, misshaping your words. Frustrated, you shake your head.

A rumble breaks out from above. The smell and the queasiness intensify. "Oof," Evie complains, holding her nose. "This *is* worse than the fat." Thick goop crashes into the corridor, flooding it. Evie grabs your wrist as the pressure change blasts you both upward. You latch on to a lump on the inner wall and scrabble up.

The walls press inward, then relax. You're standing in another canal now, horizontally oriented. Ian and Evie are stumbling ahead of you, trying to hold their balance. You rest for a moment, catching your breath, waiting for them to gain some distance. Watching them. You're defecting, and they don't even see. Whatever. You're the one who won't care. You focus on the rippled walls of the canal, searching for an opening, but there's nothing you can see. With your hands you probe the slick surface for some hidden gap to slip through.

There's a gurgle behind you. The canal is contracting again, squeezing the mass forward. You press into the ridges and stand your ground.

"What are you doing?" It's Evie, some strides ahead.

You ignore her and continue searching, plunging your fingers in here and there. The tissue yields but only so much.

"What is it?" She's at your shoulder now. "What are you looking at?"

"Nothing. Leave me alone."

"Margaret. We need to move."

You shake her off. "You don't get it."

"Get what?"

"I'm going back in."

"What? But why?"

You shrug, as though it's obvious. "We haven't solved the mystery."

"Y'all," shouts Ian from ahead. "What's the holdup?"

Evie tugs at your arm and you elbow her away. Another suction blast, this one closer, knocks you off your feet. You scramble up and away from Evie. Not much time. If there's no passage here, there must be one at the beginning of the level. Before you can think too hard about what it is you're doing, you rush at the mass, clamping shut your nose and mouth just before crashing into it. It's silty and sweltering; you can't handle the stink. Come on, come on. If it doesn't work— It works. Soon enough you're obliterated.

At the start of the guts, you wait. Will Evie and Ian rejoin you or will they wait where they are? Maybe they'll go on without you. They probably already have—made it out and back to Briarwood with whatever magic delivers them there. You hope they have. You're happy to be here, alone. You'll find every secret pathway, every hidden chamber. In the body, everything is connected. You'll investigate it all on your own.

You inspect your surroundings. Where's the narrow slit that led you here? It's gone, disappeared. The only clear passage is down, through the guts. So it seems.

On one wall of the chamber you notice a series of slight protrusions, easy-to-miss swellings of a paler pink. You begin there, probing the tissue with your hands. The protrusions are denser than the tissue around them. Hmm. They're warmer too.

Maybe this is a bad idea. Maybe you should wait for Evie and Ian. You pause, listen for voices. Aren't they coming?

Apparently not. That's fine. You'll see through this case yourself.

A few steps down from the protrusions, the tissue becomes stretchier. Porous. It gives.

You were right. There's something here. You sink your hands farther in and the tissue stretches, shifts. You press harder. Now your arms and shoulders, now your forehead is breaching the tissue until it goes taut. Is this it, the opening? You dig into the spongy matter but it no longer yields. Maybe not. You ease up.

Half-immersed, still, and holding position, you notice the surrounding tissue has begun to heat up. As it warms, it relaxes. A murmur rises, questioning, invitational. You nudge forward, and this time it loosens, opening up and absorbing you inside it. You worm in as far as you can, wriggling, burrowing. The tissue seals itself around you, and you're held fast, clung to, enwombed.

It's not what you were looking for; it's better. It's nice having some alone time. You haven't been alone, really alone, in weeks. That was the problem.

It's warm here. Snug and drowsy. Suspended and weightless, you're reminded of that moment with Carrie, the closet time. The floating, the kiss. It was serious. You were so headachy then. Light-headed. You couldn't focus, and Carrie's presence made your energy whir. You couldn't breathe or think straight. You didn't feel good. That was the problem. You weren't well.

Not like this. This feels perfect. You shift into a fetal position. There. You've figured it out. It's so nice. You'll figure it all out. You don't need Carrie or Evie or Ian. Irene or Dr. Holly. Not Davina or Eisha. Or Angie or Jina or Gretchen. You don't need anyone.

Tears stream from your eyes. That's not true.

And what if they need you? If you don't get out of here,

who will finish Eisha's mixtape and scream Tori songs with Davina? Who will IM with Evie and Ian, check in to make sure they're okay? Who will Gretchen have to forgive when she's finally ready to talk? Who will email Carrie and tell her everything you still need to say?

No. You have to get out.

"Margaret?"

"Margaret!"

Your ears feel clogged, like you're underwater. But there are voices.

"Where are you?"

Here. I'm here. The words dissolve in your throat. There's something wrong with your mouth. You struggle to move but your arms are stuck to your torso.

"Check out this bulge," someone says.

"Is it . . . moving?"

Ian? Evie? You try, but the words won't come out. Where are your eyes? You can't see anything. *Help.*

Then there's a sucking, a rupture, and light.

"She's a tumor!" cries Evie.

"Or an egg sac or something."

Gripping fingers. A gushing. Your body tumbles forward and unfurls itself. Hands again, rolling you onto your back.

"There's, like, some membrane over her face."

"Ew. It's covering her whole head."

Soft pressure on your cheeks, gentle scrapes on your mouth, your nostrils, your eyes.

Fingers tap at your mouth.

"Let me try." There's a stab, a pop, and you're gasping. "Got it!" Evie's holding a hairpin in the air triumphantly.

"Oh my god." Ian flops back on the floor with relief.

Evie helps you wiggle out of the membrane.

"Sorry," you say. "Thanks. That was dumb."

"Yep," says Evie flatly. "Extremely and positively dumb."

"Agreed," says Ian.

"I know."

Evie's not done. "You were going to leave us without even saying anything!"

"I know. I'm sorry."

"I thought we were roommates. I thought we were friends."

"Yes, but . . ."

"But what? *But what?*"

You don't say anything, stunned.

"I am really fucking mad at you."

You look to Ian, who sits up and shrugs. "Same."

Their anger is bewildering. You're at a loss.

Evie lets out a frustrated groan. "Margaret! You almost got trapped in a mutant body! And you made us follow you into a huge hunk of shit!"

"I know. I *said* it was dumb. And I'm sorry. I didn't think you'd come after me."

Evie glares. "What about the rule, *your rule*?"

You're confused. "What rule?"

"And I quote," Ian volunteers, "'While sometimes it is wise to split up for the purposes of blah blah blah, skilled sleuths *never* explore a secret passage alone.'"

They've got you there.

"Right. I just . . ." You think back, try to trace your logic but you're not sure you can, at least not in any communicable way. "I wasn't ready to leave. I am now. But I was scared"—revise, revise—"I was *worried*—It's stupid. I just didn't"—you close your eyes and force yourself to say it—"I didn't want to be left out," you mumble.

Evie scoffs. "So when you made us climb us into a pile of shit, it was so we could prove that we care."

"Well . . . yeah. But I did have realizations. While I was in there, I mean."

"Right." Ian makes a strained whinnying sound and flops back down on his back. "Realizations." He keeps up a bitter laugh. "ROFL. I am literally ROFL."

"Oh my god," Evie says. "Oh my fucking god. Margaret, you are a . . ." Exasperated, she laughs, a loud, crazed honking you've never heard from her before. "I don't know what you are."

"I'm sorry! That's what I am."

"Okay, fine. You're sorry." Evie lets her laughter die down so she can give you a formidably stern look. "Anything else you want to say to us?"

You're chastened. "Thank you. For coming after me and getting me out. And, um, it may also be worth saying that . . ." You breathe out, face hot. "I love you guys."

"We love you too, you fucking fuck," Evie says. "Wow, once you start saying 'fuck,' it's really hard to stop."

Ian, still chuckling, claps his hands together. "All right, all right. We love each other. Now can we get the hell out of here?"

Back in the colon, you hurry along—ready now. You want out. Evie and Ian want out. The mass behind you is advancing more swiftly, expressing in no uncertain terms: *get out.*

The canal curves downward. Evie pokes her head over the bend. "Great. It's backed up." You step up beside her and see another brown mass at the bottom.

Ian groans. "Okay. We've got options. Either we dive into

that shit," says Ian. "Or wait for the other shit to plow us into it. We know where that takes us."

"Yeah," you say apologetically. "Let's not do that again."

Evie grimaces. "So this is it."

There's a loud gurgle behind you.

"See you on the other side?" says Ian. You nod. He sails down with perfect form. You watch his body plunge into the mass and disappear. You glance questioningly at Evie. She steps back. "After you," she says.

You scrunch your eyes shut. Hold your nose. And jump.

Bad move. You get stuck halfway and have to rearrange your body so you're digging downward. You press through, pushing, pushing—

"Earth to Margaret." Suze waves her hands past your eyes. "Hel-*lo*." You've been shat out into the cafeteria, where it appears you are almost done with your breakfast. You're sharing a table with Suze, Evie, and Ian.

"I *said*, 'You look like you had a hot night.'" When you don't respond, surprised she's even talking to you, she adds, "Come on, spill. What are your secrets?"

"Oh." You laugh uncertainly. Evie snorts into her juice. Ian smirks.

"Whatever," Suze scoffs. "Something smells."

There's a lighter feeling in the air this morning, some bright relief. It's as if an imaginary escape hatch has been lifted. Though you won't be leaving anytime soon, you can relax just knowing it's there.

Hun / gry / hun / gry The chanting echoes in your mind.

You shove the rest of your English muffin in your mouth and keep quiet.

Suze looks curiously at Ian. "You never sit with us."

Ian clears the hair from his face and shrugs impassively. "Here I am."

"Nice job, Margaret," Irene interrupts. You've cleared your plate easily this morning, attaining a benign fullness.

Carrie's gone, you remember with a pang of guilt. How can you feel so easy, so full, when Carrie's gone, when she's somewhere else, and sicker than ever?

But the truth of it is: you do.

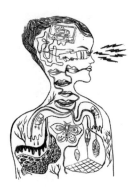

Carrie,

I know you won't read this, which is partly why I'm writing it.

I guess I need the *idea* of you reading it. The fantasy of some response. Was that what Dr. Holly meant with all those unsent letters? Giving us the idea of readers? I'm writing *at* you here. My idea of you.

Years have passed and there's still so much I want to say to you.

Here's one thing, a confession: I've been a bad, bad girl. Just kidding.

What I mean is: it's possible I'm not a girl at all.

At least, not anymore.

Yes, I know. Girls can be anything. That's what has made this so hard.

My last night in Briarwood we snuck out for the Tori show— Lana (you knew her as Ian) in makeshift faerie wings (her last art project) and me in the Lilith Fair T-shirt Irene gave me, a going-home gift. Lana requested "Butterfly" at the Meet and Greet, and when Tori played it Lana wept, a full-body shudder. I held her hand limply, ineffectually. I didn't hug her. I wish I had tried.

Got me running girl / fast as I can Tori enunciates the word "girl" in an idiosyncratic way. Sometimes "girl" becomes "gill" or "gull," something other than girl.

Butterfly / they like you better / framed and dried The internet was young and so were we. If we were late teenagers now, we might have already known we were trans. Lana got there sooner. It seems to have taken me forever. I didn't want to copy her, or wasn't sure. She's been patient, and right. I'm trans too. Or I've decided to try it. Or I just am. I don't know.

I remember my first meal back home. My mother said she'd make me whatever I wanted. I requested meatless baked ziti with low-fat ricotta and a salad with fat-free dressing. She was elated to cook for me; I let her have that. I finished my plate and thanked her, ignoring the full-throttle panic. After that I made my own meals. And we achieved an uneasy détente.

I remember graduation day: My friend Angie basking in her huge family's thunderous applause. Davina trotting onstage and nearly tripping over her own feet. Eisha flipping a subtle bird at the photographer. And me. My friends cheered. My parents cheered. (My brother was at boot camp. He'd enlisted a few months before.) I threw off my cap. I was done.

I remember graduation parties and cakes made out of senior portraits. I remember eating a slice of my face and enjoying it.

For a year I got up before sunrise to row on the lake. Crew practice was rigorous; my body hurt all the time. I joined crew to ward against the freshman fifteen but put on pounds instead: muscle. In crew culture, weight was currency and I was a buck eighty in no time. Much too much. Heavyweight.

Pounds were supposed to be currency but that was a lie. We were all dissatisfied with our bodies. Our number-two seat despaired over the folds of skin where her arms met her chest. *I don't understand how there's fat here*, she wondered aloud, pinching it. *Look.*

I've kept in touch with Evie and Lana and (surprise) Jess. Evie's become internet-famous in multiple fandoms. Lana codes video games and plays bass in a Richmond punk band. Jess is a public librarian and competitive runner. We see one another when we can.

And you? I tried. You didn't respond to my emails but your Away messages gave glimpses, let me know you were still alive. *brb calories to mercilessly slaughter   grateful for real friends like ana4me and slenderriot   gawd wannarexics are the worst* They all felt directed at me. Had I been sick enough? Had my anorexia been real? I had recovered too quickly. You were outdoing me still.

Irene called to let me know you were in the hospital. She said you asked about me, wanted to hear from me. She was probably lying. She gave me the info and gently suggested I call. For days I carried around that yellow Post-it, phone number and visiting hours scrawled in red ink. It was with me all the time, folded carefully into a small square and kept in the secret pocket of my backpack. Every now and then I pulled it out to stare at the numbers, only to fold it back up and put it away. Eventually I threw it out. I had to. I couldn't risk it.

I know. I know. I'm sorry.

Two Girls. It's a 2001 photograph by the artist Sue de Beer that depicts, using digital effects, the violent collision of two girl bodies. One girl has inserted her head through the other girl's collarbone and pushed herself down through her crotch, installing her arm in the other girl's socket so that the other girl's arm has popped off. The first girl's head is visible in the other girl's split pelvis. The girl is dead, body in pieces. But her expression is resigned, even dreamy. This may have been an experiment. A consensual act.

Anorexia is a violent breaking of the chain of desire. What might my desire have looked like without it? What kind of desire might I have had?

How do I write about something this profound without sounding sappy? When I think about this story I am telling you, this story I am sharing with the world, I think: how profoundly embarrassing. We've exhausted the coming-out story, grown weary of stories of queer repression and trans suffering. And who wants to talk about eating disorders? (I do, sometimes.) I suppose that's why I've avoided constructing any straight, or straightforward, narrative; why I've relied on camp and comedy to deflect. Which is more mortifying: Taking one's own adolescent eating disorder seriously, or meditating with solemnity about the internal and external obstacles to Being/Becoming Queer and/or Trans? Maybe neither. More mortifying still may be writing with deep sincerity about the friendships that have taught one how to love. *Maybe sappiness exists for a reason—for those situations where aesthetics are superfluous, where irony has no hold.*

Rampant nostalgia has romanticized the nineties, buffing over its rough spots, looking past lingering wounds. For many of us who lived in the category of Girl, the nineties were kind of a mindfuck. After the spirit of riot grrrl got co-opted by marketing, the slogan "girl power" became plastered on T-shirts and stickers, endorsed by the Spice Girls, sold on billboards and ads. Meanwhile the media routinely described the nation's First Daughter as "homely" and "ugly," *SNL* lampooned Janet Reno as a big ugly dyke, and the entire nation, it seemed, collaborated in slut-shaming and fat-shaming Monica Lewinsky. Lilith Fair was dismissed as an "estrogenfest" of "feminazis." The few characters of size on television included Roseanne, who was derided as disgusting by mainstream America, and Oprah, who was eternally losing weight.

You know this; you were there. I guess I'm trying to create a context for myself. To justify my responses to it.

Got a ways to go / It's a cryin' shame My last summer in college I arranged to meet singer/songwriter Beth Ditto for an interview after The Gossip show at the Black Cat. She ruled that stage, a southern punk goddess entirely in her own power. She ripped off her shirt and tore around in a black bra, her sweaty, unruly flesh confronting our gaze unapologetically. I was awestruck. When it came time for the interview, I snuck out, too nervous. I wasn't enough yet. To meet someone like that.

That's how I felt about you.

I'm beginning to think my problem was loneliness. *It describes not only a way of life but also a state of being, a social experience insistently internalized and corporeal, felt to be both essential and permanent.*

Here are some things that I missed: Not just riot grrrl, but zine culture, the birth of the fat-positive movement, the stirrings of transgender visibility. Ellen's "Yep. I'm Gay" *Time* cover. My school's first GSA, founded the year after I graduated. I look back to these years and grieve. For a long time I convinced myself I missed out due to lack of access. A trapdoor I couldn't open. *My recurring sense of myself outside the normal life and touch of human beings was again, in part, a kind of revelation.* But it was all happening, much of it right in front of, or close behind, me. I just didn't let it touch me.

The whole fucking planet is built on eating. I no longer want to miss out. When I entered graduate school I said yes to group dinners, to spontaneous meetups in bars. Many nights I'd return home buoyed by friendship, by community. I felt like I was growing back into my voice. I wanted to talk and talk, about big ideas, life, art. One night I realized: I hadn't thought about food for hours.

Instead I started thinking about gender, in a newly politicized, new-feminist way. It hovered over everything like bright yellow highlighter. Once I started seeing it, exposed and glaring, from bathrooms to bachelorette parties to the way my cis guy coeditor said *my* and not *our* magazine, I couldn't stop. When I complained to my friends that this same guy *treats me like a girl*, I meant he talked over me, interrupted me, made decisions without consulting me. I meant he was sexist and I was critically aware of it, that I didn't like being condescended to, who does. I also meant, Don't you see me. Can't you see.

Or that's a fiction. I didn't see myself. *Trans . . . wants from feminism a way of interrupting the process by which m/f reproduces m > f. Transmasculinity . . . wants this both because he loves feminism and . . . because there is as of now no better discourse he can speak to articulate the harms he incurred for failing to be f.*

I've been researching a paper on Kathy Acker, whose work I think you would love, like I do. But I'm troubled by an interview I found, where she throws anorexics under the bus by including them in a negative category of (female) body modification practices. According to Acker, women who starve themselves or get cosmetic surgery are *obeying the normal society*, whereas women who get piercings and tattoos or who modify their bodies through weight lifting are *actively searching for who to be . . . It's very different.* But we, too, were searching.

Teenage girls puke in private, they puke because they have been presented with an impossible image of femininity that is pukeworthy. A feminist understanding of eating disorders, which recognizes their contradictory performance of attachment to and rejection of cultural expectations for girls and women, was reassuring for a time. It helped me understand the problem and, more crucially, reframe it as political response. But there's Lana. Made to be a boy, she was puking too.

And what about you? *To question food is to question everything.* You were opting out of the whole fucking system. *Impossible to accept the self-destruction of a woman as strategic. . . . "The girl" can only be a brat.*

And me? The whole time I was searching, actively, for *who to be* within a context of limited-seeming options. It was (at times) a feminist act. It was (at times) a coping mechanism during a confusing and alienating time. It was (at times) another story to step into. It was (at times) an exploration of corporeal limits. *Our right to die . . . is our right to dream— and live in—a radically different present than the one we now inhabit.* It was (at times) a transgender practice.

Acker's betrayal of the anorexic is perhaps especially stinging because her work so adamantly centered the figure of the Girl. Self-destructive and frankly pessimistic, Acker's girl is also absorptive, avaricious, appropriative. She can become Don Quixote, she can become Mohamed Choukri, she can become a series of murderesses. She can die and come back to life. Over Acker's body of work, her girl mutates, defying fixity, and culminating in the figure of the girl pirate.

In her final novel, *Pussy, King of the Pirates*, her character Antigone has returned from her death in Sophocles and gone shopping. Faced with the prospect of buying one of the huge, autumn-colored chenille sweaters on the racks, *the only clothes which remain in the world*, she declares:

I refuse.
I will be _____ instead.
_____ is something impossible.
I'll be a girl pirate.

Importantly Antigone is not rejecting girlhood here but bad fashion. A temporary substitute for *something impossible*, for something unlanguageable, the girl pirate exists on some Muñozian horizon of queer—and trans—possibility. Some of the pirate girls aren't *female* (whatever that means in their bizarro context), and some are not always girls.

Acker's pirate girl is also an adult. Many of Acker's characters are perpetual adolescents, never babies but forever girls. Like I was. I was always too young for my age. Where most coming-of-age novels present protagonists who are far wiser than their years, my character is wincingly the opposite. I didn't want childhood to end. Because I needed to be _____. Something that still seemed impossible.

What does it mean when I write that I "felt" like neither a girl nor a boy? If I'm not pirate girl Antigone, neither am I Peter Pan, paragon of perpetual irresponsible boyhood. I was never a boy. If I'm no longer a cis girl, I was for a long time; indeed, insisted upon it. I pull out an old photo of myself at prom. I look triumphant, dazzling. My lethargy covered over by shimmery makeup. My smile a put-on. I am skinny and I am sick. I have just eaten pasta in a cream-based sauce and I am upset with myself. Everyone tells me how lovely I look except Mrs. Lytell, who clocks my prominent collarbone and scowls.

No one looks deeper than the flesh, do they. So practice being invisible. Learn to look in the mirror and see only the mirror. There's no sign of genderqueerness, the chubby tomboy, emergent butch buried alive. I've figured it out, haven't I? And I am reaping the rewards. My date tells me to take off my heels, I'm taller than him. And I do.

José Esteban Muñoz has written at length about performances of disidentification, that is, of identifying and not simultaneously, and the political potential of such a positionality, particularly for queers of color. The Girl is typically coded as white and feminine, cis and straight, affluent and able-bodied, often glamorous. We are all disidentifying with her, all the time.

What are the possibilities of politicizing disidentification, this experience of misrecognition, this uneasy sense of standing under a sign to which one does and does not belong? I was a kind of girl. Looking at this photograph I see that. The kind of girl: who is white; who is smart; who passes as straight and cisgender and knows how to present as normatively attractive, which in her middle-class suburban context means thin. The kind of girl who assumes power by becoming as thin and as pretty as she can be. The kind of girl who, at the same time as she is subscribing to cisheterofemininity at all costs, remains attached to the belief that she is special, is different, is exceptional; if anyone can master her body, she can. This is the ideal of white femininity, and it is sick.

Though the detective story postulates a world in which everything might have a meaningful bearing on the solution of the crime, it concludes with an extensive repudiation of meanings that simply "drop out." Where were the clues? Why couldn't I see them?

If clues are somewhat queer, then the herring is even queerer. It is both a clue and not a clue. The following may all be red herrings. That I could not keep my jeans cuffed. That my favorite hair accessory was a hideous neon-pink head scrunchie, the key detail here being either "hideous" or "pink." That I was loud until I wasn't. That I developed intense attachments to my friends. That I religiously read teen magazines and sought out the beauty products they endorsed. That I developed intense attachments to girlhood. That I privately recognized an urgent desire to be flat-chested and straight-bodied in a cultural moment defined by heroin chic. That I was not a tomboy, nor particularly butch. That I was a reader, and fat. That I was anorexic. That I loved you. That I was a girl. That I behaved as a girl. Wait. Where is the crime? I've lost track of the mystery.

The "real self" who comes into being through fiction is not the self who produces fiction, but is instead produced by fiction. The magical or otherwise exceptional girl is the most available girl narrative there is. Isn't that what anorexia is? Not a mystery or crime but a kind of magic. Exceptionality bent back on itself. A fantasy.

I've lost sight of who I'm writing as. *One of the unacknowledged limiters of the current froth of identity politics [that] cages us in as writers is the need it seems for a seamlessness between author and narrator, narrator and protagonist, between author and word.* Myself, my former self, my fictionalized self, a fiction. Words on the page. Who are you? You're multiple too. A fantasy. A construct. A ghost.

We intuitively know that everyday life doesn't conform to the simple outlines of well-made genres. A more legibly transmasculine narrative might highlight my avatar's undeniable, inevitable boy-ness, displacing and deferring the girl. A more comfortably young adult narrative would chop off this retrospective adult voice. A more knowingly adult novel would not commit the crime of adolescent unknowingness. Where detective fiction promises knowledge and order, this story is aligned with unknowing.

Every body contains in itself a phantom (perhaps the body itself is a phantom). In his experimental film *The Year I Broke My Voice*, Angelo Madsen Minax inserts transmasculine bodies into iconic young-boy narratives such as *The Outsiders* and *Stand by Me* to haunting effect. In her novel *Fierce Femmes and Notorious Liars: A Dangerous Trans Girl's Confabulous Memoir*, Kai Cheng Thom reorients girl-group and fairy-tale narratives around a trans-femme-of-color narrator. I seek to haunt narratives of the young girl—at least, the ones I grew up with—with the queer and genderqueer and trans girls and maybe-not-girls they leave out: so many missing bodies. The butch and the genderqueer, the not-yet-transmasculine and the not-yet-transfeminine, are ghosts in that body of Girl Lit. Hovering between presence and absence, barely visible, inchoate, not knowing where they fit or if they fit anywhere at all.

In my dream I'm in the kitchen watching a dark blob scurry across the sink. It's a spider. It scuttles up over the corner of the sink and anchors itself down to the floor, where it rests, growing larger the longer I look at it. I have a kitchen pot in my hand, and bring it down on the spider's back. Its armor is tough, resilient. It takes four swings to crush. Finally the spider's body splits open. Inside is a creamy yellow custard, bright as the sun. I kneel down and lap it up. Then I'm the spider.

 THE DOCTOR TOLD ME THE SHOTS WOULD MAKE ME SPIN SILK / Along with muscling out my shoulders / and dropping my voice, / they'd let me hang by my own fibers, / invade distant lands with my gossamer webs . . . I don't want to invade anything but I'm anchored and gliding further every day.

How can a person choose to be who they are? What is the difference between the fantasy of anorexic body mastery and the magic of hormone-based transition? I don't know. When I first announced a desire to take T, my partner at the time, who herself has struggled with anorexia, questioned medical transition as another way to assert control, to lose weight. I've gained it. Most days I feel humbled: I control very little about this process.

 The doctor said my silk would be / as strong as high-grade steel in six months flat, / that man *would not be right* . . . The HRT-induced hunger I'm experiencing now revives old paths with different effects. The old hunger was dull, chronic, an emptying out. It felt romantic and steadying; gave me some toxic, numbing sustenance. This new hunger is loud and insistent; if left unattended, it storms into full-body nausea. I'm eating constantly and gaining quickly; it's upsetting and it's expensive, and I have moments of new distress. But my relationship to it is changed. It's not me; it's the hormones. I'm not failing at my gender. I'm reaching for something else. And finally I see: my body wasn't missing; it's been here all along.

I still don't quite know what to call myself. When I was a girl, my mom would ask me teasingly, say, driving home from the new Walmart or on our way to my softball practice, if I had a boyfriend yet. Instead of admitting no, risking failure, I tried to explain. If I were a boy, I'd say, it'd be easier. I sound like I'm feminist, or queer, or trans. I knew, I always knew or almost knew. Or I've never known anything at all.

To learn anything worth knowing requires that you learn as well how pathetic you were when you were ignorant of it. I still don't know. Am I this or that intrinsically? Or have I simply made choices? Would I have made these choices were I *not* intrinsically this or that? Would I have made these choices earlier had I known they were available? Surely I could have found the information sooner if I had more urgently needed to find it. Did I know, somewhere deep down, and simply refuse to know? Which is worse, not knowing or refusing knowledge? Should I have known? *Could* I have known? Known what, exactly? I don't know. Did you? The shame, my foolish, pathetic ignorance, burns. *The acquisition of knowledge—especially when we are young—again and again includes this experience.*

I still wrestle, still struggle, still seek. Sometimes when I'm full, I keep eating; sometimes when I'm hungry, I don't.

But there are better things to care about. Like Lana and Evie and Jess. Davina and Eisha and Angie. The new friends I've found, and keep finding. And you. Always you. Transmasculinity hasn't solved everything. But it has made me a better friend.

The longing for community across time is a crucial feature of queer historical experience, one produced by the historical isolation of individual queers as well as by the damaged quality of the historical archive. I pursued touch in baby steps. I went on a number of bad dates with women I met on the w4w section of Philly craigslist. I "wandered into" Giovanni's Room, the local queer bookstore, where I purchased a copy of *Stone Butch Blues* from the smoking-hot dyke behind the register whose fingers almost touched mine as I passed her my money. I read the novel, and was touched.

Longing produces modes of both belonging and "being long," or persisting over time. It would be a while before I'd follow Lana's lead, because the truth is I'd never met an out trans guy before. When I did, I gawked at him, struck. Even then, the truth is it barely touched me. We were eating dinner among friends; I was focused on the food.

You almost touched me too. I missed you then and I am missing you now. I imagine what it would be like to meet now, with my power and yours intact. Another fantasy. *Is there not a longing to grieve—and, equivalently, an inability to grieve—that which one never was able to love, a love that falls short of the "conditions" of existence?. . . The fear, of course, is that in looking backward, we will be paralyzed by grief, and grief will overwhelm politics.*

But grief is politics, to the extent that politics is inseparable from history. I met you at the Briarwood Center for the Empowerment of Young Women and Girls. That's code for "we all had eating disorders." It was the nineties. "Girl power" was everywhere. So we developed our powers. We were going to take over the world.

You were right. This world is bullshit.

I wish you were still in it.

Love,
M.

NOTES

This book is indebted to and informed by many, many texts. What follows is an incomplete indexing of some that have offered models and wisdom and, in some cases, actual language.

The Girls Can Solve Anything series is inspired by my ongoing love of the Baby-Sitters Club series by Ann M. Martin; as well as Nancy Drew, Sweet Valley Twins, Goosebumps, and other similar series I gobbled up as a kid. Gabrielle Moss's terrific *Paperback Crush: The Totally Radical History of '80s and '90s Teen Fiction* also informed GCSA.

The Briarwood section draws inspiration and some direct language from Susanna Kaysen's *Girl, Interrupted* ("*People ask . . .*"; "*And it is easy . . .*"; and some lines on the "Etiology" list, which as a whole riffs on Kaysen's "Etiology" list), as well as the 1999 film adaptation. Other language is sourced from Nicole Johns's *Purge: Rehab Diaries* ("*Making yourself sick . . .*" and "*Starving, restricting . . .*") and Dodie Bellamy's *Barf Manifesto* ("*Barf is an upheaval . . .*"). A line from Radclyffe Hall's *The Well of Loneliness* also appears in this section ("*How can it be . . .*").

While Briarwood is a fictional place, it is based loosely on the treatment centers captured in Helen Gremillion's *Feeding Anorexia: Gender and Power at a Treatment Center* and the documentary film *Thin*, directed by Lauren Greenfield.

Nell's story borrows liberally from Susan Terris's 1987 historical YA novel *Nell's Quilt*. Here, Terris's Nell has been moved from western Massachusetts to Richmond, Virginia, aged up from where we leave her as an eighteen-year-old in the original novel, and reimagined as a ghost. Nell's feminist analysis on eating disorders is informed by essays in *Feminist Perspectives on Eating Disorders*, edited by Melanie Katzman, Patricia Fallon, and Susan Frelick Wooley.

One iteration of this novel brought *Matilda* by Roald Dahl and *Carrie* by Stephen King into direct conversation; while most of that version has been scrubbed out of this one, traces exist in the characters Carrie, the Grunch, and Dr. Holly.

In chapter 2 of the section titled "The Mystery of the Secret Passage," some of the hidden stories are drawn loosely from experiences chronicled in Stephanie Covington Armstrong's *Not All Black Girls Know How to Eat* and *Looking Queer: Body Image and Identity in Lesbian, Bisexual, Gay, and Transgender Communities*, edited by Dawn Atkins. Much of the language in the choral paragraphs (*"It's like you've been. . . Your body takes over. . . For yourself you have. . . You become amazed . . . The whole life . . ."; "I remember . . . You start thinking . . . You call 'fat' . . . It's kind of a . . ."; "I really hate . . . Just look at what . . . I wish I could . . ."*) is lifted from Hilde Bruch's *Conversations with Anorexics*.

In the final section, the italicized lines come from the following sources, in order:

Got me running: "Butterfly," Tori Amos, track 12 on *Music from the Motion Picture: Higher Learning*, Epic Records, 1995.

Butterfly: "Butterfly," Tori Amos, 1995.

Anorexia is: Chris Kraus, *Aliens & Anorexia* (Los Angeles: Semiotext(e), 2000), 143.

How do I write: Dodie Bellamy, "Beyond Hunger," in *Academonia* (Krupskaya, 2006), 104.

Maybe sappiness: Bellamy, "Beyond Hunger," 105.

Got a ways: "Got All This Waiting," Gossip, track 2 on *That's Not What I Heard*, Kill Rock Stars, 2001.

It describes not only: Heather Love, *Feeling Backward: Loss and the Politics of Queer History* (Cambridge, MA: Harvard University Press, 2007), 108.

My recurring sense: Cherríe Moraga, quoted in Love, *Feeling Backward*, 40.

The whole fucking planet: William Burroughs, quoted in Kraus, *Aliens*, 163.

Trans . . . wants: Cameron Awkward-Rich, "Trans, Feminism: Or, Reading like a Depressed Transsexual," *Signs* 42, no. 4 (Summer 2017): 838–99.

obeying the normal: Kathy Acker, interviewed by Andrea Juno, *RE/Search #13: Angry Women* (1991), 183.

Teenage girls: Kate Durbin, interviewed by Becca Klaver, *H_NGM_N* (2010).

To question food: Kraus, *Aliens*, 145.

Impossible to accept: Kraus, *Aliens*, 27.

The girl can only: Kraus, *Aliens*, 113.

Our right to die: Eric Cazdyn, *The Already Dead: The New Time of Politics, Culture, and Illness* (Durham, NC: Duke University Press, 2012), 7.

the only clothes: Kathy Acker, *Pussy, King of the Pirates* (New York: Grove Press, 1996), 77.

What does it mean: Eli Clare, *Exile and Pride: Disability, Queerness, and Liberation* (Boston: South End Press, 2009), 158.

No one looks: Lou Sullivan, quoted in Julian Carter, "Embracing Transition, or Dancing in the Folds of

Time," in *The Transgender Studies Reader 2*, eds. Susan Stryker and Aren Z. Aizura (London: Routledge, 2013), 134.

What are the possibilities: Judith Butler, quoted in José Esteban Muñoz, *Disidentifications: Queers of Color and the Performance of Politics*, (Minneapolis: University of Minnesota Press, 1999), 12.

Though the detective story: D. A. Miller, *The Novel and the Police* (Berkeley: University of California Press, 1989), 34.

If clues: Faye Stewart, "Of Herrings Red and Lavender: Reading Crime and Identity in Queer Detective Fiction," *CLUES: A Journal of Detection* 27, no. 2 (Fall 2009): 36.

The "real self": Muñoz, *Disidentifications*, 20.

One of the unacknowledged: Ryka Aoki, Colette Arrand, Cooper Lee Bombardier, Grace Reynolds, and Brook Shelley, "More Like *This* Than Any of *These*: Creative Nonfiction in the Age of the Trans New Wave," *Ninth Letter* 15, no. 2 (December 2018).

We intuitively know: Joan Retallack, quoted in Dodie Bellamy, "Crimes against Genre," in *Academonia*, 52.

Every body contains: Paul Ferdinand Schilder, quoted in Gayle Salamon, *Assuming a Body: Transgender and Rhetorics of Materiality* (New York: Columbia University Press, 2010), 13.

THE DOCTOR TOLD ME: Oliver Baez Bendorf, "The Doctor Told Me the Shots Would Make Me Spin Silk," in *The Spectral Wilderness* (Kent: Kent State University Press, 2015), 9.

How can a person: Jennifer Finney Boylan, *She's Not*

There: A Life in Two Genders (New York: Broadway Books, 2013), 161.

The doctor said: Baez Bendorf, "The Doctor Told Me," 9.

I still don't quite know: Patrick Califia, *Speaking Sex to Power: The Politics of Queer Sex* (San Francisco: Cleis, 2002), 393.

To learn anything: Samuel R. Delany, *About Writing: 7 Essays, 4 Letters & 5 Interviews* (Middletown, CT: Wesleyan University Press, 2006), 34.

The acquisition of knowledge: Delany, *About Writing*, 35.

The longing for community: Love, *Feeling Backward*, 37.

Longing produces: Elizabeth Freeman, *Time Binds: Queer Temporalities, Queer Histories* (Durham, NC: Duke University Press, 2010), 13.

Is there not a longing: Judith Butler, quoted in Love, *Feeling Backward*, 119–20.

The fear, of course . . . But grief is politics: Love, *Feeling Backward*, 128.

Other sources that I consulted in writing this book:

Patrick Anderson's *So Much Wasted: Hunger, Performance, and the Morbidity of Resistance*

Karen Lynn Dias's *Virtual Sanctuary: Geographies of Pro-Anorexia Websites*

Lisa Diedrich's *Treatments: Language, Politics, and the Culture of Illness*

Helen Malson and Maree Burns, eds. *Critical Feminist Approaches to Eating Dis/orders*

Shlomith Rimmon-Kenan's "The Story of 'I': Illness and Narrative Identity"

Kate Zambreno's "The Anorexic Text: Consciousness Is a Surface"

ACKNOWLEDGMENTS

This book was a tough case to crack; a team of many helped me solve it. My gratitude to:

Leeyanne Moore, for leading me to Kathy Acker and for providing important feedback at a number of stages.

The Temple 07 Fiction crew, especially Abbi Dion, Steve Dolph, Mary Hoeffel, and Andrea Lawlor; and Laura Jaramillo and Mecca Jamilah Sullivan, all of whom read early drafts. Thank you for the conversations and camaraderie, and for the patience with which you supported me as I grew into a fuller person.

My teachers at Temple: Samuel R. Delany, Joan Mellen, Sandra Newman, and Alan Singer; and at UIC: Judith Gardiner, Christopher Grimes, Cris Mazza, and Eugene Wildman.

Cynthia Barounis, close friend and ideal reader.

Andrea Lawlor (again), AWP buddy for life, beacon of generosity and good faith and go-to source for queer history and literary gossip.

The Happy Little Comets (Brooke Wonders, Rebecca Adams Wright, Dayna Smith, Alisa Alering, and Tim Susman), who gave me a reason to resuscitate this project in 2016, when I had just about given it up. Post-it plotting with you really is like blazing across the galaxy.

Laurie Weeks, whose Psychomagic Writing Workshop could not have entered my life at a better time.

Many friends who have provided invaluable feedback at various stages, including: Ayeh Bandeh-Ahmadi, Sam Cohen, Liza Harrell-Edge, Raechel Anne Jolie, Svetlana Kitto, Grace Kredell, Rebecca Novack, Casey Plett, Ezra Stone, Jeanne Thornton, Craig Willse, and Max Zev.

Liz Latty, Erica Cardwell, Marisa Crawford, Jeanne (again), and Max (again) for writerly friendship and support.

Mareen Eapen and Naga Jujjavarapu, for seeing me through high school.

My parents, Mary and Tom Milks, who have been there all along.

My agent, Rach Crawford, for seeing this project through many drafts and believing in it despite all the aspects that made it an improbable sell. This book has been improved enormously by your input. (And thanks to Tom Cho for connecting us.)

Xander Marro, for solving the mystery of this cover.

Delia Davis, for the sharp eye in copyediting.

My editor, Lauren Rosemary Hook, who descended as if on a winged unicorn from rainbow clouds just when it seemed like all paths to publishing had been sealed. Thank you for taking a chance on Margaret and for working closely with me to shape this weird, unwieldy book into its best, most cohesive form.

To everyone at Feminist Press (Lauren, Jisu Kim, Drew Stevens, Lucia Brown, Rachel Page, Nick Whitney): Thank you. I am honored to be joining the extraordinary legacy you have helped build and cannot believe my good fortune to have found this home for my book.

Amethyst Editions
at the Feminist Press

Amethyst Editions is a modern, queer
imprint founded by Michelle Tea

**Against Memoir: Complaints,
Confessions & Criticisms**
by Michelle Tea

Black Wave by Michelle Tea

Fiebre Tropical by Juliana Delgado Lopera

The Not Wives by Carley Moore

**Original Plumbing: The Best of Ten Years
of Trans Male Culture**
edited by Amos Mac and Rocco Kayiatos

Since I Laid My Burden Down by Brontez Purnell

Skye Papers by Jamika Ajalon

The Summer of Dead Birds by Ali Liebegott

Tabitha and Magoo Dress Up Too by Michelle Tea,
illustrated by Ellis van der Does

We Were Witches by Ariel Gore

amethyst editions